The Girls of Haviland

Deborah Rafferty Oswald

ISBN: 1548860085
ISBN 13: 9781548860080

For my husband, Chuck, and our daughters, Caragh, Annie, and Katie

Chapter 1

Brewster, New York
Monday, September 2, 1918

"Mother of St. Jude!" Mam shrieked. "We're being attacked!"

The slam of the porch door rattled the windowpanes. I kicked off my covers and jumped out of bed. The side my sister, Eileen, slept in, hadn't been used. I ran outside after Mam. Sullivan, my Boston terrier, raced ahead of me, barking wildly. My bare feet were soaked in dew and grass clippings as I ran past the clothesline where the shirts I was supposed to take down were still hanging. When we reached the barn, I saw Da and my brother Christie looking up into the sky, shielding their eyes against the orange sliver of sun rising above the mountains.

"Jesus, Mary, and Joseph!" Da pointed a thick, calloused finger toward an airplane soaring over our farm. "It's a German fighter plane! I think I see a gun!"

"Saints preserve us." Mam made the sign of the cross.

"No, it's American." I had noticed the bright blue paint on the wing. "It's VE-7 Bluebird."

Mam looked back toward the house. "Where's Eileen?"

"She probably stayed out all — Ow!" Christie yelped when I slapped the back of his head.

"You had a mosquito on your neck." I glared at him.

"Where is your sister?" Mam asked, louder this time.

"She's uh, she's still sleeping," I was sick of covering for Eileen, but I didn't feel like catching hell from my lame-brained sister.

The silver plane dipped low enough for us to see a tiny figure crawling toward the edge of the top wing.

"Oh, God, there's someone up there!"

1

"Where?" yelled Mam. "I don't see anything!"

"There!" I grabbed Mam's arm and jabbed my finger frantically toward the plane. Suddenly, the small form was in the air. I opened my mouth to scream, but no sound came out.

In slow motion, as if from a newsreel, the figure spun around and around, arms spread, seeming to float in mid- air. The folds of a skirt rippled against the wind as the body spiraled downward.

"It's a girl!"

Christie took off toward the north end of our property, where the airplane was attempting to land. Da hobbled behind us, swearing as he held his sore back.

The Salmons were already climbing over the stone wall that separated our farms. Mrs. Harkins was pulling her son, Ambrose, by the arm, followed by Doc Birdsall, carrying his cracked leather bag. Miss Addison, from the newspaper, was running frantically up Brewster Hill. The drone of the biplane's engine became piercingly loud. Poor Ambrose covered his ears and started rocking back and forth.

"It's the noise!" Mrs. Harkins yelled. "He won't stop for me! Calm him, Jay, please!"

I tried covering Ambrose's ears, but he let out a terrible yell and started banging his head with the heel of his hand.

Against the deafening crush of sound, I whispered, "It's okay, Ambrose, the noise will stop once the airplane lands."

He slowed down the rocking.

"We're all going to die!" screamed Mrs. Salmon. "It must be a spy plane! He'll shoot us all!" She tried to calm the screeching toddler in her arms. "Oh hush, Nell, please."

"Give her to me." Mr. Salmon grabbed his daughter who was struggling to escape from Mrs. Salmon's tight embrace. "You're scaring her!"

Sullivan, along with the Salmons' dogs, barked at the plane that was rapidly descending. Ambrose started rocking again.

"Keep those damn dogs quiet!" Da kicked Sullivan in his ribs.

"Leave him alone!" I grabbed my whimpering dog.

"Move back, everybody." warned Doc Birdsall. "He's trying to land."

A sudden assault of noxious engine fumes made my eyes water. I tucked Sullivan's head under my arm to protect his lungs.

"Mama!" Nell wriggled out of her father's arms and ran toward Mrs. Salmon, but tripped over the dogs. The little girl lay sprawled on the ground screaming as the plane came closer.

"My baby!" Mrs. Salmon rushed to scoop Nell up. She stood, eyes fixated on the plane.

"Move! It's going to crush you!" I pulled Mrs. Salmon and Nell toward me with my free hand. I held onto Sullivan as I felt myself falling backward into the crowd. Someone pushed me back up on my feet.

"Here it comes!" Christie yelled. The silver underbelly of the plane forced us all to spread out in a haphazard circle.

"Oh my God, I am heartily sorry for having offended Thee." Mam and I prayed in unison.

The earsplitting noise started Ambrose wailing and hitting himself again.

When the sputtering engine finally ceased sputtering, a young pilot emerged from the cockpit, bathed in sweat and grease. "She was right behind me, I swear! I ... I don't know what happened!"

Da charged at him. "What in God's name is going on?"

"I don't know! I don't know!" The pilot unstrapped his aviator helmet and goggles, then bent over, clutching his thighs with both hands.

I took a closer look at the biplane, noting it was a two-seater, with no gun mounted. This was no fighter plane.

"You'd better start talking soon!" Da roared. "Somebody just fell out of your airplane! Did you push her?" He scanned our frightened faces gathering around the airplane. "Who's got a rope? Let's tie him up until the sheriff gets here."

I approached the shaken pilot. "Do you know what the girl would be doing up on the wing? I mean, was she ..."

"Sheriff Stevens is on his way." Margaret Addison pushed her way through the crowd. She took a pencil that was resting behind her ear. "Sir, I'm with *The Courier*. Can you tell me exactly what happened?"

Da grunted and pushed Miss Addison out of his way. "Get out of here, you fool woman! What went on up there? Start explaining!"

"Da, you knocked her over!" I helped Miss Addison up.

"She doesn't belong here!"

He continued with his rampage. "You shouldn't be flying a plane if you can't keep your passengers' safe!"

"It was nothing like that, I swear, Mister!" The pilot panted. "I'll … tell … you … everything … if, …you'll just … let me catch … my breath."

"Well, go on then!"

"Please stop bullying the man and give him a minute to collect his thoughts, Da." I said.

"Jay, run up to the house and bring the pilot some water," said Mam.

Mr. Salmon produced a silver flask. "The poor fellow's had the stuffing knocked out of him. I reckon he needs something stronger."

"At this hour of the morning!" Mrs. Harkins said. "Is there any decency left in this village?"

The pilot took a long swig from the flask before beginning.

"Let me try to think. We were flying over Brewster at about 2,000 feet. I thought a bird hit the top wing. I looked back to see that the seat behind me was empty and … and, oh, I don't know what happened …"

"Did she say anything before climbing up onto the wing?" I asked. "Was anything on the plane broken?"

"I just remember leaning out and seeing her up there on the wing and, Oh, God, I can't believe it!" He held his head, and his voice broke. "I'm hollering and trying to grab her back in, and the next thing I knew, she was gone! Honestly, miss, no fooling, that's how it happened. You've got to believe me!" Two tears were carving clean lines through the dust streaking his face.

"Do you know where she could be? Maybe she's still alive."

"Nobody could survive that fall. We were flying over trees and rocks, for gosh sakes. Why in the world would anybody…"

Miss Addison elbowed her way back up to the front of the crowd. "Did she tell you why she wanted you to take her up in the plane?"

"Not really, just asked me to tell her when we were flying over Haviland Seminary."

Haviland! I couldn't believe my ears.

4

"Well, we've just got to look for her! Everybody spread out and search the fields! Maybe there's a chance, even if..." My orders were drowned out by the clanging bell on the Buckeye Pumper clamoring up the road. Fire Chief Harkins reined in the horses. Seated beside him, his namesake, Henry, smoothed his jet-black hair with his fingers. I hadn't yet had a chance to say goodbye to him.

"About time you got here!" said Mrs. Harkins. "Henry, go look for your brother. He's wandering around and liable to get lost."

Henry jumped down from the rig and, ignoring his mother, joined me as I ran to search for the girl.

"I saw her fall from right up there." I looked up at the sky, catching my breath as we reached the farthest pastures on our farm.

"The wind might have carried her." Henry continued on toward the Salmon property.

I ran to catch up, terrified of what we might find. We had sprinted far ahead of the others, and now we were all alone at the top of the ridge. I spotted something sparkling in the sun over by the rock wall. Slowly, I made my way through the scorched grass. I stopped suddenly, my stomach lurching. My legs went wobbly, and I staggered backward in horror.

There she was, lying on her back, her arms and legs bent backwards at unnatural angles. On her left hand was a ring, the red stone reflecting the rays of sunlight, like a beacon. I willed myself to tiptoe closer. Her grey eyes were looking up at me, but there was no life in them.

"Henry!" I felt like I was going to throw up. He was at my side in seconds.

"She's dead, isn't she?"

"Stay here. I'll get my dad."

I put my hand over my mouth. "I'm going to be sick!"

Henry led me over to the rock wall, away from the body. "Sit down. I'll be right back."

His voice sounded far away. Everything started looking all distorted and funny.

"I really don't feel good. Please don't go yet." My face and the back of my neck felt clammy.

"You're going to pass out, Jay. Put your head down. I won't leave you. Just breathe slowly, in and out." He put two fingers in his mouth and blew a sharp whistle.

Taking slow, deep breaths helped a little, but when I tried to stand up, I grabbed my stomach and retched, the raw taste of bile souring my mouth. I wiped my mouth with my sleeve and saw Henry's dad and Doc Birdsall climbing up the hill toward us.

From the stone wall, where I sat mute and nauseous, I watched Doc pronounce the death of the girl I had found among our grazing dairy cows.

❋

The leaves rustled. Someone was coming. A hint of a breeze sent ripples across our swimming hole. It was really just a pond that had been covered with thick, green algae for most of the stifling summer. Bullfrogs dotted the shore, sounding like they were plucking banjos.

The sun finally slipped behind a cloud, providing a break from the heat. Aside from the maple leaves that were starting to turn colors, fall was nowhere in sight.

"Are you alone?" Eileen's voice called through the late afternoon shade of the trees.

"Yeah. Where've you been? Da's going to kill you!"

Eileen emerged from the woods. She jumped into the swimming hole, still clad in the dress she had stolen from me last night.

To escape having to hear about her midnight adventures, I dove deep down into the water. My hands grabbed at the slimy reeds growing up from the muddy bottom. Here, in the blackness, I knew I would find some cold pockets of water. I stayed underwater for as long as I could hold my breath. It gave me a minute to digest all that had happened today, a day I'd just wanted to be quiet and ordinary before my life changed forever. I stayed in this underwater cocoon, trying to block out the image of the dead girl, until my lungs felt about ready to burst.

Splashing through the pond's surface, I shook my wet mop of tangled hair, hurling green algae onto Eileen's worried face.

"Sorry!" Water dribbled down my chin.

"What are you, half trout?" She picked strands of algae off her freckled forehead.

"Are you crazy, not coming home until now?" Although she was two years older than me, Eileen didn't have the sense she had been born with.

"Me and Artie went for a drive, and the tank ran out of gas. The jerk at the filling station wouldn't sell Artie any because of some law that says you're not supposed to go pleasure riding on weekends, so we had to sleep in the car."

"I'm sure you got a lot of sleep!" I said sarcastically. "Christie almost gave you up to Mam. I said you stayed up late sewing, but she knew that was bull. You missed everything that happened here, by the way."

"You mean how a girl fell from a plane on our farm? It's the talk of the village, simp! You need to get out more, Jay!"

"Da's furious."

"What else is new?"

"Now there's going to be a big scene between you two, like always. Mam says ..."

"Mam says, Mam says. When are you going to stop listening to everything Mam says, Jay? I can drive around with whomever I please, no matter what Mam says!" She swam away, kicking water in my face. "She can control you, Miss Goody Goody, but not me."

"Mam controls me? Ha! Artie controls you! You have no idea what he does behind your back."

"What are you talking about?"

"I saw him flirting with Cassie Salmon at Diehl's Confectionary last week, and he was all over Mabel Puglsey at the movies Friday. So now who's the simp?"

"I don't believe you. Artie would never flirt with Cassie Salmon. She's your age, for God's sake. And Mabel - she's downright pug-ugly!"

"I don't care if you believe me or not. He's no good, that one."

She gave me her usual snotty face, but didn't fire back, so I changed the subject.

"I saw her." I swept away a yellowjacket that had landed on Eileen's sunburned arm.

"You saw who? Mabel?"

"No, the girl who fell from the plane."

"Really? What did she look like?" The water had smudged her mascara, and it was running down her face.

"I can't get the picture of her looking up at me out of my head, no matter how I try."

"I can't believe you found a dead body! Does anyone know who she is?"

"Christie said she was a cousin of the Cranes. You know the family who live in that big house by the reservoir. She was supposed to start her sophomore year at Haviland."

Just like me, I thought.

"Yikes! I wouldn't want to be you going there tomorrow."

"It was so scary seeing her spinning around in the air." I looked at the sun's rays filtered by the trees, wishing today had never happened. How was I going to get up in the morning and start at a new school where I knew absolutely no one?

"Do you think you can get out of it?"

"I don't know how. It took me and Mam a whole year to convince Da to let me take the scholarship. I was kind of looking forward to going before this" I tilted my head towards the fields, "happened. All Da's been doing is ranting about the money Mam spent on my uniform and supplies. How can I tell him I've changed my mind the day before I'm supposed to leave? I have to listen to him go on about how I'm bleeding him dry as it is."

"Tell him to stuff it. It's not your fault Borden's closed down."

"I don't even know why Borden's gave me a scholarship in the first place if they knew they were moving out of the village."

Borden's bought milk from Da and other local dairy farmers to evaporate and sell as their famous condensed milk. The closing of the condensery cut off both sources of our family's income, as Mam had worked the night shift in the canning department.

"Hey, at least Mam signed you up for the scholarship. She never even mentioned it to me. She must think I'm too dopey to go to a fancy girls' school."

"You're just as smart as I am. You just don't show up at school enough."

"School's for kids." Eileen picked off some dead skin where it was peeling on the top of her back behind her shoulder.

"Hey!" I splashed her.

"No, I don't mean you. You're made for school. For me, it's just a stupid waste of time. Artie and I are in love." Her strawberry blonde hair stuck to the side of her face. Unlike my out of control curls, Eileen's hair was straight and baby fine. She had to wear rag curls to bed every night to make it look all fluffy.

"Artie and you are in love? Just like Fred and you were in love, and Wally and you were in love, and, let me think, Frank and you were in love, and before him, um, oh, now I remember, Stan and you were in love! And that's just this year! The talk is you're turning into the village floozy!"

I dunked under the water to get out of the way of her nails, lunging for my face. I'd enough scars from her scratches.

When I felt it was safe to come back up to the surface, she had calmed down, just a little.

"Just because you can't get Henry to look at you, don't make up lies about me, Jay! Artie isn't like any of those boys. His pa is setting him up to get a good job on the railroad, and I can take in sewing, just like Mam. I do most of the work as it is."

"Listen to yourself, will you? You want to end up like Mam? Slaving over a sewing machine and cowering in a corner every time Da loses his temper? You're crazy! At least at school, I'll be away from him."

"Of course I'm not going to live like Ma! Artie's a dream. He's nothing like Da! Plus, I won't have to slave over anything. I've got my eye on that nice little house next door to his. Artie says once his grandma kicks the bucket, it'll be all ours. Just wait, you'll see. I'm going to be sitting pretty in my own home. You'll understand when you fall in love - if that day ever comes!"

This time I swam away.

"Oh, I've forgot, you've already fallen for the Harkins kid haven't you? Talk about following someone around like a lost puppy!"

"We're just friends, that's all." Henry probably thought we were friends, but I considered him the most perfect creature God ever created.

"And I'm the Queen of Sheba!"

I hoisted myself up onto the grassy bank and grabbed a black tractor tire tube that was propped up against a tree trunk. I placed it over my head, taking care not to stab myself with the air valve, and jumped back in the water. Resting on the front of the tube, I paddled back over to Eileen, who grabbed onto the other side.

She frowned.

"What's wrong?"

"You're too chicken to tell Da you don't want to go. You're leaving in the morning. You'll make a ton of new friends."

"I'll see what kind of mood Da's in at supper. If he insists I go, Mam won't stick up for me. And if I've got to go, I doubt I'll make friends. Everyone there already knows each other because they all started together last year as freshmen. I'm probably the only new sophomore."

"You'll be so full of yourself when you come home for Thanksgiving. There'll be no talking to you."

"I had to promise Mam I'll come home every few weeks to go to mass so I don't turn heathen. You just *have* to go to school so you can tell me everything I missed when I come home! I want to know every detail, down to who comes in with their hair bobbed, and if George Addison still seems sweet on you, even though you're with Artie. Why don't you give George a chance? He's awful nice."

"He's a child. Don't you really want me to find out if Henry Harkins is sweet on you?"

Just to go one day without studying the back of Henry's head in class seemed like torture.

The supper bell clanged in the distance. Reluctantly, we made our way out of the water, mud squishing between our toes.

"What are you going to tell Mam and Da?" We walked through the woods back to the house. The ground was a mossy carpet caressing my bare feet.

"What have you told them, so I can be prepared?"

"Just that you were sleeping, that's all. But how are you going to explain that wet dress?"

"You're going to bring me dry clothes while I hide in the barn."

I ran off to sneak a skirt and middy blouse out of the house.

❋

The only two farmhands Da hadn't yet let go were known to us simply as Felix and Ernie. They joined us for meals. Unfortunately, tonight's supper was cold tongue and cabbage. I cringed every time my mother sliced into the large grey tongue. My stomach was still queasy from this morning.

"I wonder what it feels like to have knife slice through your tongue," I whispered to Eileen.

"Ugh, it's disgusting, isn't it? Mam, no one likes this stuff except Da. Isn't it Meatless Monday?"

"Enough of your cheek, young lady!" Da stabbed the tongue with his fork. "I put the shoes on yer Mammy's feet, and she'll cook what I tell her to!"

"Da, please don't talk that way about Mam." I was disgusted by the spittle that sprayed from his mouth when he shouted.

"Stop! Quiet, all of you!" Mam shushed us and set down a bowl of boiled potatoes on the table.

I passed on the revolting meat and helped myself to some potatoes before Mam scooped half of my portion back into the bowl.

"Control yourself, Josephine! You'll never fit into your uniform if you eat like a pig! I've the six of you to feed. Leave some for Christie. He's a growing boy."

Christie grinned at me as Mam heaped food on his plate. I shot him a look. Da and the farmhands guarded their food with both arms.

"This is why I don't like my real name. You only call me that when you're yelling at me! And I already know I'm too fat!" I slunk down in my chair. "I don't like anything but the potatoes."

"Stop acting like an arse, Josephine," Da said. "You'll eat what's put down in front of you, or you won't eat at all."

I pushed my plate away, hating everybody at the table.

"Sheriff Stevens questioned the pilot of the plane," Christie said. "Wanted to make sure he had nothing to do with the girl falling, I guess."

"Oh, no," Mam called from the sink. She never sat at the table when we ate. She just grabbed a few bites of food whenever she could, between serving us and clearing the plates. "He couldn't have. You saw the poor man. He was a wreck."

"Why was she up in a plane with him anyway?" I asked.

"Said they store military planes down at the Mahopac Airport where he's a mechanic," Christie said. "Told us the girl came up to him at dawn with a big wad of cash in her hand. Said she asked him to take her up in the plane and fly over the Haviland Seminary."

The potatoes I had managed to shove down my throat turned to lead bricks.

Felix finally looked up from his food. "Ernie and me heard they had to place a telephone call clear down to New York City to reach the girl's pa. Seems he's a doctor at some big city hospital."

"He's trying to save lives, then. And his own daughter just lost hers." Mam spooned the last of the potatoes onto Christie's plate. "Eat. You need your strength."

I mouthed "Mama's boy!" across the table.

"No thanks, Mam. I didn't want any more," Eileen said, sarcastically.

"And where the devil have you been all day, young lady?" Da said.

"Just like Jay told you, I overslept because I was up all night finishing Mam's fall dress orders. I had errands to run in the village all day today."

"The noise from the plane would have woken the dead, Eileen, and all the shops in the village were closed on account of the Labor Day Parade. More likely you were off gallivanting with that tinker, Art Hubbard's boy."

"Artie's not a tinker!"

"All the Hubbards are tinkers!" Da downed the whiskey and water Mam had placed in front of him, dribbling a brown line down the side of his stubbled chin.

"You're not to leave this house, Eileen," said Mam. "I don't want any of you going out while people are dropping from biplanes. Jay, this whole incident has been a bad omen. I've been thinking you should stay home until the police can get to the bottom of this."

Had Mam just provided me with a way to get out of going to Haviland? I prayed Da would agree with her. He was still glowering at Eileen. I was frightened by the way his face looked when he was angry, all twisted downward like a troll. Broken blood vessels made a map on his bulbous nose.

"Jay, take the kettle off the flame and pour the tea, will you?" Mam started clearing the dishes. "And bring your brother the last of the peach pie. The rest of us can have leftover soda bread."

"You're the best, Mam." Christie hugged her as she passed by his seat.

"Enough of you now!" said Da. "Didn't I tell you to fix that tractor wheel? It's squeaking worse than ever." He slurped from a chipped mug of tea Mam had placed in front of him. "Useless, that's what you are." He ripped off a hunk of soda bread and dunked it in the tea. "Completely useless."

It was at times like this that I almost felt sorry for my only brother still living at home. Almost.

"Leave the boy alone, will you? Have one of the hired men do it tomorrow." Mam motioned to Felix and Ernie, who rose and left the table.

"And that will be quite enough from you, Nonie!"

I wondered if I was the only one who noticed Mam flinch.

"We've spent money we don't have getting Jay everything on that God-blasted school list. She'll be in class tomorrow, and that's all there is to it."

Da took a wrinkled slip of paper from the pocket of his overalls and slapped it down with such force I felt my wrists vibrate from the impact. The noise sent Sullivan scrambling to the safety of my bedroom. I wished I could join him.

"And what is the meaning of this bill from Lobdell's Dry Goods? Why does Jay need to supply her own napkin ring and soup spoon for school? They're thieves, I tell you!" Da grimaced as he rubbed his right hand, disfigured by rheumatism. His knuckles had swollen up to three times their natural size, resembling four huge eyeballs. I always imagined they were looking at me.

"I assume Haviland is going to try and turn our Jay into a proper lady." Mam's voice was shaky.

So that was it. Eileen was right. I wasn't going to challenge Da.

"Coward," she whispered.

"I'm off to Wassaic in the morning." Da rose from the table. The nearest Borden's Condensery was now more than 20 miles north of our farm. "Salmon heard there are dairymen up that way looking to buy cows."

"You're not going to sell Bridie, are you?" I asked.

"Give that cow a different name, Jim," Mam said. "It's disgraceful that you named a cow after my only living sister."

"Your sister needs to shut her mouth and chew her cud!" He drained his glass. "The name suits her. And I'm not selling Bridie. Felix thinks she's with calf."

I thanked God for this small mercy. I'd much rather sell Da than Bridie.

"A trip to Wassaic will take you most of the day. You've got to get Jay and her trunks to Haviland by 8:00 in the morning."

"I'm having a God-awful time trying to sell any of the herd. I have to take as many of them as I can tomorrow. The boy will take Jay to school before making the delivery rounds."

Christie pushed away from the table. "Thanks," he said as he passed me.

"Now about this bill, Nonie," Da took out his spectacles and fit them on his large, round head.

"He's got a head like a melon!" I whispered to Eileen.

She burst out laughing, spitting tea in my face.

"Ew!"

"It's your own fault for making me laugh!"

"That crook Lobdell is trying to cheat us. Look at the price of these napkin rings. That has to be wrong." He handed the bill to Mam, who looked it over for a moment.

"This figure here is the price is for two napkin rings, not one. And look, he subtracted the deposit I gave him, so this is the price we've to pay, not the original total."

I swallowed my tea before leaning over to whisper to Eileen. "Yesterday Mam waited until Da left to explain that the war was started because of the assassination of Archduke Ferdinand, not *Bird in Hand*," like Da pronounces it."

"He's an eejit!" We both cracked up.

"Stop the roaring!" Mam said. "Jay, bring the pie plate out to the sink and scrub it with brown soap. And you left the laundry hanging outside again. Take it down before it gets dewy. What's this, the fourth night this week you forgot?" She pushed me into the kitchen. "Maybe it's a good thing you're off to that fancy school, but I still wish Da would let you wait until we find out more about the plane accident."

"When are you going to stand up to him, Mam? Why are you making me go away when you want me to stay?"

"Don't take that tone with me, young lady. You're too bold for your own good, and they won't put up with any of your cheek at that fancy school. You're cursed with yer Da's temper. Hold your tongue, Josephine. Remember that. A good education is your only hope."

"What do you mean, my only hope?"

"You're a disaster in the kitchen, you can't thread a needle, and I usually find you up on the stone wall reading those socialist books of yours when you're supposed to be mucking out the barn!"

"They're not socialist books; they're about Women's Suffrage and Fair Labor Laws. They make a lot of sense. You should read them."

"As if I have time to read a book," Mam scoffed. "I've mending to do in the parlor. Finish up out here, and for heaven's sake, take the wash down!"

"Why can't Eileen help? She doesn't do anything."

"I've got a ton of hemming orders to work on," Eileen called from our room.

I listened to Mam's attempts to appear interested in Da's reports of the day while seated in front of the unlit fireplace. I'd lose my mind if I had to darn stockings every night while Da droned on about his Dairymen Meetings.

As if on cue, just as I was putting the last dish back in the cupboard, Eileen walked into the kitchen, stinking to high heaven of perfume. I threw the wet dishrag at her, but she ducked out of the way.

"What?" She dabbed makeup over a pimple on the side of her nose.

"How do you always manage to disappear when it's time to clean up after supper?" I scraped disgusting chunks of tongue into Sullivan's bowl. He swallowed them whole before they even landed.

"It's a skill you've yet to acquire." She checked her reflection in a compact mirror, and picked some red lipstick off her teeth.

"Mam said you can't go out."

"Never you mind about that. I'll be home in an hour, tops. Not a word to Mam." She checked the freshness of her breath by blowing into her cupped hand and sniffing. "You look like you're sucking on a lemon, Jay. What's wrong with you? "

"I don't know." I poured some still hot water from the kettle into the sink to soak the pie plate. "I thought maybe Mam would do something a little special for me on my last night home."

"Didn't you get enough special attention from being in the newspaper when you got the scholarship? Sheesh!"

I peeked around the wall separating the kitchen from the parlor to watch Mam mending Da's long underwear.

"I wonder if she was pretty once, before her face got all hard like that."

"Aunt Bridie said Mam was a real beauty back in Ireland."

"Then how'd she get stuck with Da?" I removed the ash pan from the oven so I could empty it.

"Aunt Bridie and Mam had no family here. They got let go from the factory where they sewed. They were behind on their rent when Mam met Da. He basically took them off the streets."

"I would have tried my chances on the streets!" I stopped on my way down to the cellar to fill the scuttle with coal for the morning. I only took a few precious lumps. "How do you know all this stuff anyway?"

"Get your nose out of your books once in a while, and you'll learn something." Eileen put her finger to her lips to quiet me as she slipped out the door.

I laid awake in bed for much of the night, listening for Eileen to climb through our window. Sullivan slept curled up against my shoulder, snoring. My oldest brother, Jimmy Joe, had found him abandoned on a train coming into Brewster. Because of the way he fought with dogs twice his size, Jimmy Joe had named him after the prize fighter, John L. Sullivan. The scrappy little dog had taken to me instantly, and he had slept every night snuggled up with me in bed since. Where would he sleep when I was off at school? Eileen wouldn't allow him on her side of the bed, and I didn't want Sullivan going anywhere near Da.

Eventually I fell off into an uneasy sleep. Frightening dreams of the girl dropping from the airplane woke me several times before daybreak.

Chapter 2

Tuesday, September 3, 1918

"Awake, Jay?" Mam's tired voice swept up the butterflies that were fluttering about in my stomach. I inhaled the reassuring scent of Pear's soap on her skin, and was calmed by the touch of her rough hand on my back, even if it only lingered there a moment.

"I had a bad dream about the girl who fell," I said, but Mam was already dragging my trunk out into the hallway.

"At last I have this bed all to myself." Eileen's head emerged from beneath the covers. "Get this fleabag out of here." She pushed Sullivan off the bed. I had faked sleep when she had finally come in through the window sometime this morning.

"There are rashers and eggs waiting for you after you wash up and dress," said Mam. "Tie a dishtowel around your neck so you don't drip yolk all over your uniform. For heaven's sake, Jay stop dilly dallying! Christie can't wait around all day for you!"

"I guess it's time for goodbyes. Promise me you'll think about what I told you about Artie, because I just don't want you to ..."

"Jesus, Jay! Close the curtains, will you? The light is killing my eyes."

I could only get a few bites down at breakfast. I had hoped that Mam might have decided to help me settle in, but I could see she had the straining cloth out for making pot cheese. I guessed she just couldn't get away.

"Remind Christie to tell Felix and Ernie the ice man is coming today." Mam put a cardboard sign that read, "*25 pounds,*" in the window.

"I'm never going to remember that."

Ma flitted about the kitchen like a hen, opening and shutting the icebox and then dashing over to the stove to see if the can of cooking grease needed emptying. I snuck Sullivan a sausage under the table. I swore he knew I was leaving.

"Let me take a look at you." I cringed as Mam propped the corn broom against the wall. She planted her hands on her narrow hips. "That middy blouse hangs terribly on you! It's loose in the chest and tight around your waist. This is what happens when you eat too much! I was half your size at your age."

"You're supposed to tell me how proud you are of me, Mam, not make fun of my weight! You know how scared I am about going away."

She came around the back of me and grabbed my shoulders. "Stand up straight, for heaven's sake! Oh God, you look like a banshee woman with that hair. Give me the brush."

"I'm not a baby, Mam. I can brush my own hair." I wrestled the horsehair brush from her and dragged it through my knotty mess of hair, then plaited the tangle of curls into a fat braid. Picking up a hand mirror, I groaned when I saw some corkscrew tendrils already taking shape along my hairline. My hair color resembled a penny, not the shiny new kind, but the dull, worn-down brown of one that has spent years at the bottom of a piggy bank.

Ma lifted my chin with her hands. "You've got circles under your eyes. What's the matter with you?"

"I couldn't sleep. I kept seeing that girl falling from the plane."

"I'm lighting a candle at St. Luke's for the girl's poor parents." She took my plate away from me, bending and scraping the untouched food into Sullivan's bowl. He awoke from his post-sausage nap on the rag rug, sniffed the air, and slobbered up my breakfast, smacking his black lips in satisfaction.

"Saints preserve us, Look at the time! You'll make Christie late with the milk. Go on now!"

I stopped by the row of dusty work boots parked inside the door to put on my new school shoes. My right foot wouldn't go in all the way. I dug my hand in to find out what was inside my shoe. My fingers touched fur. I screamed and threw the shoe against the door.

"Stop the roaring!" Mam retrieved the shoe and pulled out a long tail. Hanging from the tail was a dead mouse. Sullivan barked and leapt up into the air, trying to catch the tasty treat. Mam opened the door and threw the rodent outside for the cats to feast upon. I heard Christie howling with laughter as he cranked the engine to start our truck.

"Leave him be, Jay. He's just having a bit of fun." Mam shooed me out the door. "You'll do fine, don't worry."

Christie was wiping tears from his eyes as I emerged, stone faced, from the house.

"Jeez, Jay, have a sense of humor, for gosh sakes! Thought you needed something to take the lead out. Check the gas, now."

I stomped angrily past the six feet tall form of him, climbed up on the running board, and swung into the passenger side. Lifting up the seat to reveal the gas tank, I unscrewed the cap on top and grabbed the dipstick.

"Half a tank left," I yelled.

"If you think I'm going to wait this long again, you're crazy. Cream's been sitting so long it's going to turn to butter before we reach Dieter's, and when he turns it away, you can tell Da we lost a day's pay! Thank God I won't have to be making this trip much longer."

"OK, Christie, you've made your point. And what are you talking about, you won't have to make this trip much longer? How am I going to get home in a few weeks?"

"No, I meant that once I ..." He stopped suddenly. "Nothing, Jay, forget about it. Make sure you're in this truck by seven o'clock from now on."

He was struggling to open a tin of tobacco when a deer darted out in front of the truck.

"Christie! Pay attention!"

"Will you relax, Jay?" He swerved to avoid the deer. "I know what I'm doing."

As we made the turn toward Carmel, Christie let go of the wheel again to pinch a plug of tobacco. The truck veered to the right. I grabbed the wheel to avoid crashing into an oncoming wagon. Christie slowed the truck to a stop.

"Get off!" He pushed my hand away from the wheel. "What are you doing?"

I ran around to the driver's side. Opening the door, I shouted "Get out!"

"You're kidding me."

"You can't drive and chew tobacco at the same time. Move over. Now!"

I climbed up into the driver's side and shoved Christie over. After I positioned my book satchel under me to give me some height, I climbed on top, got behind the wheel, pulled the handbrake all the way back, and turned the key in the ignition. Pressing down as hard as I could on the starter pedal with my toes, I adjusted the throttle with my hand. I then adjusted the spark advance and pulled back out onto the road.

"You can't drive! You're only fourteen, for God's sake!" He grabbed my arm.

"Jimmy Joe taught me so I could drive the milk cans to Borden's when he was hung over, so let go of me!" I wrenched my arm away.

"You're going to get in so much trouble when I tell Da you've been driving!" He stuck the tobacco in his mouth and pushed it against his cheek.

"And you're going to get in trouble when I tell Mam you're chewing tobacco." I made the turn up to Haviland.

A huge set of twin stairways at the front entrance opened up before us.

"Wow, will you look at that." A rush of excitement raced through my body. Our rickety truck skirted the wide cobblestoned walkway lined on both sides with Black-eyed Susans. It felt like I was entering the palace at Versailles.

"Don't know why you want to go to a school where people fall out of airplanes just so they don't have to come here. Let's not take all day getting you settled in this snooty place!" Christie spit a stream of brown tobacco juice out the window, attracting the attention of a group of students walking together. They giggled at the sight of the milk cans clanking together.

"I'm doomed." Hunching my shoulders, I tried to slink down behind the steering wheel, but then I noticed a girl on a bicycle riding alongside our truck. Her skin was golden bronze, as if she'd spent the summer at the seashore.

I tried to smooth back some windblown hair that had come loose from Mam's pins. The bicyclist glanced up at me and attempted to arrange her own black curls while keeping one hand on the handlebars. I followed the signs that led to the dormitory behind the school. The cyclist followed me. Maybe she was new here, like me. I hoped she was, even though she didn't look nervous like I did. She looked proud, almost defiant.

"You go ahead and let them know you're moving in," said Christie. "I'll unload all your junk. Go on now, you're costing me money!"

I grabbed Mam's valise, which up until yesterday had lain covered in a thick layer of dust in the attic, and turned the ornate brass knob of the door bearing a plate that read, "Strength Hall." My footsteps were cushioned in swirls of thick carpeting in the dark, hushed, vestibule. The only sound I heard was the rhythmic pecking of typewriter keys. I came upon a receptionist in a Haviland uniform, seated behind a desk.

She looked up from her work, clearly startled by my arrival. She grabbed a heavy dictionary and quickly plopped it down on her typewriter.

"May I help you?" She dabbed at her eyes with a handkerchief. Had she been crying?

"I'm Jay McKenna. I'm boarding in this dormitory."

"Oh, my word, you must be the missing student from Room 19! We've all been beside ourselves wondering what could've happened to you! We were expecting you Saturday morning with the others. Have you been ill?"

I was certain the letter informing me of the date I was expected to arrive had ended up tossed in the stove by Da or Christie. I apologized for my lateness.

"Not to worry." She extended a slim hand with tapered fingers. "I'm Lydia Penny, Resident Assistant."

I followed her down the hallway. "There was a last minute change of rooms, so I can introduce you to the student with whom you'll be boarding." She glanced nervously at a timepiece pinned to her middy blouse. "I'll acquaint you with the other students later on this afternoon, but I'm afraid you'll just have time to secure your belongings in your room before classes start within the hour. Do you need any help with your luggage? I'd be glad to ..."

I blushed crimson as I heard a loud banging against the walls.

"Jesus, Jay! What the hell did you pack in this trunk, lead bricks?" Several heads poked out of doorways.

"Where does this go? I'm about ready to drop it!"

Girls in Haviland uniforms gasped as Christie shouted a stream of expletives while heaving the trunk to my room.

"As I was saying earlier, there was an unexpected room change earlier this morning, so you'll now be boarding in Room 17. Ah, here we are." Lydia Penny rapped lightly on the door.

"Leave me alone, Mary Agnes. I've had quite enough of your butterfingers. That was Mother's good china figurine, for land's sake!"

"Evangeline, it's Lydia. Your new roommate is here."

I was terrified of who or what was behind that closed door.

Evangeline, such a delicate, apple blossom scented name, didn't suit the moon face taking inventory of me from head to toe. The thick lenses of her glasses magnified her owlish eyes.

"How old is she, ten?" Evangeline's forehead and cheeks were covered in some foul smelling white cream. Ham hock hands rested on her ample hips. Her greasy dark hair was chopped at an unflattering chin level. Flecks of dandruff were clearly visible on the shoulders of her navy blue Haviland cardigan.

"I'll be fifteen this Christmas."

Christie came barreling though the doorway, pushing Evangeline out of the way. He dumped Mam's steamer trunk on the nearest bed. Above the bed, Haviland pennants, and tons of postcards and photographs were tacked all over the floral wallpaper.

"No, not there! That's Grandmother's good bedspread!" Evangeline lifted a meaty arm and pointed at a striped mattress. "That's hers!"

I dragged the trunk to the bare bed at the far side of the room.

"Jay, get out here and help me with the rest of your junk! It's almost 8:30!"

I followed Christie out and caught the last few parcels he threw off the back of the truck. He jumped down and handed me my book satchel.

"That's it. I've got to go."

I was surprised to feel a dull pain starting in the pit of my stomach. I had a momentary mad urge to grab my things and hop back into the truck. I wouldn't even care if Christie made fun of me the whole way home.

"Good luck living with that old buffalo of a roommate you got stuck with."

"Yeah." I blinked to prevent my eyes from watering.

"Listen, I've got to get to Lakeside Hotel. Should've been there an hour ago."

"Will you ask Mam to write me?"

"Shoot, Jay. Mam should've come down here and settled you in herself. This place gives me the willies."

"Bye, Christie."

He pulled out the choke lever, cranked the engine, and disappeared down the hill.

Lydia smoothed out the paper she was typing on. The heavy dictionary must have wrinkled it. I wondered what she was hiding.

I opened the door of Room 17.

"I expect you to knock before entering my room. I was in the middle of my beauty routine." Evangeline admired her reflection in a hand mirror. "I know the Haviland guidelines discourage our bringing an elaborate toilette, but I can't resist this cream. It really works, don't you agree?"

"If you want to look like a circus clown who reeks of rotten eggs, then yes, it works!"

"Well, I never! Clearly you have never been taught manners. Anyway, back to a few ground rules for you. That chifforobe, desk, bed, and drying rack belong to you. Everything else is mine. Please do not touch any of my things."

"I'm not interested in your things, believe me, and I'm not following any of your senseless rules. I've got as much right to be here as you do."

"I'm not accustomed to being spoken to in such a crude manner." She waited for an apology. When she realized I wasn't about to offer one, she continued, taking a hand towel from a shelf in her chifforobe. Everything she touched was blotted with the revolting cream.

"I'm sure in time you'll prove companionable, once all your rough edges are smoothed over, but I don't want to repeat the same mistakes I made rooming with my idiot sister, Mary Agnes. I've done very well here at Haviland. I'm assuming you've been publicly educated, so you'll probably struggle with the coursework here."

"No I won't struggle. I was first in my class at the village school in everything but French."

"We'll see about that. Why were you so late getting here? Do you live far away?"

"No, Brewster."

"Well, that's no excuse. I live in Brewster too, and I was here on Saturday when I was supposed to be, for orientation."

"You live in Brewster? Really? Where did you go to school? I've never seen you before."

"Haviland Prep, of course, like everybody else - except you. Mother felt the public school was inadequate."

"I liked the village school."

"Let me see your schedule. Perfect! You're taking college preparatory courses like me, so we'll be in all the same classes. Now hurry up, because I'm not going to wait for you if you dawdle, and you're bound to get lost unless you follow me." Evangeline arranged her blue neckerchief so it hung just below the center of her collar. I checked to make sure mine looked the same as hers.

"Dr. Wisdom gives the welcoming assembly in Ormsby Hall, and she does not look kindly upon latecomers." I noticed she still had a dab of that awful cream under her nose. With a smug grin, I decided to let her find that out for herself.

Once outdoors, Evangeline caught up with some other girls. She didn't introduce me to anyone, so I listened to the chatter of the other students as I climbed the stairs that led to the entryway of the school. A gold engraved sign reading, "Patience Hall," stared down at me. Double French doors opened to the main vestibule. Wine colored velvet drapes blocked the sunlight. A black baby grand piano stood in front of a fireplace with a hearth tall enough for me to walk under. A grandfather clock read a quarter to nine.

"I'm not lying, Millie, she fell out of an airplane!" A girl with light brown braids, coiled around the back of her head like a cobra, was whispering to her friend.

I tapped the cobra girl on the shoulder. "Um, I just wanted to let you know that the girl fell onto my farm."

"Uh huh, sure you did, sweetheart!" She giggled with her friend as they continued climbing the stairs.

News of the girl's death traveled like lightning from the bottom of the staircase to the top, and then back outdoors across an overpass that led to yet another building. A polished, bronze sign was engraved with the words, "*Ormsby Hall of Performing Arts*."

I searched for the bicyclist among this large crowd of girls gathering in the darkened auditorium. Up on the stage, royal blue velvet curtains were closed behind a podium emblazoned with the Haviland crest. Seated on either side of the podium were several adults I assumed were the teachers. A tall woman in a brown serge suit and single plumed hat called for order.

"For those who are new to our school, I am Dr. Wisdom, Headmistress of Haviland Seminary for Ladies, and I'd like to welcome you all back to what promises to be an academically rewarding year. To begin our orientation this morning, everyone please rise as Miss Nathalia Ormsby leads us in our opening hymn, '*To God Be the Glory.*'"

Nathalia Ormsby was devoid of color except for her pearl and garnet ring, identical to the one the dead girl was wearing. White blond hair met with a face the shade of newly fallen snow. Barely enough skin stretched across her high cheekbones and narrow nose. Her eyes had just enough of a hint of blue so as to not make them transparent. She opened her mouth to release a voice far too powerful to be contained in such a fragile looking body. It filled every corner of the high ceilings of the auditorium.

I swore the floor was vibrating under my feet when she held the high notes. When she was finally finished, her lips quivering from exhaustion, the singer whispered a breathy, "Thank you," and returned to her seat.

When the applause finally died down, Dr. Wisdom continued. "Thank you, Miss Ormsby. I would next like to extend a warm Haviland welcome to our incoming freshman class." The headmistress picked up an additional sheet of paper.

"In addition to our freshman, we welcome two new sophomores who are joining us this year. Josephine McKenna, winner of the Borden's Condensery Scholarship, and Florence Bright, who joins us from St. John's School in Manhattan. Please stand to be welcomed, Miss McKenna and Miss Bright."

The other new student standing was the girl who followed us in this morning on the bicycle. She stared down at the girls in the audience, almost daring anyone to say anything about the exotic color of her skin. I heard someone behind me whisper "She doesn't belong here." I didn't know if they were referring to Florence or me.

"Finally, I would like to introduce you to our newest faculty member, Miss Lila Chichester, who joins us from Deerfield Academy in Massachusetts, and will teach Second Year Mathematics and Science." This teacher was clearly the youngest and most stylish of all the faculty members seated on either side of the podium. She was wearing one of those duster coat dresses I loved looking at in Eileen's *McCall's* magazines. I was happy to see that I was going to be in both of her classes.

"Who's she?" Evangeline whispered loudly to a girl next to her. "And where's Dr. Propper?"

Dr. Wisdom proceeded. "Reverend Courage wishes for you to join him in a closing prayer. Please stand, ladies."

A somber looking, bespectacled man wearing mutton chop sideburns and a cleric's collar approached the podium. I didn't really pay much attention until the close of his speech.

"Finally, I ask that all students and faculty bow heads and pray for Violet Crane, who has tragically departed from this earth. May God have mercy on her soul." I heard gasps and then hushed sobs from the girls around me, even among the teachers. Reverend Courage recited a few prayers for the dead, and the service was over.

She had a name now; Violet. The name invoked the memory of sweet wild-flowers, not fuel engine and dead grey eyes.

We silently filed out of the auditorium. Students wiped their eyes with lace handkerchiefs and buzzed about the news of Violet's death.

"I heard it was a plane crash!"

"No, the plane burst into flames up in the sky! I was there!"

"My pa said it was a German spy plane!"

I tried to stay quiet after the disaster on the staircase, but I couldn't hold back any longer. "No, it was an American plane!"

"Who are you?" one asked.

"Uh, Jay. It was an American plane, a V-E Bluebird."

"Jay? Isn't that a boy's name? So, you're an expert on war planes, I guess?"

My neck started feeling hot. I bolted down the hall to class, cursing my big, fat, mouth.

I inhaled the smell of beeswax on the polished desks. At the village school, I had had to share a desk engraved with the initials of former students. Here, each desk had scrolled, black wrought-iron legs. I spotted Florence already copying the notes written on the blackboard.

"Bon jour, mademoiselles. Welcome to French class. You're to address me as Madame Primrose." The dour looking instructor walked up and down the straight columns of desks. "This year, we'll focus on grammar, translation, and pronunciation. We'll pick up from where you left off last year with the conjugation of irregular verbs. Turn to page 61 in your textbooks. I need a volunteer to recite these verbs."

The verbs on the page blurred before my eyes.

"Come now, *filles*, girls, I must insist one of you begin recitation." She stopped at my desk, smelling as if she had been stored in camphor all summer.

"You look too young to be in a secondary school. Are you sure you're in the right class?"

"Yes, I'm in the right class."

"Begin here."

"But I ...I haven't -"

"*Non*, No, we'll have none of that. How can you expect to speak French if you don't practice French? Do you expect French verbs to fall out of the sky? Now, stand up, and begin reciting these verbs."

"Listen, I've had a year of Latin, but only six months of French." Somebody behind me giggled.

"Mr. Digbee, my French teacher last year, was forced to retire in January after he was found passed out in the janitor's closet. So, you see, it's not my fault, but I never really learned the language!"

The giggles grew to a wave of muffled laughter.

"Proceed, please, Mademoiselle McKenna."

I phonetically pronounced the unknown jumble of words in a stumbling recitation. "*Je veux, Vous voulex, Il veut, Elle veut, Nous voulons, Ils voulent*. I want, you want, he wants, she wants, we want, they want."

"Oh, no, that will never do!" Her teeth clacked when she talked, like they were going to fall out of her mouth. "I was under the distinct impression that two years of French study was a prerequisite for admission at Haviland. The standards have evidently relaxed since I started here in '88."

Mercifully, she gave up on me and moved on to her next victim. "Let's see, you there, please take over for this poor young lady."

I took my seat and tried to become invisible, vowing to despise Madame Primrose for the rest of my natural life.

"I told you it was hard!" said Evangeline.

Madame had called on Florence. She looked directly at me while she recited the verbs by memory in flawless French accent. Her eyes sent me a warning: *"Don't let them think they can get to you."*

Straightening my shoulders, I sat up taller in my chair for the duration of this miserable class. When the round bell at the top of the wall at last clanged, I looked for Florence to thank her, but she had already left the room.

Chapter 3

Room 27 smelled faintly of fish, rotten eggs, and gunpowder. Microscopes sat atop high black laboratory tables stained with some kind of white, powdery residue. Biological charts lined the walls. In one corner hung a human size skeleton. A display case with streaked windows was filled with what looked like real fossils, along with a dead baby shark floating in formaldehyde. Along the shelves beneath the tall windows, overgrown green ferns basked in the sun in red clay pots. Guppies and black mollies swam in fish tanks filled with cloudy water and algae. Beakers, containing dried rings of some chemical, sat upon rusted Bunsen burners.

A signed photograph of Marie Curie hung above the teacher's paper strewn desk. There were never pictures of anyone other than George Washington and Abraham Lincoln in my old school, and they were certainly not autographed!

Miss Chichester appeared gleefully immersed in writing a row of smudged numbers, letters, and parentheses across the crowded blackboard. Her high-pitched voice, accented with broad R's from New England, was animated as she neared her solution. She disappeared in a cloud of chalk dust, and used her sleeve as an eraser.

Once the fog cleared, a beaming Miss Chichester, nose and chin covered with chalk, explained "This is the way we use inverse operations to isolate and solve for the variable in algebra!"

I studied the elegant way she had arranged her chestnut curls, all expertly pinned up the way the Gish sisters sometimes wore theirs in the moving pictures. Hanging from her tiny ears were two drop earrings! I had never known anyone with pierced ears.

The door opened, and the girl who sang at the assembly entered the room.

Miss Chichester stopped explaining the algebra equation. "You there, are you enrolled in this class?"

The girl at the door checked her schedule. "Yes, Ma'am, I believe I am." She waved to someone in the back of the classroom.

"Kindly share with us why you weren't here on time. This school has a clear policy on tardiness, Miss …?"

"Begging your pardon, please, I'm Nathalia, Nathalia Ormsby." I think she gave a slight curtsy. "I'm sorry I'm a bit late. Reverend Courage sent for me after my first class. I'm singing a solo with the choir tonight." She handed the teacher a paper. "I've a note from the Reverend excusing my tardiness." Her voice was whispery, like a little child.

"Be seated, Miss Ormsby. Right here, up front."

After algebra, Miss Chichester began the science class by sharing some of her ideas on education with us.

"Ladies, as Dr. Wisdom announced prior to class, I am new to Haviland, having just joined the faculty a week ago. Yes, Miss, what is it?"

The unmistakable drone of Evangeline's voice could be heard from my left.

"What happened to Dr. Propper? He was our science teacher last year, and he said he was going to be moving up here with us to Second Year Science."

"I'm sure I've no idea. The reason behind Dr. Propper's departure was not made known to me. Now, as I was explaining, while many find my method of teaching science unorthodox, I believe that the study of biology must be done among living things."

"Where are we supposed to learn?" asked Evangeline.

"We are going to conduct our studies outdoors, where we can observe plant and animal life up close in their natural environment. We'll take field notes and bring our data back here to the laboratory to analyze. You will be expected to dress for the weather, with adequate footwear and clothing suited for the out … yes, what is it?"

"But what if it should rain? We're liable to catch cold."

"Nonsense. Weather has nothing to do with disease. Germs that are spread in confined areas cause sickness. Therefore, you're at far less risk of catching a cold outdoors than when you're cooped up inside this classroom. We'll review the process of scientific analysis for the first few weeks of school, and begin conducting our stream study at the end of the month."

I was sorry to hear the bell ring at the end of the hour. My schedule told me it was time for lunch. At my previous school, the students simply opened their lunch pails and ate at their desks. Students who lived close to the school went home for lunch. I didn't know what to do, so I just followed Evangeline down the hallway.

I sucked in my breath when I entered what looked like a banquet hall. Rows of rectangular tables, covered in white linen, were graced with vases of chrysanthemums. Sunlight flooded through tall, grated windows draped in heavy gold portieres.

Students paired off, dropping books to claim seats at tables. I got on a line that was forming at the far end of the room. Older women wearing headscarves and white aprons served dishes of pork chops with sauerkraut, applesauce, and potato pancakes. My mouth watered at a tray of ripe peaches.

None of the girls on the line were carrying any money.

"Um, how do you buy lunch?" I asked a girl in front of me on line.

"Oh, you're one of the new girls. Meals come with your room and board. "Just give the clerk your name."

I thanked her and looked for any sign of Florence. It was impossible to spot her as everyone was dressed the same. Several girls from my algebra class were seated together, so I took a deep breath, and approached the group. There was just enough of a space between the last girl seated and the wall.

"Um, is anyone sitting here?"

No one answered, so I squeezed into the small space.

"Violet Crane fell out of a biplane!" Evangeline jammed herself in on the bench, forcing me flat against the wall. She leaned her head in and tried to lower her voice, spraying chunks of pork chop all over everybody.

"Who's Violet Crane?" asked an anemic looking girl with mousy, lank hair, who sat across from me.

"She was a student here. She ..." I started.

"Try to pay attention, Mary Agnes, for once in your life!" So this poor soul was Evangeline's sister. If they were twins, they looked like polar opposites.

"Violet Crane. She wrote for *Sage and Lavender*. I told you already on the lunch line, for Pete's sake!"

"I forgot. Sorry."

When the bell rang, I was once again able to disappear among the column of girls leaving the dining hall. A silent army of kitchen staff scraped the dirty dishes that had not been returned to the used tray window. I saw a tired looking worker removing the pits from discarded peaches, and tossing them into a barrel clearly marked with the sign, "*Toss your peach pits here. Peach pits are used to make filters for our soldier's gas masks.*"

I dug into the soft flesh of the peach on my plate, removed the pit and dumped it in the barrel. I took the wet cloth offered to me by the worker.

"Thanks," she said.

I looked at the sign. "My brothers are over there."

❖

When I arrived at English class, there was an older teacher tearfully consoling a group of students at her desk. "She was a lovely girl and a gifted writer. Pray for her family, ladies." I took a seat while she composed herself.

"Welcome, ladies. I'm Mrs. Westcott. While the second year English curriculum requires that we cover rhetoric, diction, and figures of speech, I've discovered an exciting way we can explore thematic writing this year. Let's write about issues that strike a fire in our hearts. Our first theme will be courage in the face of adversity. Write from your heart, ladies. Write about a cause or a subject you feel passionate about."

I knew instantly I was going to write about Alice Paul, Lucy Burns, and all the suffragettes who had braved picket lines in freezing weather last winter to try and convince President Wilson to give the vote to women. Maybe I could also write about the shirtwaist factory workers who picketed for a union and fair wages. If they didn't face adversity, I couldn't say who did.

"I'd like you now to pair up with a peer editor. You will exchange papers with your peer editor each Friday, and perform some editing and revising for your partner. When your work is at its very best, we'll share our essays at a writers' tea at the end of each month. We'll create our own writing community here at Haviland!"

I looked around, but it seemed as if everyone had already paired up. Then I saw Nathalia Ormsby leaving poor Mary Agnes alone and walking towards me.

"Do you want to work together?" she asked.

I agreed, shocked.

True to her word, Mrs. Westcott told us to close our textbooks 15 minutes before English class was over. My pen flew across the page. Nathalia was tapping her pen against her paper, splattering dots of black ink across the page.

"So you survived the first day!" Evangeline had sauerkraut wedged in her teeth. "Come on, you're bound to lose your way back to the dorms."

The late summer gardens were awash with purple asters and goldenrod. A custodian was trimming back ivy bursting with star shaped red flowers that crawled up the side of the dormitory. Tiny baby rabbits darted in and out of patches of pachysandra lining the many walkways on campus.

Once inside, I heard singing.

"That's Nathalia! She asked me to be her peer editor."

"Well, bully for you! See for yourself what a showoff she is."

We approached a door that had been left ajar.

"She does that on purpose so we can all tell her how good she sounds. Miss High and Mighty, that's what I call her."

Nathalia was practicing scales while Reverend Courage played the piano.

"Her voice is so beautiful."

"She gets private vocal lessons because she insists the walk to the studio during harsh weather harms her voice. "Harsh my foot! It's got to be 85 degrees out today."

"I just said she has a nice voice, that's all. Relax, will you?"

I checked my satchel. "Oh, I don't remember. Are we supposed to have a key?"

"You ninny, we don't use keys. We're on the Haviland Honor System! I guess I'll have to tell you everything."

She prattled on about Haviland protocol while I busied myself putting middy blouses and skirts on hangers. After I hung up everything I had brought with me, the chifforobe still looked kind of empty.

"You don't have much, do you? I guess you haven't much use for nice clothes on a farm. I brought a ton of frocks to wear to church services and orations. I suppose I could lend you one if you promise not to ruin it. I'm guessing we are about the same size."

"In a pig's eye, we're the same size!"

" Evangeline took a bag of penny candy from the top drawer of her desk and started popping root beer barrels in her mouth.

"Your mother lets you buy candy with the sugar shortage going one?"

"Father handles loans and mortgages at the bank in the village. Customers these days will pay with anything they have, even sugar!"

I thought to myself that Mam might have to pay off the mortgage in sugar if Da didn't get more customers soon.

I made up my bed with one of Mam's red and white fan print quilts, folding the matching afghan Aunt Bridie crocheted for me at the foot.

"Grandmother had my bedspread specially made up to complement the furniture. See how the floral print has a touch of the mahogany color of the wood?"

"I like mine better."

"Didn't you bring a desk lamp? How're you going to do your homework if you can't see?"

"I'll be working in the library most nights." She certainly didn't need to know that at home I completed my homework by the light of a kerosene lantern.

"What do you think of that uppity Miss Chichester? The airs put on by that woman! "

"I love her! She's my favorite teacher, although Mrs. Westcott is nice, too."

"That's just because you didn't know Dr. Propper. You heard Miss Chichester. She wasn't hired until late August. Something must have happened to him, and Dr. Wisdom had no choice but to hire someone in a hurry. She'll be fired once Dr. Wisdom finds out she plans to have us traipsing outside in the mud in all kinds of weather."

"I can't wait to have science outside. It'll be fun."

❀

It felt so strange getting ready for bed on my first night away from home.

"Can I ask you something?" I fidgeted with my neckerchief.

"The lavatories are down the hall, and you're only allowed ten minutes in the baths. Don't hog them or you'll get a demerit."

"I know where the lavatories are." I hoped I could figure out how to use a flush toilet. "Have you heard anything about the girl who fell out of the airplane?"

Evangeline unscrewed the cap of that revolting complexion cream. "Why, do you know anything? No, of course you don't. Violet was a bookish, quiet thing. I think she tutored girls. Everyone said she was smart, but I didn't see it. I should tutor you in French, but I haven't the time."

"Of course you don't."

"She'd won a prize for an essay she wrote. Of course it was rigged. It should've gone to a senior. But, Mrs. Westcott is the faculty advisor for *Sage and Lavender,* and Violet published a bunch of poems in the magazine, so naturally, I think she was teacher's pet."

"What's '*Sage and Lavender?*'"

"Haviland's literary magazine, silly. Don't you know anything?"

"Violet didn't grow up in Brewster, did she? I've never heard of her."

"I think she came up from the city to live with her cousins when she started at Haviland. My mother plays whist occasionally at their house, although Mrs. Crane, Violet's aunt, leaves a lot to be desired as a hostess. She keeps her dining room draped in heavy damask in the heat of the summer. Can you imagine?"

"Can you imagine eating cold tongue with farm hands at supper?" I thought.

"That new, dark girl is in Violet's room now. I guess she was going to room with Violet, but I can't imagine the Cranes allowing that living arrangement!"

"So, no one knows why Violet went up in the biplane on Monday?"

"You're awful curious all of a sudden, aren't you?'

I practiced Eileen's innocent look to keep her talking.

"From what I've been able to find out, no one knows why on earth Violet would get up at the crack of dawn to go up in an airplane. She kept to herself, so she could've been hiding something. A good student from an upstanding family, so called. Who knows?" She yawned. "We'd better get to bed."

I took my nightshift with me to the baths down the hall so I wouldn't have to undress in front of her. When I returned, Evangeline was snoring as loud as the 5:20 train out of Brewster. I covered my ears with my pillow.

Sleep didn't come for hours. I tried to block out the vision of Violet's dead eyes staring up at me. I felt around my bed for Sullivan, and blinked back tears when I remembered he wasn't there.

This was to be my experience every night during those first weeks at school.

Friday, September 20, 1918.

I dragged myself to French. We'd taken our first test the previous day.

"70! Ugh. You've got to be kidding me."

"*Non*, No, you're showing some improvement, Mademoiselle McKenna. I'm reasonably encouraged by your progress." Madame Primrose gave me a shriveled smile revealing botched dental work. No wonder her teeth clacked. It would be a long haul to get up to speed in French, but I vowed to improve, even if I died trying.

"Now, *jeune filles*, young ladies, take out your homework so I may place a check next to your name in my book."

"*Merci*, Thank you, Mademoiselle McKenna, *tres bien*, very good."

I heard Madame Primrose ask Nathalia for her homework..

"Begging your pardon, Madame Primrose, but might I've just one more day? I promise to have it to you by tomorrow."

"*Non*, No, Mademoiselle Ormsby. You will receive a black mark. It is my policy that homework be completed in a timely manner."

"But, Madame, Reverend Courage has requested that I sing at a special church service tomorrow night to honor the local war dead. He insisted I practice late every night this week! Please, just one more day?"

Now, even I knew that Madame Primrose had recently lost her only nephew. He had been killed fighting with the troops stationed in France.

"Of course, dear. Bless you for doing God's work. You may have another day."

As we filed out of the dining hall after lunch, I caught sight of the dining hall worker with the weary, lined face clearing off what students left on the tables.

Evangeline's tray, heaped with dirty dishes, remained at her place. I grabbed the tray, and took it over to the receptacle.

"That's a first," she said.

❖

I watched the sun set that evening from the entrance to Haviland. I had been waiting for a solid hour alongside Mam's valise bulging with dirty laundry. Christie and the truck were nowhere to be seen. When I realized no one was coming to get me, I started walking.

I had hoped the summer would finally give way to a cool autumn, but the air felt close and sticky. There was still a faint line of hazy pink light slashed across the horizon, so I figured I could use that to guide me home.

As I made my way down toward Seminary Hill, I saw a pair of headlights race up and come to a skidding stop in front of the school. Mary Agnes Sprague jumped out of the automobile, raced by me, and flew up the left staircase to the school.

Evangeline yelled from behind the steering wheel of a Mitchell Six Roadster "You don't deserve to pass French if you can't remember to bring your book home, you dingbat! I declare, you'd forget your head if it wasn't attached."

Mary Agnes pounded on the main doors. "It's no use! It's locked!"

A light went on in one of the windows.

"Hey! There's someone in there!" I made my way to a side entrance near the lit window and knocked. Mary Agnes ran down the stairs and joined me, shouting for someone to open the door.

"What's all the hollering about?" A custodian pointed his wet mop at Mary Agnes, dripping water all over the floor. "Hey, You there. Haven't I caught you sneaking in and out of classrooms after school hours at least a dozen times? What are you up to now?"

Mary Agnes looked panic stricken. I shoved her through a narrow opening in the door as I stalled for time. "Um, excuse me, sir. I'm sorry to bother you, but she left her textbook in school. If she doesn't hand in her homework Monday morning, she'll get a zero."

The custodian's eyebrows descended in skepticism.

"I, uh, I'm sure she'll be back soon." Her rapid footsteps echoed down the empty hallways.

It seemed like she was gone forever.

The custodian checked his pocket watch and started tapping his work boot on the wet floor. "I've got to lock up soon, miss. That friend of yours is here all the time. She needs to tie a string around her finger to help her remember her books."

After what seemed like ages, Mary Agnes appeared at the far end of the hallway. She almost slipped on a puddle next to a bucket, but steadied herself and rushed back out through the front door.

"Good luck with your homework, girlie! Name's Gallagher, by the way." He turned out to be an okay fellow after all.

"Bye, Mr. Gallagher, and thanks for letting us in." I said.

"Why didn't you just use Evangeline's French book?" I asked.

"I don't know." Mary Agnes got into the back seat of the roadster.

"Your luck's going to run out one day, nincompoop." said Evangeline. "Jay, what in Sam Hill are you still doing here? Don't tell me you forgot something too!"

"Are you driving to Brewster?" I was so desperate for a ride home that I'd even put up with another hour of Evangeline.

"Why, yes! Father let me drive his roadster. Isn't it divine?" She unwrapped a full size milk chocolate bar. My mouth watered at the sight of it.

"Could you give me a lift to Brewster Hill?" I couldn't stop staring at the chocolate.

Evangeline's teeth dripped chocolate covered drool. "That's out of my way, and Father will have my head off if I leave the tank low with gas shortages and all. But I can take you as far as the village."

"Thanks. Mary Agnes, don't you want to sit up front?"

"No!" said Evangeline. "She's too annoying!"

She started off toward Brewster. "Jay won the Borden's Scholarship, did you know that Mary Agnes? Mind you, I would've won that award easily, but Mother said Borden's need to give money away to poor people, so I guess that's why they had to pick you."

"No, Evangeline, they picked me because I'm real smart." I imagined what my hands would feel like around her neck.

❋

"You'll have to get out here. We live up on Prospect Street."

"This is fine. I can get a lift home from someone. Thank you."

I crossed the street to Milano's Dressmaking and Milliners to admire the new fall dresses in the window. Seated at a sewing machine, pushing down on the foot levers in a perfect rhythm, was none other than Eileen. I tapped on the glass door. She looked up startled, and quickly shoved some purple satin in a box.

She grinned and slid the deadbolt lock over to let me in. "We're closed, Miss La De Da in your snooty uniform!"

"What are you doing here?"

"I work here! Isn't it divine?" She swept her hand across the front of a buttery silk tea dress.

"What about Mam's sewing jobs?" I fingered the lapel of a military styled jacket.

"I do them at night and on weekends. I answered an ad in *The Courier,* and they hired me! I'm making nice money!"

"But, what about school?"

"I finally convinced Mam I was old enough to leave school. They like me here. Maybe I'll have my own shop someday." Eileen grabbed a bolt of silk and wrapped it around her. "Mam doesn't work with fabric like this. And I'm sick of letting out Mrs. Shove's dresses every season. We have some high class customers in this shop!"

"From Brewster? I doubt that." As if on cue, Mrs. Salmon and Mrs. Harkins, clad in tea dyed housedresses and stained aprons, came waddling down the street.

"Not like them! Sophisticated customers come up on the train to have their winter wardrobes made here."

"Sure they do. I can't believe Mam let you leave school. And I thought you had set your sights on getting married."

"Oh sure, but that's down the road a little bit. I'm putting away a little nest egg so Artie and I can decorate our home real nice."

"Well, if this is what you want, I guess." I tried on a close fitting black hat trimmed with lace cutwork. "It sure is swanky in here."

"Fancy enough for you, Miss Stuck Up Private School?"

"I have the most awful roommate!"

"Good! I want to hear every last detail. Don't leave anything out. Want a cream soda?"

"I'd love one. Oh, Eileen, you wouldn't believe this school. They have electric lights, toilets that flush when you pull on a chain, bathtubs with taps for both hot and cold running water, and everything!" I touched the lacy edge of a petticoat. "Oh, look at this!"

"You're going to wish you had something from here tomorrow night."

"Why?"

"It's Mam's turn to host the Pot Luck for Christie's baseball team."

"Good God, is Henry coming?" I smoothed out the wrinkles in my skirt.

"Of course he is, brainless! Christie has a game against Katonah, and Mam said the team can go swimming after the game because it's been so hot. And that means…"

"Henry's going to be swimming at our house!" I cursed myself for eating an ice cream sundae every day for lunch these past few weeks.

"Yup, and Artie too!"

"Oh, lovely, wouldn't want to leave him out." I cringed at my sweaty shirt-waist. "Can I please borrow that green print dress of yours, you know, the one you admitted looks better on me?"

"I never said that!"

The train whistle signaled its arrival in the depot down the street.

"Yes you did!" I shouted as the train screeched to a halt.

"If I did, I was only trying to spare your feelings."

"You've never tried to spare my feelings! Oh, whatever. Please, please can I wear it, just this once? I'll wash it and iron it, I promise. You never return my clothes, and you have to admit I'm right. Oh, I hope he doesn't like someone else."

"I'd be worried if I were you. Artie's sister told me Cassie Salmon's been all over Henry since you left. She's been telling him you thought you were too good for him, and that's why you went off to your snotty girls' school."

"Well I hope you stuck up for me, at least! You've got to let me wear that dress!"

A rush of weekend visitors spilled out from the train depot and snaked their way through the throng of pedestrians, wagons, and automobiles clogging Main Street.

"Yeah, you better wear that old dress. It's your only hope. Besides, it's way too big on me, except in the chest."

"That's a lie, and you know it."

"Relax, Jay, can't you take a joke? Sheesh!" She handed me a cream soda. "Now, tell me more about that awful school of yours."

I rubbed the cold bottle against my sweaty forehead. I filled Eileen in on Miss Chichester's earrings, Evangeline's obnoxious personality, and Nathalia's voice.

"I should get my ears pierced. What did you find out about Violet Crane? It's all anyone's been talking about around here."

"Nobody can figure out what happened. At least that's what I can tell from eavesdropping. No one really talks to me. Even Evangeline can't ..."

"Did you tell her you saw it?"

"No. I don't trust her. She'd tell everybody I made it up."

"But you didn't make it up, goofy! There's no way I could keep a secret like that, but you're weird that way. Anyway, I have something you're definitely going to want to see."

She climbed under the sewing machine and grabbed the box with the purple silk.

"This morning, this white Saxon roadster pulled up right in front of the shop. Then, this short, dumpy looking lady got out of the driver's side. I couldn't believe she was driving that gorgeous car. She looked like someone's grandmother!"

"What'd she want?"

"Well, here's where things get interesting. She owns a summer home on Lake Mahopac. Now get a load of this. Turns out she's an advisor to Al Smith. He's running for Governor, you know."

"I know that. He's been in the papers all summer." I spilled some of my drink down the front of my shirt." Don't you read?"

"Shut up and let me finish my story. That's why she came into the shop. Apparently, she has to go to a fundraiser for him in Albany on Monday, and doesn't want to make a trip back to the city in this heat to get a dress she forgot to pack. She asked if I could do a rush order on a dress. Of course I said I would."

"Is that what's in the box? Show me. I bet it's very ..."

"No, the dress is kind of plain. I thought we'd finished when, out of nowhere, she asked me if I was interested in sewing about fifty sashes for her. I asked her what she needed fifty sashes for, and guess what she told me?"

"I've no idea."

She slowly pulled one out from the box. "They're for a Women's Party demonstration in Washington, D. C. at the end of the month! What do you think of that, smarty pants?"

I examined the purple, white and gold sash with the message, "*Votes for Women*," sewn onto the fabric. "She's going to be in a suffrage demonstration? I've wanted to do that for like, forever!"

"A-hah, and guess what else? She's having a Women's Party meeting at her lake house Sunday. She asked if I could deliver the dress to the meeting."

"Eileen, you wouldn't! Not when you know I've wanted to join the suffragettes my whole life."

"Relax, Jay, I told her I couldn't get away from the shop. You know I'm not interested in all that junk like you are. I told them I had a date - but my kid sister could make the delivery."

"Oh my God! Really? Wait. How am I going to get Mam and Da to let me go to a Suffrage meeting? And on a Sunday, no less! Who holds a meeting on a Sunday? They'll think I've turned revolutionary."

"You don't have to ask them anything. I lied, of course, and told them I needed to deliver the dress to the house and collect the money. You know how nervous Mam is about anyone doing business with strangers, especially city people. She said you'd drive me to Mahopac Sunday after mass and dinner."

"Drive! I can't believe Christie told on me. Mam's going to kill me."

"She said she's known all along. Had you followed to Borden's every day until she was convinced you drove better than all three boys, even Da."

"Wow! Christie must have been good and mad when she said that. Hope Da heard her too."

"Now listen. All you have to do is drop me off at Artie's Sunday afternoon, and you can deliver the dress and sashes yourself. They're expecting you!"

"Why are you doing all this for me?"

"Because you're going to help me finish these sashes. I promised to have 50 delivered to the meeting. And I get all the money for arranging everything. Agreed?"

"No way! We split 50/50, fair and square, or I'm not sewing one sash! How many do you have left to do?"

"49!"

Chapter 4

"Well, look what the cat dragged in!" Mam wiped her hands on her apron. "I was about to give your supper to the dog."

"Sullivan!" Kneeling down, I scooped up my wiggling dog. When I scratched under his saggy chin, he grunted and sloppily smacked his lips, arching his neck to remind me to scratch there as well.

"Aww, doesn't that feel good boy? I hope you missed me as much as I missed you."

"So you figured you'd stop and visit Eileen on the way home when I've been counting on your help for the Pot Luck, did you?"

"Sorry, Ma." I snuggled Sullivan's square head against my shoulder. "I had to get a ride to the village, and then me and Eileen hitched home."

"Fine thing, my daughters traipsing all over the village. Tongues will be wagging for sure." Mam winced at the meager offerings in the larder. "Thank God people are bringing food tomorrow night, because we've little to spare." She handed me tin buckets to fill with water from the hand pump above the well. "Can I trouble you to heat water for washing, or is that too much to ask?"

I took the kettle off the stove.

"You'll sluice out the cows' stalls and milk them as well, to give poor Christie a break after you drive Eileen to Mahopac on Sunday. Now get going, because there's plenty of work to do."

"OK."

"No grumbling about how tired you are? They're teaching you how to mind your elders in that fancy school, I think."

"Guess so."

❀

"Eileen, Jay, set the trays of hot food down here." Mam shooed mosquitoes away from the picnic table the following evening. I weaved my way through the bustle of mothers setting out covered dishes.

"Another whiskey and water, Jay! Heavy on the whiskey, light on the water." Da was wearing his derby at a ridiculous angle. It was too small for his big, round head.

Mr. Salmon tilted the hat to the side. "You look like Fatty Arbuckle in that hat, McKenna."

In the kitchen, I smoothed Eileen's glorious dress and tried to fix my hair. To save myself extra trips, I brought the whole bottle of whiskey out with a pitcher of water. On my way out to the porch, I literally walked into Evangeline and Mary Agnes Sprague.

"What the …?" I spilled whiskey down the front of the dress. "Great! I'm going to smell like a drunk!" I poured water on the dress to dilute the whiskey. "Now I look like I've wet myself. This is a disaster! What are you doing here?"

"Oh thank heavens it's you!" Sweat poured down Evangeline's face. "We were on our way to visit our cousins on Farm to Market, when the roadster broke down. We saw your last name on the mailbox. Mary Agnes insisted you lived here, and for once, she was right. Mother went ahead earlier, so I must let her know we've been detained." She peered dubiously inside the kitchen window. "I don't suppose you've a telephone?"

"No." Da had refused to install what he referred to as, "that invention," in our home.

Evangeline rolled her eyes. "Well don't just stand there, Mary Agnes. Go find a house with a telephone and call Mother."

"The Salmons have a phone. I'll walk you over." I showed Mary Agnes the shortcut to their house and introduced her to Mrs. Salmon, who was dressing little Nell for Mam's Pot Luck.

"I'll visit with Mrs. Salmon while you make your call." I helped hold Nell still while Mrs. Salmon tied her bonnet.

Mary Agnes picked up the receiver. "No, you go on. I know the way back."

"It's no bother, I'll wait."

"Really, I'm fine. I'll meet you back at the house."

I made my way back. Crickets were calling to each other. I passed Eileen coming out through our kitchen door, her sleeves soaked in dish water. I leaned my head over in the direction of Evangeline, who was helping herself to a dish of peach preserves set out on the table. "She's the roommate I was telling you about."

Evangeline wagged a jelly coated finger at me. "What's with the fancy dress? Are you expecting someone?"

"Oh, just some neighbors visiting. Nobody you know."

"Our brother's baseball team is coming over after their game for a Pot Luck. We'll introduce you to the boys if you want," said Eileen.

"The ... the baseball team is coming to your house?" stuttered Evangeline. "The Brewster Bears are coming here?"

I prayed to God that she and Eileen would be swallowed up into a sinkhole.

"I was just asking because Clarence, uh, I mean, a couple of the boys on the team are my neighbors. It would be nice to catch up."

Mary Agnes returned from the Salmon's house. "Mother said everyone's low on gasoline, so they can't come for us."

"Perfect." The excitement over the night deflated like a pricked balloon. "Come on, I'll make the introductions."

"Pleased to meet you, Mr. McKenna! I'm Evangeline Sprague, Jay's roommate at Haviland. I live up on Prospect. Jay invited me over to visit with some friends on the baseball team."

"God Bless the Mark!" shouted Da. He said that whenever he saw an ugly woman. Luckily, no one understood his meaning, aside from Eileen and me.

"Sprague you say? From the bank?"

Evangeline beamed. "One and the same."

"Huh. One of those crooks at the bank who wouldn't give me a dime towards the ice house. I say to hell with the whole lot of them!" He knocked over his glass. A circle of whiskey spread across Mam's good tablecloth. "Fetch a rag to sop this up!"

"Oh, God! Evangeline, I'm sorry. He doesn't know what he's talking about. Just ignore him." I tried to steer her away from the table, but she wrenched her arm from me and stood her ground.

"I will not ignore him. Father's a fine, upstanding member of the community! You, sir, on the other hand, are a ..."

"Get this big-mouthed lout away from me. We're talking business here, can't you see?"

"Come on Evangeline." I led her over to the table where we were going to eat with the boys.

"Why is your father so rude?"

"It's not worth fighting with him when he's like that. Let's go. The team should be on their way by now."

"*And it won't be over till it's over Over There!*" Eileen sang as she cranked the handle on a gramophone

"Where'd you get that?" I poured some iced tea. Evangeline fanned herself with a napkin.

"Artie swiped it from his granny's parlor. Said she'd never miss it."

"Jeez, you two sound like you're trying to wipe the poor woman out!"

"You sound like an old lady yourself. Why don't you go and knit socks with Artie's granny while I hang out with the boys?"

I ignored her and went back up to the house to try and get the stain out of her dress.

"That's some dress you're wearing," Mam took a stack of dishes from the cabinet. "It's Eileen's, no?"

"She said I could borrow it." The bar of gritty soap broke in half when I scrubbed it against the dress.

"Slop the gutter! Give me that soap before you ruin the fabric." Mam gently rubbed the material until the stain was gone. "I didn't realize Pot Luck Night was an occasion worthy of such fancy attire."

"What do you mean?"

"Make sure the lanterns are out when the boys leave. I hear them coming up the road now. And Jay,"

"Yeah, Mam? "

"The party's over at ten sharp. Make sure Eileen knows that!"

I heard "*K-K-K-Katy*" coming from the gramophone. I peeked out. The entire baseball team was serenading Eileen as they trudged up Brewster

Hill. She ran and jumped into Artie's arms, kissing him all over his face and neck.

"Good God Almighty, Eileen. Control yourself, will you?" Mam hollered out the window. "Jay, go get your sister off of that tinker, will you?"

I hadn't heard a word Mam said. There he was, Henry Harkins, standing with the rest of the team in my backyard. His features made even more perfect with sweat and grime.

Eileen chatted easily with the boys. "This win makes you guys 6 and 0, doesn't it? This is the second time you beat Katonah, and by five runs this time. Who got the homer?"

"That was me." George, Miss Addison's younger brother, played first base. "You sure know a lot about baseball - for a girl, that is."

Artie shoved George off the end of the bench. "Hey, what's the big idea, moving in on my girl?"

"Don't be such a jerk, Artie." I helped George to his feet. "He was just talking to her about the game, for heaven's sake."

Evangeline promptly positioned herself next to Clarence on the bench.

"The Danbury Fair is coming up. You simply must take me Clarence, I insist!"

Ignoring her, Clarence said, "Tonight was Christie's game. He pitched a one hitter!"

"Yeah, but Henry wouldn't let any of those Katonah boys get home!" Christie reenacted Henry's catch at third.

"I had to throw hard to help you catch that runner. He was a fast one!" Artie played shortstop.

"I'm still feeling it!" Henry shook his hand to get the blood circulating.

I struggled to hold Sullivan back from jumping up on the table once everyone had filled their plates with food.

"Anyway," said Evangeline, "I hear there's going to be a Harvest Dance at the Danbury Fair this year. Do you dance, Clarence?"

I choked on my iced tea, because I swear she batted her eyelashes.

Clarence changed his seat. "So Christie, show me where that girl fell out of the plane."

"Never saw anything like it in my whole life. We were standing right here when we saw her fall. The plane landed over there."

Evangeline jumped out of her chair so abruptly her glasses fell off her nose. When she bent over to pick them up, I'm pretty sure I heard a seam rip in her dress.

"You never told me Violet Crane fell to her death on your property!"

"You never asked!"

Christie looked up toward the stone wall. "Jay and Henry found her right up there. Doc Birdsall said she probably broke every bone in her body."

Evangeline was nearing a fit of apoplexy. "You found her, Jay? How could you keep this from me? I swear I'll never ..."

Clarence cut her off. "Has anybody figured out what happened?"

"She was in all of my classes last year at Haviland. And I hear there's an investigation going on. Of course there are rumors flying all over school, but I'm not one to spread gossip. This place gives me the creeps." Evangeline shuddered and moved her chair over to Clarence. "I'm afraid a body is going to land on my head. Can I count on you for a ride home later? I'm rather stranded on this haunted farm."

"Christie's giving me a ride home." Clarence shrugged Evangeline off his shoulder.

"Aw, c'mon, Clarence, invite the little lady to ride home with you." Christie shoved him.

Christie slapped mosquitoes on his arm. "It's getting buggy. Let's go for a dip."

As the boys started for the swimming hole, Henry tripped over a baseball mitt.

"What are you, a half wit like your brother, Harkins?" Artie did an imitation of Ambrose's unsteady gait. "Don't you know how to walk?"

Henry got up, his ears burning an angry red. "Leave him out of this." His face darkened, his voice low.

"Make me, half wit!" Artie shoved Henry.

Eileen screamed as Henry lunged at Artie, knocking him to the ground. Artie covered his face as Henry clenched his fist, pulled his arm back behind his head and punched him in the mouth.

"Get off of me!" Artie yelled.

"Still think I'm a half wit?" Henry continued pummeling his face.

Artie grunted and swore as he tried to push Henry off. They rolled over and over, like two dogs fighting in a cloud of grass, dust, sweat, and blood. Christie came running, and yanked Henry up by the back of his shirt.

"Break it up, you two!"

Henry was panting. He spit grass, wiping the green slime dripping down his chin with the sleeve of his uniform. Dirty black hair hung over his eyes.

"Jeez Louise, Harkins. Can't you take a joke?" Artie's lip was swelling. Eileen held a cloth napkin up to his nose to stop the bleeding.

Come on, guys, knock it off." Clarence stood in between Artie and Henry. "I want to go swimming."

"You're nothing but a couple of big babies!" Eileen said..

"Jay, bring these dishes in, and take Henry with you to clean him up. I'll take care of Artie." She covered his bloodied face with kisses. "Come here baby, and let mama make it all better."

"Sorry about that," said Henry. "Let me give you a hand with those dishes."

"Are you hurt?" His knuckles were scraped and bleeding.

"Na, I'm used it by now. I've had to fight lots of guys on account of Ambrose. I just go crazy when somebody starts on him."

"It must be hard."

Through the window, I was able to make out Henry's parents having coffee and dessert at the table. Mr. Harkins had a droopy black mustache that gave his entire face a morose look. When he took a slug from his coffee cup, I was sure most of what he drank would be dripping from his mustache when he set the cup back down.

"Don't let the door slam." said Mam.

"What have you done to my boy?" Mrs. Harkin's had a high pitched squeal that resembled an angry cat. "Son, come in here and help me with Ambrose."

I deposited the dishes in the sink, fetched some supplies, and found Henry waiting on the porch. He was blowing through a reed he had picked out of the garden.

I poured peroxide over Henry's cuts. It bubbled on the scratches. When I used a cloth to stop it from dripping, my hand brushed against his skin. It felt rough, but warm.

"You don't have to do all this."

"There, you're all set."

"Henry, come in here and get your brother," Mrs. Harkins whined.

I peered through the screen door and saw Ambrose echoing "Henry, come in here and get your brother." He was tapping the tips of his fingers together in a pattern that kept time with his rocking.

"Take Ambrose outside. He doesn't like the noise in here," said Mrs. Harkins.

"Ma, my friends are waiting for me down at the swimming hole."

"Do what your mother says." Mr. Harkins didn't even look up as he pressed down cake crumbs with the tines of his fork.

Henry tried to usher Ambrose out by resting his hand against his brother's back. Ambrose flinched and murmured louder now, "Henry, come in here and get your brother."

I came inside and spoke softly to him, keeping myself at a distance.

"Would you like to come with us to see the cows?"

Ambrose didn't look at me, but started walking toward the door, repeating, "Would you like to come with us to see the cows?"

Henry followed. "I'm sorry. They should've left him home."

"He's fine." I grabbed a lantern, and we made our way up to the barn.

Ambrose stood silently and studied Bridie. Occasionally he would tilt his head to one side, but he didn't rock.

"Aren't you going swimming?" asked Henry.

"I, uh, I don't know. Do you want to?" How was I going to wear my hideous bathing costume in front of Henry? It was one of Eileen's hand me downs, and I looked like a five year old in it.

"Yeah, I want to go swimming with you." He could've asked me to climb Mount Everest and I would've agreed.

"Okay. I'll change and meet you down at the swimming hole in five minutes."

Henry took Ambrose's hand and led him down toward the pond.

❈

A full moon shimmered on the black water, and the night was alive with the boys' hoots and hollers. There was Eileen in the middle of the action, yelping on the rope swing. She hadn't bothered to change into her bathing suit, and her wet underwear left nothing to the imagination.

"Geronimo!" Eileen let go and plunged into the water. Evangeline gushed at Clarence from the water's edge. Mary Agnes stood silently by her side.

"Here goes nothing!" Henry jumped and tucked into a cannonball, creating a huge splash when he landed.

He swam back toward me. "Coming in?"

I could see his teeth, white in the dark.

"Sure, but ..." I looked around.

"What?"

"Where's Ambrose?"

"He's sitting over there on the tire tube waiting for me."

"He's not there!"

Henry was on shore in seconds. The others followed. Each boy grabbed one of the lanterns and headed out in a different direction, calling out Ambrose's name. Sullivan, who had been perfecting his doggy paddle, climbed up on the muddy shore. He shook his stout little body, spraying me with water.

"I'll go tell his parents," said Evangeline.

"No, Evangeline, not yet."

I started off on my own. He wasn't up at the barn, so I kept walking.

A figure up near the stone wall caught my eye. Sullivan gave a warning growl that a stranger was nearby.

"Ambrose!" I came closer, holding out the lantern. His wide set eyes showed recognition.

"Hi. Are you looking for stray cows? They're all back in the barn, I hope."

Ambrose looked down at his cupped hands.

"What have you got there?' I started toward him. He turned his back to me.

"Ambrose, do you have a surprise? I can keep a secret."

He studied at me for a moment, then raised his soft, chubby hands to my face, opening them just enough to reveal a fluttering white moth. His round face lit up with pride.

"It's beautiful Ambrose. You may want to set it free now. It won't live very long if you keep it in your hands."

"Ambrose, get back here!" Henry was running toward us. Startled, Ambrose uncapped his hands, releasing the moth. His lips started to tremble

"I told you to wait for me!" Henry had to look up to reprimand Ambrose, who had several inches on him. "You almost got me in a lot of trouble! What if you got lost like last time?"

His voice softened as he saw his brother's eyes fill up. "It's okay, buddy, just come back with me." He took one of Ambrose's large hands in his own.

"I'm sorry, Jay."

"No harm done. Ambrose caught a moth." We started back.

Eileen ran up to us. "I'll take him back to your mother, Henry, so she knows he's all right," She left us alone.

I walked alongside Henry back to the house. He stopped suddenly. I held my breath.

"Thanks for being so nice to Ambrose. Most people just make fun of him."

He reached for my hand, and held it in his. We stayed there for a few minutes watching the full moon.

"How's the new school?'

"I'm still getting used to it. The only person I really know is Evangeline."

"That's too bad."

"I'm going to try to make a friend this week."

"Good. You can tell me about it next time you come home." Henry gave my hand a little squeeze.

When we arrived back at the house, I spotted Henry's parents following Evangeline. Mrs. Harkins waddled over to Henry, reached up, and cuffed him on the back of the head.

"What's the matter with you, leaving your brother alone by the water? He could've drowned on account of you!" She stood a full foot shorter than Henry..

I shot a look at Evangeline.

"What did you expect me to do? She asked me where Ambrose was."

"Get in the truck," Mr. Harkins growled.

"It's getting late," Mam called to me. "Party's over." She spotted Eileen's wet camisole clinging to her skin. "Mother of Christ, Eileen, get inside and put some clothes on, now!"

"Who's coming with me?" Christie started up our truck. Clarence jumped in the back. Evangeline extend both of her arms up toward Clarence.

"Would you help me up?"

Eileen and I cracked up at the sight of Clarence hauling Evangeline up into the bed of the truck. It took such force she went flying, and landed sprawled on her stomach in the truck bed. Mary Agnes climbed in and sat in a corner by herself.

"I have to change out of these wet clothes," Eileen kissed Artie way too long. "I'll meet up with you later, sweetheart."

"Eileen! Mam said you can't ..."

Mind your own business, Jay!"

Artie's stale breath hit me like a brick wall when he whispered in my ear. "How 'bout I swing by for you later, instead of her, and we'll keep it our little secret?"

I wrenched away from him. "Stay away from me, you slimy little snake!"

"What?" His hair tonic had beaded up on his wet hair.

"I swear to you if you ever ask me that again, you'll live to regret it."

"Is that a threat, sweetheart?"

"That's a promise. And stay away from my sister."

Christie got out of the truck. "What's going on here? Are you coming or not, Hubbard?" He looked over at me. "What's the matter with you?"

"Nothing." I glared at Artie and walked in the house.

❧

"Eileen." The moonlight allowed me to see her slipping a middy blouse over her night shift.

"Go to sleep, Jay."

"Don't go out, please!" I checked my alarm clock. It was one o'clock in the morning.

"Leave me alone!" She was struggling to button her skirt in the dark.

"I have to tell you something."

"What is it, for God's sake? You're going to make me late." She was rubbing way too much rouge on her cheekbones.

"Artie said he wanted to come back for me tonight. He didn't want me to tell you. He's a creep, Eileen."

"You little ..." She threw her shoe at me.

"Hey!" I threw the shoe back at her.

"You're a spiteful little child! How dare you make up such a lie!"

Sullivan yelped from the bed and charged at Eileen, growling.

"Are you that jealous that I'm much prettier than you? Are you trying to get back at me because you have no friends at school except that fat cow Evangeline?"

Sullivan barked and bit Eileen's ankles.

"Keep that mutt away from me!"

"Sullivan's not a mutt, Artie is! I'm not jealous of you! I'm telling you the truth! He's no good!"

Eileen's lipstick looked garish in the moonlight. "Just because your precious little Henry had to go home with his Mommy and Daddy, don't go trying to steal my man." She climbed out the window.

"You don't know anything," I called after her. I opened the box of sash material, and started sewing.

Chapter 5

"Well, thanks to your lies, Artie and I got in a big fight last night."
Eileen was riding shotgun on our way to Lake Mahopac Sunday
afternoon. "Did you at least finish the sashes, Little Miss Troublemaker?"

"Stayed up all night while you were out gallivanting. They're in the box. So,
you two called it quits then?"

"No. We made up. Stop!" There was Artie, leaning against the front of the
Southeast House. "Let me off here."

❊

The house was set back from the road. I sat for a minute after turning off the
engine, and watched the ripples moving across Lake Mahopac in the afternoon
sun. Sullivan jumped down from the truck as I grabbed the dress box and
sashes.

I pushed what I figured was a bell or buzzer on the side of the door, but
nothing happened. It had some kind of Hebrew letters printed on it. I knocked
and called "Hello! I'm here with the Votes for Women sashes!"

The door opened slightly. "Shh, Jay! Don't announce that! The neighbors
will call the sheriff!" Miss Addison from the newspaper poked her head out,
looked around, and ushered me inside to an entryway. I could hear jazz music
playing on a gramophone.

She looked completely different than she did at the newspaper office. Her
bobbed hair was styled in finger waves. A crystal beaded bandeau was tied
across her hairline, and her eyes were rimmed in black liner.

"Miss Addison, you look like Theda Bara. Why don't you wear your hair like that all the time?"

"Folks like your Pa think it's bad enough having a woman run the village newspaper. Imagine if they saw me like this."

"Well, I like it!" I handed over the large box. "Sorry about talking too loud. But we have the vote already in New York. These sashes are for federal suffrage. Why would they get you in trouble?"

"You always ask too many questions, Jay McKenna. A cop lives three houses down, and he's already suspicious about our Women's Party meetings. We've got to keep it down."

"Please don't tell Mam I'm here. She'll have my head."

"My lips are sealed. Now get in here and meet Ruth."

"Uh, I don't know. I've got my dog with me."

"Bring him in. Ruth has two pugs."

"That might be a problem." Sullivan started wriggling in my arms, whimpering to get free.

"Sullivan, stop!" He leapt from my grasp and took off toward the dogs, running over the laps of the women sitting on overstuffed sofas, knocking over a silver tray of canapés on a coffee table.

"Get back here, now!" I took off after him.

A woman smoking a cigarette in a black holder scooped Sullivan up with her free hand. "I've got him!" Sullivan squirmed his way out of her clutch, sending a samovar of tea crashing down upon the parquet floor. The pugs charged him, barking and nipping at his jowls. An all-out fight broke out over an overturned dish of smoked whitefish.

A short, squat woman wearing a frowsy brown dress clapped her hands. "Alice! Lucy! Down girls!"

"I am so very sorry." I grabbed Sullivan and attempted to clean up the remains of the sandwiches, which by now were crushed into a Turkish rug. "I'm Jay McKenna, Eileen's sister. I've brought your dress and the sashes. I'll put my dog out in my truck."

"No, leave him be. The girls in the kitchen can clean this up. I'm Ruth Lefkowitz, by the way." She grabbed one pug under each arm and wiped cream cheese from their pushed in snouts. "They need to run around outside, so they can all get to know each other. You're staying for our meeting, I hope?"

"Well, I, uh, I'd love to, but I don't want to barge in on you."

"Wonderful." She called to two uniformed servants speaking with thick brogues at the far end of an enormous kitchen.

"Kitty, Peggy, please go over the floor with the carpet sweeper."

"Come, Jay I have a few minutes before the start of the meeting. We can let the dogs get some fresh air while we get acquainted."

Sullivan leapt from my arms to join the pugs running across the neatly clipped lawn.

Miss Lefkowitz clapped loudly. "Alice, Lucy, not too close to the water!"

"Did you name your dogs after Alice Paul and Lucy Burns?"

"Yes. Their mommy belongs to Alice. I got first pick of the litter, and I couldn't decide among the two of them, so I took the pair. She laughed as she scooped up one pug and nuzzled it against her face.

"You actually know them!" I couldn't believe I was having this discussion with Al's Smith political about the founders of The National Women's Party. This surely had to be a dream.

"Know them? I went to jail with them!"

"You were arrested with Alice Paul? Did the wardens force feed you in jail?"

Ruth patted her ample girth. "Do I look like I'd have to be force fed?
I stifled a laugh.

"Can I ask you another question? What's that thing on your door?"

"It's a *mezuzah*. You touch it when you enter or leave a Jewish home, kind of like for good luck."

"Oh, okay. I thought it was a doorbell."

"Everybody does."

A pair of swans glided across the lake, which glistened in the late afternoon sun. Six scruffy grey cygnets followed in a single row.

"Hey, are you ready to sit in on our meeting? They're a real lively group, and we're not going to let the senate shoot down the amendment again like they did in June. Kaiser Wilson is going to address them on September 30, and we'll be out in force making sure he states his full support for women's suffrage. That's what the sashes are for."

"Kaiser Wilson as in President Wilson?"

"One and the same."

❖

After the meeting was adjourned, Miss Lefkowitz invited me to take tea with her in the gazebo.

A blue heron swept its wings wide with a whoosh, taking off from the branch of a dead tree half submerged in the lake. It glided through the air until it swooped down to catch a small trout in its beak.

"I wish I was old enough to go to that Women's Land Army Camp at Wellesley College. You know, the one that Miss Addison went to over the summer. I could have helped the farmers while the boys are overseas."

"Let me talk to Edith Diehl. She operated the training station. I know there's a camp in Bedford, not far from here. Maybe we can get you in. I've heard, though, with the war winding down, they might not continue funding the project."

"Thanks. I'd love to help any way I can."

We admired the black outline of a sailboat against the sun, now low in the sky. The dank smell of the lake reminded me of the swimming hole. Water, dark with black grass and algae, lapped against the shore.

"I watched you Jay, during the reports from our members at the meeting. You've got a real fire in your belly for our causes, don't you?" Ruth sipped her tea out of a glass, which seemed kind of odd.

"I couldn't follow everything, but I've always loved to read about women's suffrage, and the rights of factory workers, you know, for decent pay and hours. And I'm interested in the plight of immigrants, and fair housing for the poor, and child protection laws. Mam thinks I'm a communist."

Her big features softened a bit. "You'll have to get used to comments like that if you plan on advocating for women and children. You need a thick skin if you want to promote change."

"I just have a problem with men who bully women, and I want to do something."

"It seems as if you've had some experience with them, Jay. That's a good thing in some ways, for you will encounter many bullies if you decide to pursue a career in social work."

Social Work. I rolled the term around on my tongue a bit, savoring the sound of the words. Ruth gave a name to the passions that did indeed set a fire in my belly. But then again, looking at Henry Harkins had quite the same effect. I blushed, hoping this learned woman did not guess at my indecent longings.

"I'd say the Women's Party would be lucky to have someone with your spunk among its ranks. Say you'll try to make our next meeting, won't you? Margaret Addison or I can pick you up at school and drive you back. And call me Ruth, please."

"I'd like that. I don't think Mam would approve, but okay, Ruth."

Sullivan finally stopped gamboling to lounge in the last of the sun's rays. His fur held the warmth of the day. The time between the cricket chirps slowed down a bit. Dusk was deepening into the last purple and deep indigo slashes of sunset, leaving the lake in semi darkness.

"Mam doesn't want me out with the truck at night, so I'd better go. Thank you. This has been one of the best afternoons of my life, I mean it."

Ruth took my two hands in hers. "I know you mean it. We're going to be good friends."

The pugs followed Sullivan out to the truck. I gave the crank a hard swing down and around with all my might. The engine started on my fourth swing. I rubbed my sore left arm.

"I can't believe you drive! You are certainly a modern young woman, Jay McKenna."

"So are you." I struggled with the gear shift to put the truck in reverse.

"Not so young, I'm afraid. Goodbye, my new friend." Ruth held one of the pugs' paw up and helped it wave to Sullivan on my lap in the truck.

"See you." I turned the headlights on and headed for home.

When I was well away from the house, I realized Ruth was not exactly the kind of friend I had promised Henry I would make, but she could teach me how to live life on my terms.

❊

"Hold on there, girls, I've got to muck this place out before Mam kills me!" I grabbed handfuls of wilted greens from scrap barrels to temporarily pacify the cows while I set down my lantern. Pulling on a pair of muddy boots, I slid the heavy doors open and threw on Christie's flannel shirt hanging on a nail. I picked up a pitchfork and tried not to breathe through my nose as I removed the strong smelling hay from the cow stalls. By the time I finished sluicing out the stalls with buckets of water I hauled up from the well, I was covered in grime, sweat, and manure. Sullivan chased the few chickens we had left out into the yard while I scooped feed from sacks piled along the walls. I got down the milking stool and rinsed the bucket to milk Bridie and the other cows.

I was hauling the filled milk cans out to the ice house when I froze at the sound of raised voices Da was yelling at someone. I ran back inside the barn, closed the door, dimmed the flame in the lamp, and hid behind Bridie. From my hiding place, I recognized the other voice as Christie's. I peeked ever so slightly around the stall to see what was going on. The door slid open, banged against its frame, and flooded the barn with lantern light. Christie stormed in, marching dangerously close to me. I crouched down and tried to make myself as small as possible. There was a tiny slit in Bridie's stall that allowed me to watch everything.

With his chin raised and his arms folded in front of him, Christie maintained a defiant glare. Da ranted furiously, stabbing the pitchfork in a pile of hay.

"It's not enough that I've two sons who might not make it home from this bloody war. You're not satisfied with that. No, you've got to make it three. Have you thought about what this will do to your mother? No, of course not! Do you want your sisters in the fields all day, taking up the slack while you're off playing hero?"

"How can you expect me to stay home with girls while Jimmy Joe and Packy are off fighting? How can I be a man and stay here?"

"You're not a man. You're nothing but a spoiled little boy, hiding behind yer mammy's skirts. They're not even going to let you in."

His face chiseled in stone, Christie produced an envelope. "They already did." He slid his finger across the edge to break the seal and handed Da his enlistment papers.

Feeling sick and dizzy, like when I found Violet, I waited, motionless, until I heard Christie storm out of the barn and start the truck. I poked my head out, but didn't see Da. I ran as quietly as I could back to the house and stood on the porch for a few minutes, trying to regulate my breathing before going inside.

Ma sprinkled some water on my middy blouse. She pressed an iron, hot off the stove, down upon the collar, working out the wrinkles. I stared at her bony frame bent over the supper table. Not even the comforting scent of steam and starch could calm my anxiety. Mom was humming "*Molly Malone,*" blissfully ignorant of the fact that the last of her sons was going off to war.

She looked up. "Jay, you look as if you saw a ghost!"

"I'm fine, just tired from mucking out the stalls."

"Sit down for supper. Mr. Maher from the butcher's sent over this good blood pudding after I made over his daughter's dress."

I closed my eyes, letting everything sink in. We just went through this a year ago when Jimmy Joe and Packy left. The paralyzing fear, the agonizing months between letters, Da snapping at Mam for no reason; I was so sick of it all.

The congealed white spots of fat in the blood pudding made me feel like puking.

Mam filled the kettle and glanced out the window up toward the barn. "Jay, you didn't leave a lantern lit when you finished milking, did you?"

Oh God! Da must still be up there. "No," I whispered.

"Turn the flame off when the water boils, and pour the tea." She lit another lantern, draped her apron across a chair, and went out into the dark.

I sat at the table and attempted to concentrate on my French homework. Mostly I was distracted by the ticking of clock in the parlor. After two hours, the door opened. Christie stumbled in, glassy eyed.

"What are you doing here?" He wobbled toward the icebox, opening it with such force that the door almost fell off the hinges.

"I live here, remember?"

He picked up my plate and started shoveling food down his throat.

"Sit down at least. You're going to choke."

He slumped into a chair and continued cramming food into his mouth. He guarded his plate with his left arm, not bothering to use a knife.

"You eat like a Viking."

"Get me a beer."

"Don't you dare order me around!"

He leaned forward, attempting to rest his chin in his hand. It didn't work. His elbow landed hard against the plate, sending it sliding off the table on to the floor. He swore under his breath and crawled around, trying to pick up the pieces of the broken plate. Sullivan ran over to slop up the spilled food.

"He's going to cut his paws!" I grabbed the broom and swept up the broken pieces. "I heard you fighting."

"What did Mam say?"

"I didn't tell her." I checked Sullivan. "She's up at the barn with Da. How could you do this to her?"

"You don't know anything!" He got up and grabbed the back of the chair to steady himself. "Da tells me I should be more like Jimmy Joe and Packy. Then, when I sign up, he has the nerve to tell me I'm not a man! I'm going to kill me some Germans. That'll show him I'm a bigger man than he is, miserable old cripple!"

"Christie, your papers aren't even legal. You lied about your age, and forged Da's signature."

"What are you saying? I'm not good enough to fight?" He stumbled toward me.

"Sit down before you break something else, for Christ's sake! "Da's not going to let you go through with this. He's going to let the Army know you're underage."

"Shows what you know. Da's not going to do anything because he's never gotten around to becoming a citizen. Mam neither. Last thing they need are the Marines checking into my background. They'll ship them both back to Ireland."

"Really?" Maybe I could turn Da into Immigration myself.

Christie trudged off to his room. I brought the lantern to my room and packed my things for school.

Sometime later, I heard the kitchen door opening. Two pairs of footsteps stormed through the house.

"If you won't stop him, I will! The papers were forged!" Mam flew into Christie's room, dragging him out bed by the back of his neck. I heard a slap, and then Christie howling.

"How could you do something so foolish and deceitful?"

Sullivan rushed out of my room, barking at the noise. I ran after him.

"Josephine, take the dog!"

I grabbed Sullivan and backed into my room, making sure to keep my door open just enough so I could hear everything.

"How can you sit by and listen to Da criticize every blessed thing I do to help keep this farm going? Huh, Mam, did you ever think of standing up to him? No, of course not!"

Da pounded his fist against the wall. "Don't you ever speak to yer mammy like that or I'll give you something to yell about, so help me!"

"I can't do anything right in your eyes! I signed up to get away from you." Christie lowered his voice. "I'm sorry, Ma, but I'm leaving. Da doesn't think I'm a man, and the United States Army wants to make me one. I report to Camp Upton on Long Island in a week."

With that, I heard a chair being pushed from the table, then the kitchen door shutting, probably Christie leaving. I heard another chair pushed back, then another door closing. This time Da, I figured. Everything grew quiet. Satisfied that everything was over for the night, I went to bed. Sullivan snuggled up against my back. A kerosene lamp shining through my open door prevented me from falling asleep. I waited for as long as I could before going out into the kitchen to turn off the flame.

As I stepped out of my doorway, I froze. Someone was crying. I peered around the corner and looked into the kitchen. It wasn't my mother. Da's shoulders heaved. He held his large head in his gnarled hands and sobbed at the table. I had never until this moment saw Da shed a tear, not even when he got the telegram from Ireland letting him know that his mother was dead. The man we all feared looked broken.

Chapter 6

Monday, September 23, 1918

*T*here was still no break in the heat when Christie and I started back to Haviland Monday morning. Sullivan jumped onto my lap after I got behind the wheel.

The sun was just coming up over the mountains. Purple heather growing along the paddock fences mirrored the shades of indigo and lavender painting the morning sky.

I slid forward to set the hand brake and lower the throttle.

"Get that dumb mutt out of this truck." Christie slurped coffee while holding a cold rag to his forehead. "I've got a ton of deliveries to make, and I should be driving."

"You owe me after last night. Give the engine a few cranks while I hold the choke out."

"Girls don't drive," he said. But he did as I told him.

"Release the choke!" he roared, but I already had. The engine sputtered to life. Christie jumped into the passenger seat, cursing.

Sullivan craned his neck to feel the breeze blowing by.

"Well, I guess you won't miss this trip anymore," I said, relaxing my foot a bit on the pedal as the car coasted along the road.

"Nope," he said.

"Are you scared?"

"Nope."

"Have I done something wrong?"

"No. Mam hasn't said a word to me all morning."

"You gave her the shock of her life. You're her favorite, you know that."

A breeze greeted us as we came upon Lake Gleneida. The fish must have been biting this morning for there were rowboats scattered about, lines in the water. I counted ten men fishing along the shore.

Christie tapped the ashes of his cigarette, the wind spreading them all over my skirt. "Well, she's just going to have to get used to the fact that I'm leaving. There's no use trying to stop me."

"Who's going to make the deliveries?"

"What about you, Miss High and Mighty? Why don't you leave your snooty school and help out for once in your life?"

"It's okay if you're a little nervous about leaving, you know."

Christie's hair was that same dull copper color as mine, and his face was ravaged with even more freckles. "You know I'm only pulling your leg when I complain about driving you to school or, rather, sitting here like some bozo watching you drive."

"So you've decided to treat me like a human being now that you're leaving."

"You're really going to have to help out Mam more. Da cut Felix and Ernie's hours. The money's running out, fast. You know that, right?"

"I'm not an idiot. I know how bad things are. No one's going to hire Da. He looks about 100 years old. You know, I get it if you're afraid about leaving home and going overseas, don't you?"

I drove in silence until we pulled up behind my dorm.

Christie looked at me hard as he took the wheel. "I'll deny ever telling you this, but the truth is, I'm scared to death."

❧

Miss Chichester wore a crimson belted jacket over her ankle length skirt. When her back was to us, everyone gasped as we admired the scalloped edges of her back collar. When she stepped out from behind her desk, I saw that she sported a pair of rubber boots muddier than my own.

"Onward to the great outdoors, my fellow biologists!"

We proceeded down to the edge of a wooded area lined with benches. I heard a stream gurgling behind us and made a note to explore it when I had a chance.

Crammed together on the benches, we took out our notebooks and shielded our eyes from the mid-morning sun.

Miss Chichester paced back and forth, commanding as much respect as General Pershing. "We'll conduct our first laboratory activity today. You will each be assigned a lab partner, and together you will be required to turn in a detailed lab report in exactly one week. Time is required in the classroom and outdoors, taking field and observation notes, forming hypotheses, collecting and analyzing data, summarizing results, and drawing conclusions." She took a sheet of paper and held it tightly in her gloved hands against the wind that was starting to blow up from Lake Gleneida. "Listen for your names as I announce the lab partnerships."

I tried to get Nathalia's attention to ask her if she had finished her English essay, but she was talking to Mercy Flanders.

"Helen Starr and Florence Bright," Miss Chichester said. "Start making your way toward the stream to collect your water samples."

Nathalia's friend Helen approached Miss Chichester.

"I can't," she said.

"Excuse me, Miss Starr. What exactly do you mean?"

"I can't be partners with a, a..." Helen motioned at Florence.

No one spoke. Florence maintained steady eye contact with Helen.

"Proceed with extreme caution, Miss Starr," said Miss Chichester.

"I'm sorry, but my parents would be furious with me if I kept company with ... I mean, they wouldn't approve if I ..."

The only sounds were grey doves cooing from the apple trees.

She tilted her head toward Florence. "You know."

"Miss Starr, you will work on this lab alone, and I will be reporting your refusal to collaborate with Miss Bright to Dr. Wisdom."

Miss Chichester rubbed her temples. She returned to the list on her clipboard. "Josephine McKenna."

I walked purposefully toward Florence. "Hi."

Florence's eyes were the color of green sea glass, with bright yellow coronas encircling the pupils.

"Do you have a problem working with a colored girl?"

"No."

"Are you sure? Let me know now so I don't waste my time."

"I don't have a problem."

"All right, then." She took out her notebook. Together we edged as close to edge of the stream as we could, our boots sinking deep into the black mud, and collected water in tin buckets.

"Maybe we should try and scoop up water from the bottom so we can see more under the microscope."

She said nothing.

I scooped up a sample thick with algae. Wordless, Florence did the same. I heard rushing water somewhere downstream where it curved into the forest. Florence picked up the heavy bucket from where I had set it down and carried it back to the classroom.

"Carefully take your stream samples and begin your observations," said Miss Chichester.

We found a lab table for four with two empty stools. When we sat down, the two girls sitting at the table left and found another table.

"Have a nice day, ladies!" said Florence.

I'd never met anyone like her.

"I can't wait to use the microscopes." I gently adjusted the lens at the top until I could see clearly.

Florence squeezed a dropper to release some stream water onto a thin glass slide.

We worked in silence until class ended.

"Uh, Florence, do you think we'd better meet up in the library after class, to work on our lab report?"

She looked at me like I had two heads.

"You're kidding me, right?"

By the time I caught up to her, she was on the lunch line.

"Hey! What do you mean? Don't you think we should work together to get this first lab right?"

"Listen, go find another charity case, will you?" She took silverware, and handed her plate to a dining hall worker ladling chicken and dumplings.

"I don't know what your problem is, but I have to ace this first lab to keep my average up. We've got to do this together so we get everything right!"

Evangeline tugged on my sleeve. "Let's go slowpoke! The food will be all gone by the time you're finished yakking. Hurry up, and save me a seat."

"I'm sitting with Florence."

"Uh, no you're not." Florence had reached end of the line.

"Oh, yes I am!" I followed Florence to a table with a few empty spaces on the benches.

Florence yelled, "Bye, girls!" to the group of students who got up and moved to another table.

"They're just being jerks."

"Listen, I can take care of myself. What are you trying to prove anyway? Buzz off, will you?"

"I don't have anything to prove! I'm just having lunch with you to talk about the lab. Jeez! Why are you being so hostile?"

She looked around the dining hall, and then back at me. "Either you're trying to show off, or you're just plain half baked."

"I don't know what you're talking about. Listen, I don't need this. Just forget it! We're going to get a lousy grade if we don't work together, and it'll be all your fault!" I got up to leave, but she grabbed my arm.

"Sit down. You really don't have a clue, do you? What are you, some kind of hayseed?"

"I must be, because I don't know what you're talking about!"

"Listen, I don't know many white people, but I heard of girls like you, girls who want to show everyone they think black folks are the same as white folks. You don't have to prove anything by sitting with me. Do you have any idea how much trouble you're borrowing, hanging around with the only colored girl at Haviland? Any idea at all?" When she squinted, the space between her eyebrows wrinkled up a little. "Or were you raised on a farm or something?"

"As a matter of fact, I was raised on a farm, if you must know. And even though you think I'm a hayseed, I went to school with a black boy in Brewster. But you don't look like him. Your skin is kind of gold, actually."

"The kids in my old neighborhood used to tease me because I was lighter than everyone. They'd say, 'That Florence Bright, she thinks she's better than everyone else.' I guess the girls at Haviland don't think I'm better than them, though."

"They don't think much of poor farm girls here on scholarship, either. Look, I don't want to borrow trouble. I'm just sick of eating alone."

"Beat it, Josephine McKenna. I don't think you understand what you're signing up for."

"I have nowhere else to sit, and we need to work together on this lab." I scooped up a forkful of chicken. "Where's your old neighborhood?"

She sighed heavily. "Okay, it's your funeral. I'm from Manhattan. My mother's been a cook for this man, Mr. Crane, since before I was born. This summer, one of his sons asked him to come live with his family in Brewster, because he's old and his heart's been acting up. Mr. Crane insisted my mother come with him, cause he's kind of set in his ways. So we moved up here in July."

"Did you say Mr. Crane?"

"Yes."

"Is he related to Violet Crane, the girl who..."

"We were supposed to room together. Our things were all moved in the weekend before school started, and Violet was going to show me around campus, but when. . ."

"I remember on the first day of school, you were following me on your bicycle."

"Mama didn't want to bother the Cranes with driving me, so she told me to just ride one of the bikes. I had forgotten where the school was, so when I saw your uniform, I just followed your truck. How'd you learn how to drive?"

"It's a long story."

A chamber orchestra of three girls set up their music stands in the corner of the dining hall and began to play. The strings sounded mournful. We listened for a few minutes before I started up the conversation again.

"You must be devastated."

"I felt like I was finally starting to get close to Violet before she.... died." She sipped her tea. "She made coming to a new school easier for me. I was so relieved when she invited me to room with her. Now I'm all alone in there."

"Ugh. Did you even want to move up here?" Through the floor to ceiling windows overlooking the lake, I spied a Dieter's bakery wagon broken down on the side of the road. Mr. Dieter was gesturing to a livery man shodding the horse.

"I had no choice. Mr. Crane paid for to me to attend Haviland with his granddaughter, Violet, and he gave Mama a big raise. Anyway, now it's just all so sad with what happened and ..."

"Have Violet's parents been here to collect any of her things?"

"Violet's mother died when she was 11. Her dad's been too preoccupied with other things, I guess, to come for her stuff."

I thought about telling Florence I saw Violet fall, but I decided to wait.

"What was she like?"

"Quiet. Not that I'm a chatterbox or anything, but she was really shy. She stayed to herself. I usually found her holed up in the gazebo on the front lawn writing poetry. She couldn't have been nicer answering all my questions about Haviland, but she never really told me about herself."

"What possessed her to go up in an airplane by herself?"

"I don't know. It doesn't make sense."

We sat quietly for a few moments. I thought about the ring sparkling in the sun on Violet's finger that terrible morning.

When the bell rang, I placed my tray along with some others in the out-stretched wiry arms of the worker with the tired eyes.

"Run along now." Her voice was rough.

After school, I stood in awe of the endless rows of high shelves stacked with books. Rows of low green lamps lit tables where students were studying in groups. I spotted Florence sitting alone at the far end of the library.

"Mind if I join you?"

I took her shrug for a yes.

"What's the silly grin for?"

"I was just thinking of how different this place is from our library in the village. It's above Hickman's butcher shop, and the floors are covered with the sawdust people track up the stairs."

"Hayseed!"

Nathalia came in with Helen and Mercy. They were handing out flyers.

Florence made her voice sound all breathy. "My daddy sent me to private school to get away from people like that."

"You sound exactly like her!"

"I know."

"What's she doing here? She told me she has choir practice every night."

"She's playing you for a fool, girl."

"I'll be right back." I approached Nathalia and tapped her on the shoulder. "Can I speak to you for a minute?"

"I'm kind of busy handing these out for the Liberty Bond Drive. Would you like one?"

"I really need to talk to you right now."

She called to Helen and Mercy. "Apparently there's a fire that needs to be put out! We'll catch up in the dorm, ladies."

I pulled her out into the hallway. "Where's your essay? It's due Friday."

"I've been so busy I haven't had a minute. You're such a good writer, Jay. Be a dear and just write something for me, just this once, please? I'll write yours next month, promise." She tried to kiss me on the cheek, but I pushed her away.

"I'm not doing your work!"

"I don't think it's asking too much when I'm so busy. You do nothing outside school!" She ran off.

"Told you, she's playing you," said Florence.

"You try turning Nathalia Ormsby in for cheating. She's Reverend Courage's prodigal child!"

"Mm hm."

We worked for hours, sharing our parts of the lab report, and then finishing all of our other homework. I tried to rub the fatigue out of my eyes.

Finally, Florence sat back. "You're useless when you start falling asleep, so I guess we'd better stop."

I inhaled the smoky autumn night air as we headed to the dorms. A doe was nibbling on rotten apples that had fallen from a tree. When it sensed us coming, it leapt like a gazelle back into the woods.

Florence walked ahead of me toward the dorm. She hesitated as we approached her room.

"Do you want me to come in with you?"

"Suit yourself." She opened the door to a room much larger than my own. Cold goose bumps rose up on my arms. Against a wall covered in floral print paper was a bed covered in a pink chenille spread, piled high with throw pillows. She switched on the electric lamp sitting atop a nightstand.

"Violet's bed?" I moved slowly inside the door.

"Yes." Florence sat on her own bed, which was covered in a quilt that looked like mine.

A chocolate velvet chaise longue sat against a bare wall.

"Am I allowed to sit on this?"

"It doesn't belong to me." She moved over on her bed. "I don't want anyone accusing me of using Violet's things."

I huddled in beside her on the bed. "Are you ever, uh, a little scared in this big room all yourself?"

"Not really."

We stayed quiet for a bit.

"I wish someone would come for her belongings."

"Do you ever, uh, have trouble falling asleep in here?"

"You get used to it."

"Really?"

"It'll get better once someone comes for all of this." She gestured toward Violet's bed. "Mama says Violet's Aunt Adelaide has her hands full with the little ones, and Dr. Crane's been busy with the investigation."

"The investigation?" Evangeline mentioned something about an investigation at the Pot Luck, but I just figured she was showing off.

"Mama told me Dr. Crane's hired a detective from the city to look into Violet's death."

"Like a murder investigation? Wait until Eileen hears about this!" I wanted so badly to tell Florence what I knew, but it was too soon. I had to gain her trust.

I looked longingly at the set of Louisa Mae Alcott books on top of Violet's desk. "Imagine owning all of them."

"You can look at them if you want. Just put everything back the way you found it."

I spied *Eight Cousins*, the only Alcott book they didn't have at the Brewster Library. I gently took it from its place in the row and admired the cover and red binding.

Some framed pictures caught my eye on the shelves above the books. There was a portrait of a couple I assumed were Violet's parents. Next was a group picture of a solemn girl, about my age, surrounded by children in sailor suits. On her lap sat a stout baby boy with black curls. She was wearing the ring I had seen on her finger in the field past our barn. Her eyes, just like the ones that stared up at me that day, belonged to an old soul, as Mam always said. Florence joined me at the desk.

"This is…" I couldn't even say her name.

"That's Violet. She was a pretty little thing, wasn't she?"

Chapter 7

Friday, September 27, 1918

"Welcome to our September Writing Tea, ladies." Mrs. Westcott's orchid corsage drooped over her ample chest. "Help yourselves to some tea and lady fingers." She bit into a cookie. "My compliments to our fine dining hall staff."

I spotted Nathalia coming through the door with Helen.

"Where's my essay?" I tried to keep my voice down.

"I think you forgot to give it to me. I've looked all over, and I can't find it."

"That's a lie!" I almost grabbed her arm, but something in her icy eyes made me draw my hand back. "Just give me your first draft now. I'll read it fast and try to come up with something."

"Maybe it's back in my room. I'll go look."

"Oh, for the love of Mike, hurry!"

I rifled through my satchel, but all I found was a messy rough draft. My right knee began shaking with nerves. I pressed down on it to stop the tapping noise my foot was making on the floor.

Mrs. Westcott chose Evangeline to go first. She read her lengthy essay, which bought me time to try to invent some editing comments.

"Frankly, I disagreed with every comment my peer editor made," said Evangeline before Mrs. Westcott cut her off.

"Remember, Miss Sprague, we accept feedback with grace. Miss McKenna, may we hear from you now?"

Nathalia returned empty handed.

I tried to read my rough draft aloud, but I couldn't make out half of the words because of all the cross outs. The room fell silent.

"I, um, that is … I think everything, uh, Nathalia told me about my essay was helpful." I sat back down so hard the desk slid a little bit across the floor, making a loud squeaking sound.

"Was there anything specific? It would help us all greatly if you'd share more."

"No, Mrs. Westcott."

"Very well then. I'll take your essay and your checklists."

I handed her my wrinkled first draft, covered with ink spots. Her forehead wrinkled in confusion. "This is the draft you wish me to grade, Miss McKenna?"

"Yes, Mrs. Sprague."

"But Miss McKenna, I don't understand. Where are your checklists?"

"Nathalia never gave me anything to edit."

Evangeline whispered something to the girl next to her, probably that I had just committed social suicide.

"Miss Ormsby, can you explain this?"

"I have my essay memorized by heart, every word of it, Mrs. Westcott. I simply repeated it to Jay."

"Really? What did Miss McKenna say that was so enlightening?"

Nathalia stood and cleared her throat. For a minute I thought she was going to sing.

"The most helpful feedback Jay gave me is that I should continue to develop my writing with specific details."

"How am I to grade your essay if I do not have a paper to correct?"

"I must have fallen asleep before I finished. I guess I was just overtired from the extra choir rehearsals."

"But why didn't you edit Miss McKenna's essay?" She held up my horrible draft. "Clearly she needed help."

"Reverend Courage asked me to sing at the veteran's memorial services this weekend. Which meant extra practices."

"Of course, you couldn't refuse Reverend. Get some rest, but please, hand everything in as soon as possible. Miss McKenna, you should have come to me earlier and let me know Miss Ormsby was unable to edit your paper. You're going to have to stay after class and rewrite this so it's at least legible."

❖

Monday, September 30, 1918

Brewster

Morning sunshine streamed in through the kitchen window. I woke up on the sofa in our parlor. Someone had thrown an afghan over me. Sullivan's tailless body was curled into a black and white ball on top of a half-finished muffler in Mam's knitting basket.

"Get off of that!" I whispered hoarsely, heaving myself up from the sofa. My back ached from crouching in such a narrow space all night. Sullivan was snoring loudly. At my touch, he opened one bloodshot eye in disgust. His ears twitched as I gathered him up in my arms. One ear flopped forward, while the other flopped back. I gently placed him down on my afghan, which had fallen to the floor. As he nestled down into the blanket, his rubbery, mackerel jowls exhaled in bliss.

Why hadn't someone sent me to bed? It took a few seconds for the dull thud of reality to hit me. Christie. Staggering toward the kitchen, I banged my bare foot against the heavy coffee table. My toes throbbed as I made my way to the kitchen window.

The truck was gone. I tried the bedroom doors. Christie's room was empty. I ran outside onto the front porch.

Ma was sitting in her rocking chair with a cup of tea. "We didn't want to wake you. He left on the 5:50 train."

"Did he say anything?"

Ma stared at the activity on the farm. A wood colored rabbit scuttled along the dewy grass, seeking shelter beneath a gooseberry bush. Two grey doves and a striped chipmunk were nibbling on berries and seeds. All were content until a bully squirrel came and chased them away, hogging the feast all for himself.

Deer stared at us from the fields with large, wary eyes.

"He said he already spoke to you." Mam tucked a strand of hair behind her ear. It was stubborn in texture. When did she get so grey? There was even a white patch above her right temple.

That morning in the truck on the way to school, Christie had admitted he was afraid. I didn't know that was going to be our only goodbye.

"How was he?"

"Hard to tell. Feels he has to prove something, I suppose." She sighed. "Anyway, it's all in God's hands now. They're all three in God's hands." She sipped her tea. Her rosary beads rested in her lap. "Get ready for school. There's tea and toast on the stove."

After I dressed, I came outside with my satchel and laundry. Mam remained on the porch, still clad in her wrapper.

I heard horses coming up the drive. Maybe Christie had come to his senses and changed his mind at the last minute. A rig appeared pulled by the sorriest pair of horses I had ever seen. One looked to be at least 25 years old, with rotted teeth and a matted brown coat. The other horse had a visibly hunched back, with a scruffy, beaten down blond coat. They grunted, snorted and whinnied at each other like an old married couple.

Henry snapped the reins and call to the horses, "Come on, Sam, come on, Martha! Only a few more feet!"

"He offered to make the deliveries and bring you to school," said Mam. "Da stacked our rig with the milk and cream deliveries to make before he left for Wasaic with more cows to sell this morning. Tell Henry to rest those ancient horses before they drop dead. Hitch Maisie and Mulligan up to the rig for the trip. Go along now. I'll see you in a few weeks."

Henry settled Sam and Martha up in the barn while I brought our horses out from the stalls.

"Thanks for doing this," I said. "Don't you have your own deliveries to make?"

Henry's father owned the Feed and Supply Store in the village where he worked delivering grain and coal.

"I finished already. There were only three farms that needed feed deliveries today, and with the war shortages, there's hardly any coal to be had anywhere. Anyway, you don't need to thank me. I was all too happy to volunteer."

I felt my cheeks growing hot.

❖

We took off down Brewster Hill as the sun soaked morning deepened the saffron colored leaves on the maples. Maisie and Mulligan held their heads high as they clopped along the dusty road. I swear they knew they had been swapped out to replace the older horses.

"Did you get to say goodbye to Christie before he left?"

"He was gone by the time I woke up."

"That's too bad. How are you doing?" He ran his hand through his thick hair. It didn't work because his long black bangs fell back over one eye, kind of like Sullivan's ears this morning.

"I'm okay. It's just going to be strange coming home to just Eileen, Mam, and Da."

I was sad to see Haviland come into view. As we approached the dorm, the strains of "*Blessed Assurance*" could be heard coming through an open window.

"Who's that?" asked Henry as he hitched the horses to the post.

"Nathalia Ormsby." I stared at her through the window, my stomach knotting up.

"She's got some voice." Henry looked at her a little too long. I hopped up onto the back of the rig and tugged at my laundry bag.

He finally came around. "Here, let me get that for you."

"I don't think men are allowed inside."

"Oh, uh, sure. I understand." He started back toward the rig. "Well, bye then."

"Bye," I said, underwhelmed.

"How about I come and get you next time you come home?"

"Sure." I admired the veins in his arms where he had rolled up his sleeves. "Thank you."

"I'll try to skip out of school early!"

I wanted him to tilt my chin to kiss me like he did on the night of the Pot Luck. His lips had been cold from the swimming hole, but heated up as the kiss lasted.

"Jay?"

I snapped out of it.

"You look nice in that uniform."

"Thanks, Henry." I tucked in my shirtwaist. "I'll see you in a few weeks." I attempted a Mary Pickford sweetheart look, but it came off looking gawky.

"See you then." He guided the horses around and started down toward the lake.

After taking one last breath of the spicy autumn morning, I made my way inside, humming a song Eileen had played on the gramophone.

"Goodness Gracious, Jay, you startled me!" Lydia ripped the sheet she was typing on from the roller. She tossed a pile of papers in a dustbin before clasping her hands.

"I wonder what she's wearing today." I walked with Florence to math and science. "I love the dark green dress with the ivory edging on the cuffs."

Florence ignored me and read over her lab report sections.

Today we were treated to a cream colored shirtwaist with gold trim. While Miss Chichester's skirt was plain grey wool, its length was high enough to reveal suede pumps with criss-cross straps and gold buttons.

"I've graded the lab reports that were due last Monday. Overall, I was pleased. Be sure to carefully read the comments I've made in the margins."

I closed my eyes and turned mine over. I got a 90. "Impressive evidence of collaboration" was written across the top of the cover page.

"Now, please take out the soil study lab reports that were due today. Stand when I approach your lab table."

I stood and solemnly handed mine to her.

"Very well, and now yours, Miss Bright." She took Florence's sections and moved on.

From the row just to our right, Mercy Flanders and Nathalia were summoned to turn in their respective sections.

"Thank you, Miss Flanders, Yes, yes, very well done. Everything seems to be in order. "Now your sections, Miss Ormsby."

"I gave Mercy my sections on Friday before I left for choir practice."

Mercy's lips drained of color."No. You never gave them to me."

Nathalia's breathy voice, still composed, persisted, "I specifically remember handing my sections to you on my way out to meet Reverend Courage. I was in a rush.

"You never gave them to me."

"Perhaps you should check your satchel."

"Don't believe her, Mercy!" I blurted out.

Nathalia's eyes shot daggers into my skin. I checked for wounds in my chest.

"Enough!" ordered Miss Chichester. Her grey eyes were stone. "Miss Ormsby, as of this moment, you've received a zero. You've until the end of the school day to submit your sections for partial credit."

"Begging your pardon Miss Chichester, but if you'd allow me to explain…"

"No excuses. Miss Flanders, you've lost ten points for failing to collaborate with Miss Ormsby"

When would I ever learn to be quiet?

Chapter 8

Thursday, October 17, 1918

Someone was shaking my shoulder. I must have fallen asleep cramming for the French test.

"Get up, you slugabed!" said Evangeline. "You're going to be late for the test."

"What time is it?" I stared at her, groggy and disoriented.

"7:30! Pick your dirty clothes up off the floor right now! You're such a slob!" She abruptly stopped. "What's that racket out in the hall?"

I bolted out of bed, grabbed my wash bucket and opened the door. Stumbling over a pile of empty whisky bottles, I fell face first into a crowd of girls.

"Get out of the way!" Florence pushed her way through the girls. "Help her up."

The whiskey bottles all bore the label of the brand Da drank.

"Oh God, no!" Frantically, I grabbed up the bottles. "Who put these here? Who did this?"

"If this is some kind of joke, Jay, I swear I'll...." Evangeline said.

"You think I did this?"

"Let me through!" Lydia Penny shoved Evangeline out of my way. "Everyone go to class. Now!"

"I demand to know what's going on!" said Evangeline

Lydia's face was stone. "Go to class, now, or I'll charge you with insubordination."

I grabbed as many bottles as I could and ran outside, down to the entrance way, hurling bottles one by one into the bushes, listening to them smash on either side of me.

"Jay! Stop!" Florence and Lydia were running after me.

My lungs were bursting. "Go back! Just leave me alone, please!"

"Fine, be a fool, then!" Florence roared.

I couldn't run any more. Bending over to try and to catch my breath, I realized I was still wearing my wrapper.

Lydia helped me up. "Come back, Jay. We'll help you."

I wiped my eyes. "I can't go back! They'll never ..."

"You have to. Look, you're hurt. You must have cut yourself when you fell."

Blood was trickling down both of my calves, and bits of broken glass were embedded in the heels of my palms.

"You've got to get to the nurse. Come on, we'll take you." Lydia put her arm around my shoulders.

"Florence, you have to go to French for the test. I'll go myself."

"Don't tell me what to do. I can think for myself."

"I'm taking you, and we're going to report this to Dr. Wisdom," Lydia said. "Evangeline has to come as well. We have to find out why someone piled those bottles in front of your door."

"They weren't put there for Evangeline."

"What makes you so sure?" asked Florence

"Because my father drinks that brand of whiskey - all the time."

"A lot of men drink whiskey," Lydia said. "Who would go to the trouble of finding a bunch of empty whiskey bottles just to pile them up in front of your door? Someone could have really gotten hurt, worse than you did."

"I can think of someone," Florence said.

❀

"What is the meaning of showing up late for an examination?" Madame Primrose looked down at my bandaged hands. "And what have you done to yourself?"

"I had a ... uh ... accident, and I had to go to the nurse."

"I will not allow you to disrupt the others who cared enough to arrive on time. You'll have to make up the test on your own time." She pushed her glasses up on her spindly nose.

"Thanks for being so understanding." I stormed away.

"And your impertinent tone just earned you detention this afternoon. You can take the test then.

❊

By the time I finished the blasted test, the dining hall was closed. I sulked as I made my way back to the dorm.

"You've got to learn to hush once in a while, girl. Your sass lands you in hot water all the time." Florence was waiting outside my room for me. She handed me a plate of meatloaf and carrots.

"How'd you manage that?"

"One of the workers in the dining hall asked me where you were. You've been the talk of the school all day."

"Wonderful."

Helen and Mercy slowed down to get a better look at me.

"Something wrong with your eyes?" asked Florence. "That's right, keep on walking."

"You have no fear of anyone, do you?" I let her in my room.

"Nope."

I practically inhaled my dinner.

"Here, you get cranky when your sugar's bad." Florence opened her book satchel handed me a napkin filled with molasses cookies.

"Please don't feel sorry for me. I can handle anything but pity."

"I don't feel sorry for you."

"I think it was unfair of Madame Primrose to punish me just because I had to go to the nurse. And how could anyone here know which brand of whiskey Da drinks?"

"Someone sent you a message."

"For what?"

"Think about it."

"If I knew, I wouldn't be asking, would I?"

"Don't get nasty with me. I'll leave now and never say another word to you."

"Sorry."

"You've crossed Nathalia. You ratted her out to Mrs. Westcott and Miss Chichester. The bottles were a warning for you to keep quiet."

"You're right."

"Of course I'm right." She loosened her neckerchief. "She's thinking she can get away with this because nobody's going to care what happens to girls like you and me."

"Girls like you and me." This was progress. I didn't say anything, though. It was best to let that chip on her shoulder continue to smooth away on its own.

"Do you know what those pearl and garnet rings stand for?" she asked.

"Everybody here wears them, except us."

"They're passed down from mother to daughter. Some of these girls are fourth generation Haviland students. Nathalia's mother gives plenty of money to this school. That girl could shoot a hole clear through the roof and wouldn't receive as much as a day's suspension."

"Violet was wearing one."

"And how would you know that?"

"She had that ring on when she fell out of the plane." Maybe it was fatigue, but I suddenly wanted Florence to know everything.

"Why would you know what she was wearing?"

"Because I found her."

"What the hell are you talking about? Don't you dare play games with me!"

"She fell from the plane on our farm. I saw the whole thing. Her ring was sparkling in the sun. That's how I was able to find her."

Florence stared openmouthed at me for a few moments.

"I can't believe this. Why didn't you tell me earlier?"

"I was afraid you would think I was making it up if I blurted it out when we first met." I grabbed my pillow and hugged it to my chest. "I wanted us to be friends before I said anything."

Florence stayed silent for a few moments.

"Did you, um, I mean, did you get to see her alive?"

"Only when I looked up at the biplane. I saw her climb out of the cabin onto the wing, and I couldn't say for sure whether she fell... or jumped. She wasn't alive when I found her."

"It must have been horrible."

"It was. I've replayed it a million times in my head. Sometimes I dream that she's screaming at me to help her, but when I wake up, I realize it's too late."

"We both have a connection to Violet. It's… What's the word I'm looking for? Surreal."

"It is."

"Dr. Crane's investigator should talk to you, you know, for clues."

"I'll tell him everything I saw."

❀

Friday, October 25, 1918
I pounded on Nathalia's door.

"Stop that banging!" shouted Mercy.

"Where's Nathalia?"

"Calm down and I'll tell you, Jay. She went to the infirmary after choir practice. She hasn't been back since."

I pushed my way inside the room, which was strewn with shirtwaists, nightgowns, and stockings.

"Hey, you can't just barge in here like that!"

"Where's her essay?" I shuffled through papers on Nathalia's desk. All I found was sheet music.

"She didn't tell me anything about her essay. Please leave, now, Jay. I'm editing the last part of Helen's."

"At least you have an essay to edit. I've got nothing!" I snatched the papers atop Mercy's desk. "Helen's essay? Give me a break! These are Nathalia's lab sections! You're doing her work for her!"

"Give me those papers and get out of here! I'm just helping her. If you were her friend, you'd do the same."

"Yeah, right. You're as bad as she is."

❀

My sleep was haunted by images of Mam and Da standing over three coffins draped with American flags. I saw myself apart from my family, looking over a fourth coffin, unadorned, except for the portrait of Violet from Florence's room.

A knock at the door woke me from my night terrors. The room was grey with the dull light of a rainy dawn. My eyes felt gritty.

"Who's there?"

"It's Nathalia. May I come in?"

"Evangeline's sleeping." I grabbed my wrapper. "I'll come out."

She was deathly pale, holding a mustard plaster to her chest. It smelt God-awful.

"I'm sick with the grippe." She coughed. "The nurse has ordered me to bed."

She swayed a little. I reached out to steady her.

"Thanks. I feel so weak. Can I sit down?"

"Come in, but for God's sake, be quiet."

"Nathalia, please tell me you have your essay."

"I haven't been able to sleep all night, Jay!" Tears pooled in her cerulean eyes. "I'm sick, probably from all the pressure."

She convulsed into a wracking coughing fit. "I'm completely exhausted, and now I'm ill. Won't you have a heart and help me, please? You're much better than me at writing."

"Why don't you just quit the choir?"

"Reverend tells me my voice is a gift from God."

"Go to bed, Nathalia. I have to think."

She clenched my arm. "So you'll help me, Jay? Just this once, you'll write my essay for me, won't you? I've told you almost all of it, remember? You took notes."

I shook myself free of her bony grasp. "Get out of here."

When I opened my door, I spied Lydia's typewriter atop the reception desk down the hall. I had only an hour before she reported on duty. I waited until Nathalia disappeared, ghostlike, into her room. Grabbing my English papers, I tiptoed toward the reception desk.

I could barely see in the dark hallway. I gently removed the cover from Lydia's typewriter and lifted it along with a stack of onion skin paper. Great balls of fire, it was heavy! My arms were ready to buckle under its weight when

I finally reached the student lounge. I took out the parts of the essay Nathalia had dictated to me on *"Doing God's Work through Song."*

"Why aren't the keys in alphabetical order?" I pressed down on the key marked with the letter A. It made a very loud "click." This would surely attract attention.

The furnaces hadn't yet been stoked, so the floor felt like ice beneath my bare feet. I thought of Henry delivering coal on this still dark morning, and felt ashamed of what he'd think of me, sneaking around. I was no better than Mercy. I padded down the hall to my room and grabbed my crocheted blanket. Back in the lounge, I threw it over my head to muffle the sound the typewriter keys made when I hit them. Rain began to drum on the roof. I hoped it would help to cover the sound of my crime.

I had pieced together Nathalia's disjointed dictations as best I could when I heard the door open.

"Who's in here?"

Oh Jesus! My heart was beating so hard I swore it was going to rip through my chest. I poked my head out from under the blanket.

"What in heaven's name are you doing under there?" Evangeline lifted the blanket off me. "And what are you doing with Lydia's typewriter? This is a direct violation of the Haviland code. I'm reporting you!" She marched back down the hall.

"No, I can explain!"

She reappeared with Lydia and Miss Avery, the resident director.

"I caught her hiding underneath that blanket like a thief in the night! This is what happens when the school accepts scholarship students!"

"Enough, Miss Sprague." Miss Avery focused her attention on me, still cowering under my blanket. "Miss McKenna, please return Miss Penny's typewriter."

"Jay was just borrowing it," Lydia said. "She told me she needed it to finish up a paper."

"Oh, really?" Evangeline looked over my shoulder. "Then why is she typing an essay on *"Doing God's Work through Song?"* She ripped the paper from the roller. "This is Nathalia Ormsby's paper!" She pointed her finger in my face. "I thought I heard you two talking in our room a little while ago. I figured something fishy was going on. Turns out I was right!"

Lydia stood beside me. "Miss Avery, Nathalia's been taken with the grippe. She's assured me she completed her essay. Jay's just typing it for her. They spoke to me last evening."

"Why not just write it for her, Jay? I smell a rat, and I think you, Lydia Penny, are in on it. Well, Miss Avery, you have your evidence. What are you going to do about it?"

"I said that's enough, Miss Sprague," said Miss Avery. "Miss McKenna, please get dressed and report to Dr. Wisdom's office. Writing another student's paper is a serious offense and must be dealt with accordingly. Miss Penny, you were charged with the responsibility of adhering to the Haviland Honor code. I'm afraid I must report you to Dr. Wisdom as well."

"Why, Evangeline?" I asked as I draped my blanket over my shoulder. "What have I ever done to you?"

"I must uphold the Haviland Honor Code, Jay. There can't be any exceptions, especially from your lot."

❈

Assembled in Dr. Wisdom's office were Mrs. Westcott, Miss Avery, Lydia, and Nathalia, who had perked up considerably since earlier on.

"This is the second time I've met with you within the span of a week, Miss McKenna," Dr. Wisdom's eyeglasses had perfectly round frames. A mustache hovered above her thin upper lip. Eileen knew how to pluck her eyebrows with tweezers, but I didn't think this was the time to suggest Dr. Wisdom try something like that.

"The first time wasn't my fault," I explained. "Someone put those bottles in front of my door on purpose. Know anything about that, Nathalia?"

She whipped up another coughing spasm.

"Be that as it may, Haviland has no tolerance for one student writing another student's paper. I've called Mrs. Westcott and Miss Ormsby in here to make sure I'm hearing all sides of this unfortunate story."

"I've been ill all week," Nathalia said. "I was just too feverish to write my final copy, so I asked Jay to finish the last few lines. It won't happen again, you have my word."

"I see." Mrs. Westcott placed her bifocals at the tip of her nose. "And you can vouch for Miss Ormsby, Miss McKenna, that these are her words, not yours?"

"I certainly will not vouch for her. She asked me this morning to write her essay. Tell them, Nathalia. Let them know the truth, please."

Nathalia collapsed in tears on Mrs. Westcott's lap.

"Miss McKenna, remember yourself, please! This behavior may be commonplace where your people come from, but this is a religious institute of higher learning." Dr. Wisdom offered Nathalia a handkerchief.

I saw how this was going to turn out.

"Very well then. Once you're recovered, Miss Ormsby, I request that you complete your essay with no assistance from Miss McKenna," said Mrs. Westcott. "I must tell you, Dr. Wisdom, that this is the second time Miss Ormsby's essay has been late. However, I'm satisfied with her explanation of how illness prevented her from completing this assignment."

"Thank you. You may go. Miss Ormsby. I wish to speak to Miss McKenna privately for a few moments." Lydia and Miss Avery left as well.

She folded her hands on her massive desk. "You are certainly not off to a very good start here. May I remind you that your tuition is being paid for by the Borden's Company?"

"Yes, I understand, and I'm grateful. However, I'm trying to explain to you that Nathalia has asked me several times to do her work for her. No one seems to believe me. I'm telling the truth."

"Miss McKenna, you should have come to me immediately with this information." She took off her glasses, rubbed her eyes, and shook her head. "I'm afraid you must be held accountable for taking school property and committing forgery. Your parents will be contacted, and I must assign you a one day suspension. You must be off school property today." She checked her desk calendar. "You may return Monday, October 28."

I shook my head. "This isn't fair. I told you she never gave me her essay. Why didn't you suspend Nathalia for lying?" Hot tears slid down my face. "Mercy Flanders wrote Nathalia's lab sections just last night. Why isn't she being suspended?"

"You're blaming students who are not here to defend themselves. You are dismissed. Please send Miss Avery and Miss Penny in here."

"I'm guessing Mercy's parents give money to the school just like Nathalia's. Is that how you dole out punishments here, Dr. Wisdom? Are they on a sliding scale?"

I walked out of her office with every ounce of dignity I could muster.

❄

"I've hidden all mother's collectibles in case you decide to get sticky fingers again." Evangeline lay sprawled across her bed, sucking on horehound drops.

I controlled myself and placed, rather than threw, my hairbrush on the desk. "Evangeline, why do you feel you are above me, or your own sister for that matter?"

"I have to ... "

I put my hand up to stop her. "I know, the Haviland Honor Code. What gives you the right to be both judge and jury to people? My Da may not be a banker, but I'm a human being, and deserve respect as such. You've seen Nathalia pressuring me to do her work. As a new student, I could use a roommate who supports me. Is that in the honor code, Evangeline?"

She popped another horehound drop in her mouth.

"And would it kill you to offer me a candy when you're eating them in front of me?" I threw dirty laundry in my valise, grabbed my book bag, and left. I was a little proud of myself for speaking rationally rather than lashing out at her.

❄

"Take the wheel. I'm so angry I can't see straight." Mam slammed the truck door shut on the passenger side. "When Carrie Salmon told me the school called about you on her telephone, I thought you had come down with the Spanish flu. I warned you to curb your wicked tongue! You've shamed me to no end, Josephine. I didn't raise you to be a thief or a cheat."

"I'm sorry, Mam. Nathalia never wrote her paper, and I ... "

"Spare me your sorry excuses. Things aren't bad enough with the boys gone, and the bills piling up, and I'm terrified Eileen may ... oh never mind..."

"What's happened to Eileen?"

"Nothing, forget it. The minute we get home, young lady, you're to take down the laundry and hang it in the kitchen because there's a storm brewing. After that, peel the vegetables for supper. No complaining. And be sure to confess your sins to Monsignor O'Brien."

"What did Da say?" I cringed.

"I told him you were sick with your monthlies and the school told me I had to bring you home. There's no need to get him started. You just make yourself useful and keep quiet about it."

We were nearing Brewster Hill. The air was thick. A drum roll of thunder marched across the sky, unusual for late October. The edges of a gunmetal cloud were tinted coral. At our backs, a sickly gold sky appeared in the east, poised to battle the storm clouds in the west. The heavens were confused.

Ma shooed me toward the clothesline once I had parked the truck. I tore down as much as I could, snapping clothes pins in half as I pulled on still damp bed sheets. Balancing the laundry basket on my hip, I hurried toward the porch to escape the fat raindrops that were plopping down on my head. Lightning electrified the storm cloud to a luminous white, resembling a full moon. I made out Da standing on the porch each time the lightning flashed.

My heart quickened when I saw his stony face. I ran, taking steps two at a time.

"What's the matter?" There was an ear-splitting crack of thunder. I searched Mam's terrified eyes for a clue as to what was obviously so terribly wrong.

"Did they bring a telegram?" Mam grabbed the papers Da was holding. A fractured bolt of lightning sliced across the horizon, casting a garish pallor of false daylight on her face.

"Two," Da said. "Packy's missing in action. Christie's got the influenza they've been talking about in the newspapers. He just left, for God's sake. He was fine."

The next bolt of lightning tore a silver tear across the sky. The thunder now came in an ear shattering explosion that threatened to split the house in two. I just stood there, the rain soaking my uniform. The storm had arrived.

Chapter 9

Sunday, October 27, 1918

I awoke to the sound of someone vomiting.

"Evangeline? Are you throwing up?"I rubbed my eyes and reached down to touch the black and white mound on top of the quilt. 'Oh, Sullivan, I'm sorry. I thought for a moment I was in the dorm." The storm had washed away the stale air overnight. I opened the window to let in the bracing morning air.

I froze when I heard Da yelling in the kitchen. "You filthy harlot! I knew this would happen with you and that tinker!"

"What's going on?" I jumped up out of bed and ran out to the kitchen. Mam was holding Eileen's hair behind her head as she violently retched into the kitchen sink. Da pushed Mam away. She fell back and landed hard against the table.

"Look at me, you tramp!" He backhanded Eileen across her cheek.

"Da, no! Don't hurt her, please!" I tried pulling him away from her as hard as I could, but his bulky frame wouldn't budge. He hit her again.

"Get him off of me!" Eileen shielded her face with her hands.

"I'll call the sheriff! I mean it, Da!" I was crying now. Sullivan raced out and charged Da, yelping and biting his arms.

"Get this blasted animal away from me, or I'll take it round back and shoot it!"

"You touch that dog, and I'll kill you myself, you bloody eejit!" Mam got up to her feet. "Let go of Eileen, now!"

"Help me, Jay! Eileen screamed.

Mam and I pushed Da with all of our might, sending him flying across the kitchen. I grabbed a frying pan to defend myself.

Da got up, brushed a string of saliva from his mouth, and wrenched the pan from me. "I'll have no Hubbard bastard here to shame us! This one's going off to the nuns, now!" He took Eileen roughly by the arm.

"Leave her be!" Mam screamed. "You're out of your mind!"

"Get out of my way!" He dragged Eileen out to the truck. I ran after him, begging him to let her go.

"Stop him, Jay!" Eileen screamed as Da threw her in the truck. I swung open the door to get her, but Da shut it on my hand.

I cursed, shouting the vilest words I knew until Eileen opened the truck door from the inside. I fell back on the ground, rolling around, swearing and grabbing my crushed fingers.

Da pushed her back into the truck, started the engine and pulled away, spinning dust in his wake. Eileen screamed my name, pounding on the sides of the truck bed.

"Follow them!" I ran halfway down Brewster Hill when I heard a cry from behind. Mam lay sprawled in the road. I stopped and went to her.

"It's no good. They're long gone by now," said Mam as I helped her to her feet.

"Where's he taking her? What's he talking about, the nuns?"

"I've no idea." Mam winced as she tried to bear weight on her right foot. She leaned on me as we started back. "He could've been planning something behind my back, for all we know." Her voice broke. "I've suspected Eileen's been with child for some time now."

"Oh Christ! Foolish girl! I told her Artie was no good!"

"Don't take the lord's name in vain, Josephine. I've heard her getting sick all hours of the night, running to the outhouse, eating like a bird."

I heard horses coming up behind us.

"Truck broke down?" Henry pulled in the reins and slowed his rig to a stop.

"Thank God you're here! Mam tripped. I think she's sprained her ankle."

He jumped down and helped Mam up onto the bench.

"Hey, what happened to your hand?" He grabbed it, and I cried out in pain.

He pulled me up by my good hand. "What's going on here? You better have Doc Birdsall take a look at that. I think you broke your hand."

"Da took Eileen ..."

Ma cut me off. "Mr. McKenna took Eileen with him to sell some cows, and wouldn't you know, one of the calves left behind wandered off. Jay and I have been looking for her everywhere. I'm afraid we're a little worse for the wear." She shot me a warning look.

Henry snapped the reins on poor old George and Martha. "I'll get you to Doc's in a two shakes of a lamb's tail."

"You need to catch up with Da's truck, please!" I kept my voice low to avoid another look from Mam. "Just cut him off in the road and grab Eileen. We'll get a ride home from Doc's."

❀

"No broken bones for either of you." Doc Birdsall bandaged my swollen hand. "Badly sprained ankle for you, Mrs. McKenna. You'll need to stay off it for a week at best. And you, Miss Jay, have some severely bruised fingers. Ice them to keep the swelling down."

"What do we owe you, Doc?" Mam leaned on my arm to stand. "I've no money on me, but when Mr. McKenna comes home, I'll send him over."

"I know you will, Mrs. McKenna. Might you give us a minute while I have a word with Jay?"

"Why would you need to speak to my daughter alone? There's nothing you can say to her that you can't say to me."

"Please, Mrs. McKenna? Just for a moment."

Ma stared at me, hard. "Be quick about it, Josephine."

Doc shut the door behind Mam.

"Everything all right at home?" His eyes were light like Nathalia's. His, though, held not malice, but wisdom.

"Sure, why?" I fidgeted with the end of my bandage that was already unraveling.

"Where's your pa?"

"He's gone off to bring Eileen to the nuns." There. I said it.

"Your sister with child?"

"Who told you that?" Jeez, did everyone know but me?

"Doesn't matter. Did your pa close the truck door on your hand, Jay?"

Through the window I could see Mam with her ear pressed against the door.

"I'm worried about your ma. Once you're back at school, she'll have no one to protect her from him. She have any kin she can stay with?"

"Aunt Bridie lives down the city, but Mam's too stubborn to ask for help. I don't even know if I should go back to school."

"You'd break your mam's heart if you don't go back. It's all she lives for." He washed his hands with carbolic soap. "And you can't stay with your pa now, seeing what he's done to you."

"I need to find Eileen. Where could he have taken her?"

"I'll make some phone calls. I'll send word to your mam when I find out."

"Thanks, Doc." I went to the door.

"You tell your mam I'll be by to check up on her from time to time. And tell her to call on me if there's trouble at your house." He handed me his business card.

I went outside to find Henry pulling the horses up alongside Doc's office.

"They're long gone," He whispered in my ear. "I couldn't catch up to any truck driving these two." He nodded at the two old horses. "I put the word out to look for the McKenna truck."

Henry gently held my swollen fingers while he guided Sam and Martha with his free hand. He carried Mam into the house.

"I'll be by for you later. You should sleep at school tonight."

I went to the icebox. My fingers had swelled up to twice their normal size.

"Airing our dirty laundry in front of strangers." Mam packed my fingers in ice. "The nerve of you!"

"Doc already heard about Eileen, He knew it was Da who shut the truck door on my hand. He's a doctor, for heaven's sake." My fingers started throbbing as the icy coldness bit into them. I cradled them in my good hand. "Besides, Mam, he's going to find out where Da brought Eileen."

"God, I hope he can bring our Eileen home to us." Mam rested her ankle on a kitchen chair as she kneaded some bread dough. "Headstrong girl, she's gone and gotten herself into some kettle of fish now."

"What are you going to do about Da?"

"What do you propose I do, Miss High and Mighty?" She was pounding the life out of the dough.

"Da's getting worse. He could have killed somebody. Doc Birdsall's worried about you being alone with him."

"Well, tell the good doctor to mind his own beeswax, Josephine. I've managed for twenty two years, haven't I?"

"Give me that." I pressed the dough in a bowl and covered it with a dish towel to let it rise.

The tense silence during our supper was punctuated only by ticking of the parlor clock and Mam drumming her fingers on the kitchen table. By the time Henry came around to pick me up around four, there was still no sign of Da.

I grabbed my satchel and valise with my left arm. "You'll get word to me if you hear anything about Eileen, or Packy, or Christie, right?"

"You're not coming home either, are you?"

"I'll stay here and help you, Mam. I'll leave school if you want." I tried to put on my school sweater and hat with one hand. "But I won't stay here with Da, and neither should you. You've got to get rid of him or get away. Doc said you ought to go live with Aunt Bridie, and I agree with him. Please write her."

Ma limped over to help me into my sweater. "And give her the satisfaction of being right? Have her pity me? I think not."

"I don't know what you're talking about, but I'm not coming back if he's here."

"Go on then. There's nothing for you around here. I can take care of myself."

❀

"I knew that runaway calf story your mam fed me was a bunch of horse crap." Henry guided the rig through the rustling swirl of russet, maize, and crimson leaves dancing along the shores of Lake Gleneida. I held my good hand in front of my eyes to shield them from the setting sun.

"I'm not going home anymore. I don't like school, but I can't go back into that house if Da's there. I'll never forgive him for taking Eileen away." I allowed myself to cry now that I didn't have to be strong for Mam. "He should be thrown in jail."

Henry moved the reins to his left hand, reached around my back to my shoulder, and pulled me close against him. He played with my curls as I leaned against his chest. I liked the rough feel of his wool jacket against my cheek.

"Word's all over the village about your dad taking Eileen. He won't get away with it."

"Promise me you'll come get me if you hear anything about Eileen, Christie, or Packy." I tore a sheet of paper out of my notebook. "Here's the main office phone number. Just ask them to get me."

"I'll let you know the minute I hear something Scout's honor."

I stopped crying. "Thanks."

"Why don't you like school?"

"Nathalia Ormsby seems hell bent on getting me kicked out. I've been in the headmistress's office twice already, and I detest my French teacher."

"But you made a good friend at school - that girl Florence. You can't give up just because of a few spoiled rich girls. You're made of tougher stuff than them."

"You sound like Eileen."

"If you're not going to come home, can I at least visit you on the weekends? We could go for rides around the lake."

"That'd be great." I took my satchel from him once we pulled up around the back of the dormitory.

"Jay,"

"Yeah?"

He leaned in and kissed me. He smelled like hay, feed, and soap. I wanted to stay there forever.

❊

Monday, October 28, 1918

"Your father did that to you?" Florence and I were listening to a brass and wood-wind quartet above the chatter in the dining hall at breakfast.

"He's gone crazy," I licked some nasty war substitute for maple syrup from my lips. "I tried to stop him from taking Eileen away." My fingers were bruised dark purple.

"He sounds mean. You should get your mama away from him."

"I tried. She's either too proud or too afraid to leave him."

"Probably both."

"I'll bet you have a nice father. He raised you to be confident."

"It's always been just Mama and me."

"I envy you."

The flautist in the quartet started playing a hauntingly beautiful piece. I was mesmerized by the sorrowful yet captivating strains of music. The oboe and French horn players joined her and lowered the music an octave. It was the most exquisite piece I'd ever heard.

"*Pavane, Opus 50*, by Faure," said Florence.

"How do you know that?"

"I know a lot of things."

The music made me feel the spirit of Violet.

❀

Mercy handed in her lab sections to Miss Chichester. Her cheeks and ears were burning red, and she burst into tears. "I didn't want to get caught and end up in trouble like Jay. I'm sorry, Nathalia."

"Be quiet," Nathalia hissed.

"Am I missing something here, ladies?"

"I wonder if I may speak to you privately, Miss Chichester."

Miss Chichester stiffened into a vertical line. "Certainly you may, Miss Ormsby. However, I need your sections of the lab report now."

"That's what I wanted to speak to you about."

Some thick coils of Miss Chichester's hair escaped from their pins. The loose curls softened her angular jaw line. "Either you have your sections or not. If you do not, you receive a zero. Your last report was late and incomplete, Miss Ormsby, as was the one before that."

Her pen violently scratched across the page in her grade book. "You've left me no other choice but to speak to the head of the science department to secure a tutor for you. I'll also be contacting your parents. A fine way to start off the week, indeed, young lady."

"But Miss Chichester, if I could only have an extension…"

"That's quite enough. This partnership has proven ineffective." She scanned the classroom. "From now on, Miss Flanders, you'll be Miss Bright's lab partner. Miss McKenna, you will work with Miss Ormsby."

It felt like someone just pulled my arm out of its socket.

"Miss Chichester, I'll work with Nathalia. Jay can work with Mercy. Would that be all right?" asked Florence.

"No it would certainly not be alright!" said Nathalia.

"Are you afraid the colored girl will turn you in for cheating quicker than any of these white girls?" asked Florence.

"That's enough! All of you! I make the final decisions involving student partnerships. Miss Flanders, I trust you will not have any objections to working with Miss Bright?"

Mercy just made a snotty face.

Florence scrunched up her face, mimicking Mercy.

Outside, Nathalia chatted with Helen while I took measurements of our corn stalks.

Nathalia approached me. "I wonder if you'd mind if I visited the nurse. I'm not a hundred percent yet."

I looked over at Florence working with Mercy. "Sure," I said, jealous as hell.

"If I could just lie down for a little bit, I'm sure I'd feel better, and you seem to be far more experienced than I at measuring corn."

"I am worried, actually. This is too late in the year to be measuring corn growth. This experiment should have been conducted back in …" I stopped when I saw her amused face. "You were just making fun of me, weren't you?"

❧

I plunked my tray down next to Florence's and scowled through most of lunch.

"Go away if you're going to sit there all day like a jellyfish with the miseries. You saw I tried to work with you."

"It's not your fault."

"I know it's not my fault. I just don't feel like looking at your pissy face all day."

"I can still work with you on my lab sections, right?"

"I guess so." She burst out laughing when she saw my horrified reaction.

"What a disaster. I copied my notes for Nathalia. I guess I'll give them to her tomorrow and ..."

"Girl, you're a bigger fool than I even thought."

"What else am I supposed to do?"

"Either tell Miss Chichester everything, or stop wasting my time complaining about Nathalia. If you let her sweet talk you again, you deserve anything you get."

That evening, in the library, I told Florence about Eileen and the telegrams we had received about Christie and Packy.

She gazed at me with those hypnotic green eyes.

"I don't know how you're even functioning here at this ridiculous school, with its cliques and special treatments. I could never be as strong as you."

I didn't know what to say. Florence was the strongest person I knew.

❧

"Oh, why are they making her carry all that by herself?" The elderly dining hall worker was struggling with a stack of trays. No one was helping her as she tried to push open the door with her elbow.

"Those trays go to the girls who get their meals delivered," said Florence. "If you're sick, or busy studying, you can get your meals taken to your room for a dollar."

The worker's bony arms struggled to keep the trays from toppling. I made my way over to her.

A group of students came bursting through the door, sending the worker falling backward. I rushed and grabbed the stack of trays from her hands, but not before she fell. All of her meager weight landed on one arm. I heard a sickening crack.

"Are you hurt?"

"No, it's just my bum back. It gives out sometimes." She wiped her hands on her apron, grimacing with pain.

"Let me help." I placed the trays down on a nearby table. "I'm going up to the dorm. I can deliver them for you." I grabbed at my own bruised fingers. They started throbbing again.

"No, thanks all the same. You've done enough." She was missing a front tooth.

She attempted to pick up the trays, but almost dropped them again. I took them from her. "You better get that wrist looked at by the nurse to make sure it's not broken." I tried to flatten out the palm of my left hand beneath the trays so my poor fingers didn't have to bear any weight.

"Doesn't matter if it's broken or not. If I take time off, they'll replace me with someone younger, and I need the pay. My man was thrown out of work when Borden's closed."

"My Da and Mam, too. How about you tell me where these trays need to be delivered, and the nurse can look at your wrist? Maybe you can get it wrapped up so you can still work."

"If you insist. I'm obliged to you, miss." She handed me a crumpled sheet of paper with some room numbers hastily scrawled on it. "Name's Mrs. Bumford, by the way."

It was a spectacular late October day. My feet swished through piles of butternut colored leaves. The air smelled dank, sharp, and musty, all at the same time.

I had no feeling in my arms once I reached the dorm. The first three girls pressed dollar bills into my hand like they were pennies. I recognized the last room number.

I plunked the heavy tray down on Nathalia's desk.

"Are they making you work for the dining hall as part of your suspension, or do you have to deliver meals because you're here on scholarship?"

"Just helping out a friend. That'll be one dollar, please."

"Of course, and here..." She handed me an impressive stack of papers secured in a portfolio. I glanced at the front page, astonished by what I saw.

"Are these your ... "

"Yes, my sections of the lab report. Look them over to make sure they support what you've done so we get a good grade."

"I, uh, I can't believe, I mean, thank you, Nathalia! I'm still putting together the conclusions section of my report. Mine will be handwritten, though, even though you've typed yours." I just had to get one shot in. "I've got myself into enough trouble with typewriters."

Maybe something was finally going to work out.

❀

Thursday, October 31, 1918

Miss Chichester was explaining our next lab on growing moss when she was interrupted by a tap at the door.

Miss Edna Biddle, the highly efficient yet perpetually nervous school secretary appeared through the paned-glass upper half of the door. Birdlike in stature, she pittered in.

"Sorry, so sorry to interrupt." Her sensibly heeled shoes clicked across the floor. Miss Biddle cleared her throat and pulled up her bifocals from the chain that secured them around her collar. She adjusted them on painful looking indentations across her spindly nose.

"Miss Josephine McKenna?' The secretary's ink-stained hands shook as she read her note.

"Yes?" Had I broken a rule when I had taken the breakfast tray to Nathalia's room? What if I got poor Mrs. Bumford fired?

"Gather your things and come to the office at once, my dear." Miss Biddle held out a shriveled arm to summon me. My knees felt like they might buckle under me.

When her skeletal hand rested on my back, I recoiled from her touch.

Struggling with my book satchel, an impending sense of doom overtook me. Something was very, very wrong. My footsteps, echoing in the hallway, sounded like I was walking through a haunted house on this Halloween day. I heard students chattering away in the dining hall. I longed to join them instead of being led away by this ghoulish crypt keeper. Violet's warning pounded in my head, "Have courage."

When I saw Mam standing in the office, wearing her old crushed black hat, I knew one of my brothers was dead.

Chapter 10

Brewster

I parked the truck in front of St. Luke's and tried to digest this hurricane of loss.

Ma handed me the telegram that had arrived at our house early that morning. I read that Christie had succumbed to influenza, or as it came to be known, The Spanish Flu, which was now ravaging American soldiers.

"They've already put him in the ground, Josephine! They told me trains won't transport flu casualties home." She twisted the handkerchief in her vein-lined hands "He probably got infected on a transport train from Camp Upton to Spartanburg, South Carolina, for final training before his unit shipped out. His lungs filled up with fluid, and he suffocated to death."

"We've got to talk Monsignor O'Brien into giving a memorial mass for your brother Saturday, after Bridie can get here." Mam opened the car door and started over to the rectory.

"Mam, the church isn't holding any services because of the flu."

"Enough about the horrid flu, Josephine!"

We were led into Monsignor O'Brien's office by his busybody secretary, old Gran McCree.

"I'm so sorry for your loss, Mrs. McKenna, and I feel terrible, but the public health laws have prohibited funerals from lasting longer than fifteen minutes," said Monsignor. "There's fear that the corpses of the dead can still spread the disease."

"We've no body to bury! We can't even hold a proper wake! How can we say goodbye to our Christie without a mass?"

Monsignor invited us to take a seat and proceeded to close the door. I watched Gran McCree linger a bit in the hallway, furious that she wouldn't be able to eavesdrop on our misery.

"I'll come to your house and give a blessing for the dead on Saturday. That'll give you time to gather your family and neighbors. If we can't hold a mass in the church, we'll have a service in your home."

"Oh, thank you, Monsignor!" Mam's lip started to tremble. "And you'll stay for supper."

"I'm already breaking the law by attending a public gathering of any kind during this flu outbreak. I'll stay as long as I possibly can."

"I understand, Father. But I have to ask you one more favor. Will you write a letter to help us try to bring Jimmy Joe and Packy home? Won't you give us the chance to mourn as a family?"

I doubted the army would listen to a priest.

"Three sons away serving their country, the youngest one gone up to heaven. I'll write some letters. That's the most I can promise. God be with you."

Monsignor O'Brien knew people. He came from the city. That gave me an idea. I drove home, dreading the next few days. Jack-o-lanterns of all shapes and sizes lined a stone wall along Brewster Hill. Big black crows were pecking at pumpkin seeds through their rigor mortis noses and crooked smiles. There were none of the usual kids dressed as ragamuffins setting bonfires. The Spanish flu prohibited all of that.

If I was driving the truck, it meant Da was home. "When did you let him back in the house?"

"Stevens the cop brought him home yesterday. He was in some kind of fight. Henry drove the car home from the jail." She dabbed at her red eyes with a frayed handkerchief.

"That's great. Fighting and getting thrown in jail at his age. The neighbors must be loving this."

"This isn't the time, Josephine."

I couldn't deal with Da right now. I needed to be alone with the grief that was forcing its way up my throat, threatening to choke me. I pulled the truck around the back of the house.

Sullivan had no idea this day was any different than any other. He greeted me by jumping at least two feet up into the air over and over again, gaining height on each jump. I scooped him up and cuddled him like a baby, caressing the layers of loose skin under his jaw. He wriggled out of my arms to run around. It was at that moment I heard the sickening roar of my father's rage.

"What's all that racket coming from inside the house?" Mam hurried toward the kitchen door.

"Jim McKenna, you may be able to bully my sister, but now you're going to deal with the likes of me!" Aunt Bridie was nose to nose with Da. She outranked him in height, bulk, and freckles.

"What in the hell are you doing here, anyway?" Da's right eyebrow was stitched up, and his eye was swollen almost shut. Someone had finally given him the beating he deserved.

Aunt Bridie blocked Da's way out of the house. I got out of her way, pulling Mam with me.

"Come inside, you poor things! Jim, get out here and bring Jay's bag inside, right now!"

"Why in God's name did you bring that god-awful woman into my house, Nonie?" shouted Da.

"Bridie's here because she's my sister, and her nephew, my son, is dead. Don't start any trouble with her, so help me." Mam's voice was stronger than I had ever heard it in my whole life. Da opened his mouth, shut it, and picked up my satchel. I grabbed it back from him and walked inside.

I put the kettle on and went to my room, with Sullivan at my feet, to listen to the fireworks between Aunt Bridie and Da.

"Where's Eileen? Answer me now, you spineless little excuse for a man!"

"Nonie, get this fat cow out of the house, now!"

"No, Jim. You'll leave before she will." I'd never been prouder of Mam. "Bridie's staying to help me when the mourners start arriving. You took Eileen away, and you drove my beloved son to his death. Bridie's not going anywhere."

Sullivan growled low.

"Nonie, you're a saint for putting up with the likes of him for this long." Bridie took the whistling tea kettle off the burner without using a pot holder, and turned down the flame. "I'll not be leaving you all alone with this eejit!"

"What filthy lies have you been spreading about me, Nonie?" shouted Da.

Sullivan ran out, barking. I followed him.

"Where's my Eileen? Tell me, please Jim." Mam sobbed.

"None of your business, you daft woman!"

Bridie raised the kettle full of boiling water over Da's head. "Just give me a reason." She turned to Mam. "After Christie's service, you're leaving with me to find Eileen. And my hand to God, Jim, you try and stop us, and I'll have the law on you. I swear I will."

Saturday, November 2, 1918

I dreamed vividly of Violet for much of the night. This time, however, the dead girl was comforting me. I heard the song from that day in the dining hall. What did Florence call it? *Pavane, Opus 50.*

I awoke feeling a hazy, dull ache. Something was wrong. I tried to recall what it was. Pulling the quilt over my head, I just wanted to sleep all day. Then I remembered. Christie was dead. I snuggled closer to Sullivan's warm body. I wanted so bad to scream and throw things, but I already heard people coming up from Brewster Hill. I rolled over and saw the plumped pillow and neatly tucked sheet on the other side of the bed.

"Where are you, Eileen? I need you!"

I willed myself out of bed, but the ache just grew stronger. Heaviness consumed me. I felt it in my bones, and saw it in my reflection in the mirror. It was the same ruddy face with the spray of milk chocolate freckles that marched across my nose and cheekbones. I saw the scar across the bridge of my nose from rubbing it too much whenever I had a cold. I saw my puffy lips and my fright-wig hair. All the light had gone out of my eyes.

I emerged from my safe room to face this miserable day. Aunt Bridie, Mrs. Salmon, and Henry's mother had taken charge of the kitchen, which was crammed with baked hams, floral arrangements, and mass cards. I'd grow to detest the smell of gladioli in the coming days.

Mam and Da sat on opposite sides of the parlor. Mam prayed with Monsignor O'Brien. No one was speaking to Da. The brief service commenced with prayers for the dead. Mam and I accepted condolences from just about every family in the village.

Eileen had always been so much better than me in social situations. I made mindless small talk with Cassie Salmon and some other friends from the village school, but it felt different. Some of them gave me polite smiles; others just stared. What had happened to everybody? Where was Henry?

When I spotted Doc Birdsall out on the porch, I was grateful for the chance to escape the oppressive crowd.

"Have you found out where Eileen is yet?"

"I know where she isn't, and that's any convent for unwed mothers in Putnam, Rockland, or Westchester County. I'm calling and writing parishes in the Bronx. I won't give up, Jay, I promise you."

"Ma's leaving with Aunt Bridie to look for Eileen. She probably doesn't even know Christie's dead." I pressed my fingers hard on my eyelids to keep back the tears.

Doc hugged me. "She'll be safe there, Jay. I can't imagine how you're keeping up with your studies." He took my hand examined my fingers, now bruised purple, and yellow. "You're going back to school, right?"

"I don't know." How could I concentrate on French with Christie dead and Eileen missing, pregnant, and alone?

"You've got to go back, Jay. Your pa spent the other night in jail for beating up Artie Hubbard. Almost killed him. The Hubbard's are pressing charges."

"No wonder everybody's looking at me funny. I'll write down Aunt Bridie's address so you can contact Mam if you find Eileen. Just wait here so I can get some paper."

Monsignor O'Brien interrupted us. "I'm sorry, but I have to get back to the rectory before Gran McCree notices I'm gone. Doc, I was wondering, might I get a lift from you into the village?"

"Sure, Father, I was just leaving myself. I'll just say my goodbyes and be back in a few minutes."

"Monsignor, I have to talk to you. Just wait here until I come back out."

I gave Doc the address and addressed the priest. "I need your help. Da took Eileen away, and he won't tell Mam or I where he's brought her, and we're frantic. You see, she's uh, she's going to have a baby, and uh ... "

"I'm not sure you should be telling me these things, child, without your parents' consent, especially at a time like this. You know the church doesn't approve of such ... "

"Just hear me out, Monsignor. I need you to help me find my sister. You came up from the Bronx, so you must know all the parish priests down there. Surely they know where people send girls to have babies, you know, to convents somewhere. Please, I need your help!"

"But you're just a girl, and I have to talk to your parents before I... I have to see what their wishes are."

"I've never missed mass or confession, except now that I'm at school, but I go to Sunday services at Haviland Methodist, and that's close enough, right Father? Anyway, now Mam's leaving, 'cause Da's gone daft, beating up Artie Hubbard, Christie's dead, Packy's missing, and I can't find Eileen, and ..." I started crying, despite biting the insides of my lips until I tasted blood.

"All right, all right, Josephine. Hush now child. Just give me an address at school where I can reach you." Monsignor gave me a handkerchief. It smelled like incense.

"I know something of these, ah, establishments for wayward girls. I'll find out what I can. And I'll pray for your poor mother."

"Thank you, Father."

After he left with Doc Birdsall, I spotted Ambrose, up at the rock wall. He must have wandered off again. I ran up to fetch him.

"Jeez, he was right behind me not five minutes ago!"

Manna from heaven wouldn't have been a more welcome sight. Henry loosened his tie.

"I...I don't know what to say, except that, I'm so sorry about Christie. He was the greatest guy in the world, and a good ballplayer, too."

"I know, Henry. You two were good friends."

"Mam made me stay home to watch Ambrose until service was over. I'm sorry we're late."

Most of the neighbors had gone inside the house for dinner. Henry reached around my back and rested his hand on my shoulder. For a long while he said nothing and let me cry.

"You know I'll do anything for you. Just ask. Please."

"Ma's leaving. She's going to stay with Aunt Bridie so they can look for Eileen down in the city. Doc Birdsall just told me Da spent a night in jail for beating up Artie Hubbard."

"Yeah, I know. Beat him to a pulp."

"Everybody around here is looking at me like we're tinkers. When Mam leaves tomorrow, can you bring me back to school?"

"Jeez, of course I will! I wish I could take you away from all this." He placed his hands on my shoulders. "Folks may be talking about your da, but they don't think of you that way, I swear." He looked down toward the house. "Someday, I'm going to take over my dad's place, and make it my own," He wrapped his arms around my waist and drew me in close to him. "And then you'll never have to worry about anything ever again, I promise. I'll stay with you forever."

I mouthed a silent, "Thank you," into his chest.

We fetched Ambrose and walked back, my hand securely enclosed in Henry's.

"I'll be by tomorrow for you." He kissed me, soft, and long. I tried to commit his perfect face to memory.

That night, I dreamed about Christie gasping for air on a filthy cot amid thousands of other dying men. I saw Packy, horribly disfigured, lying near death, God knows where. I had no idea whether Jimmy Joe, my eldest brother, was, alive or dead. I saw Eileen, abandoned, pregnant, and alone. And always, there was Violet, falling, screaming for help, with no one to catch her fall.

I woke up sometime before dawn. My mind played a cruel trick on me. Christie's face appeared, crystal clear. He was teasing me for crying. It was as if I could reach out and touch him. Here, alone in the dark, the sudden, jolting realization that Christie wouldn't be coming back, ever again, ripped my heart apart and left it in torn, ragged fragments. The dull haze in which I had functioned throughout the last few days was lifting now, leaving me with nothing to buffer my raw pain. I didn't think I could bear it.

Christie was dead. I was terrified by the sorrow that threatened to bury me alive. I started to sob, heaving, gulping, moans, heavy with the weight of suppressed grief. I cried over all the fights we had had; all the times I cursed him and told on him, even when it wasn't his fault. Despite the name calling, he was my brother. I missed him so very much that just the thought of it was pure agony.

❂

Sunday, November 3, 1918

I drove home after dropping Aunt Bridie and Mam off at the train depot.

As crowded as the house felt with all the mourners, it now had an air of eerie silence, punctuated only by Sullivan's snoring and the ticking of the parlor clock.

Da was sitting in the kitchen with his feet propped up inside the oven. The heat eased his rheumatism. Balanced upon his lap was the one meal he knew how to prepare, a fried egg sitting atop a plate of corned beef hash.

I gingerly approached him. "Where's Eileen, Da?"

"Go 'way and leave me alone." He knocked over an empty bottle, sending it rolling across the floor. I stopped it with the toe of my boot.

Sullivan growled low in his sleep.

"Please, Da, everyone is so worried. Tell me where you brought her."

"Don't start with me."

"Doc Birdsall's looking for her. So's Monsignor, and Mam, and Aunt Bridie. Won't you please tell me so I can put everyone's mind at ease? We just want her home."

"Everyone'd do well to mind their own business. A man's got a right to rule his own house."

"No, Da. A man doesn't have the right to crush his daughter's hand in a car door." I showed him the second joints of my fingers, stubby and misshapen. "Or take his children away against their will, like poor Eileen. Or drive them away, like Mam, and Christie." Boldly, I came closer to him. "You're all alone now. I'm begging you, tell me where you brought her."

"All that school's teaching you is disrespect. You'll not be returning. And tell that Harkins boy not to come around here anymore."

"Henry's coming by to bring me back to school any minute." I forced myself not to show the heart stopping fear I felt.

Da stood up and threw his plate across the room. Sullivan started barking, loud and fierce. The hash splattered against the wall as the plate spun around and around on the floor, slowing until it came to a stop. "I said you're staying home!"

"Leave her alone, Mr. McKenna." Henry stood in the frame of the open kitchen door. He ducked a bit when he came inside, just like Christie used to.

"Get your things ready for school, Jay," Henry said.

Da glared at Henry, but Henry glared right back.

"If you step one foot out that door, Jay, don't bother coming back!"

I wasn't afraid anymore. "Goodbye, Da."

Henry picked up my valise and satchel. "Let's go."

Sullivan whimpered and pawed at my shins.

"I can't leave him here!"

"Bring him." Henry shoved his food bowl in my valise. "I'll keep him for you."

"Oh, thank God!" I scooped him up in my arms. "I'm ready, then. Let's go."

❊

I stayed in my dorm room all evening catching up on the assignments I'd missed. It was quiet as everyone had gone home for the weekend for fear of the Spanish flu. When I checked Nathalia's lab sections, I couldn't believe what she had accomplished on her own. They were perfect. Maybe Miss Chichester had finally put the fear of God in her.

Cold weather had arrived while I slept Sunday night. Pulling on heavy wool socks, I padded around the next morning getting ready for class. I guessed I hadn't noticed the last of the shriveled brown leaves falling, for now the trees surrounding Lake Gleneida stood stark and bare as I gazed from my window. Evangeline had gone down to breakfast, so I had the room to myself.

I took my navy Haviland coat down from a thick wooden hanger in the chifforobe. The weight of it surprised me. I ran my fingers down the double breasted brass buttons and across the buckled belt. It looked military. I studied my reflection in the mirror. I was on my own now. I walked to Florence's room to see if she wanted to get breakfast.

"I'm sorry to hear about your brother. How are you doing?"

"It's good to be back, you know, to have a little break from everything. Oh!" I noticed the bare space the moment I entered her room. "Violet's bed is gone!"

"Dr. Crane moved her things out over the weekend. It seems a little empty in here. "

"I'll spend time in here with you every day to keep you company."

"Ugh, every day?"

I threw a pillow at her.

"You're never going to guess who came by this morning."

I couldn't guess.

"Nathalia! She gave me this because she didn't know if you'd be back today. Mrs. Westcott postponed the Writing Celebration on account of your sad news." She handed me Nathalia's essay as well as three completed editing sheets. "I looked it over for you, and it's good."

"This is amazing. She gave me her lab sections, all typed. I looked them over on Saturday night, and they're all perfect. I guess she's finally decided to pull her weight."

❈

"Oh, no, are they making us wear those awful masks, now?" Florence walked with me to French. Nathalia, Helen, and Mercy, along with several other girls, were wearing white masks that covered their noses and mouths. I had seen pictures in the newspapers of people wearing them as protection against Spanish flu germs.

"Oh no, Jay, don't look! Wait outside!" Florence flew down the aisles to my desk, but she was too late.

I was able to read the bold, black uppercase print on the notice nailed to the chair attached to my desk "*INFLUENZA: These premises are under QUARANTINE. No one permitted to enter or exit due to threat of exposure to INFLUENZA by order of the Putnam County Department of Health.*"

"No!" I ripped down the notice.

"Get those masks off, now!" yelled Florence.

"My brother died and was buried a thousand miles from here!" I grabbed at Evangeline's mask. "I'm not contagious!"

"Stop, Jay! Listen, please!" Evangeline removed her mask. "When we saw the sign, and the masks on our desks, we thought the school wanted us to put them on, honestly!"

I stopped, and stared at her.

"We didn't know this was about you. Take the masks off, everyone. This must be some kind of sick prank, like the bottles.

Madame Primrose entered the room and rapped on the chalkboard with a ruler. "Will someone please tell me what is going on?"

❦

Madame Primrose placed my test on my desk "You're making steady progress, Mademoiselle McKenna. I am quite pleased. We'll make a French student of you yet, it appears."

I gave her a snotty face.

"Get over yourself. She's trying, you know," said Florence.

"I can't help it. She could have done more to find out who put the sign on my desk."

"You know who put it there."

"But why? She's doing her work now."

"Wants to keep you on your toes, I guess. She saw an opportunity with your brother dying of the Spanish flu and wanted to take advantage of it. Who knows?"

Later on, in the library, I took out my French test to review the words I had spelled incorrectly. There was an envelope clipped to the last page of my test. I hadn't noticed it in class. I unfolded a sheet of fine stationary embossed with the initials EPE in scrolled print at the top. It read

> *"Dear Miss McKenna,*
>
> *I was saddened to hear of the loss of your brother. I recently lost my dear nephew, Austin, who was killed serving in Europe. I share your pain. May God comfort you during your time of bereavement.*
>
> *With sympathy,*
> *Ellen Eliza Primrose*

"And I was so cold to her in French this morning," I said.

"You were," said Florence.

"I should apologize."

"Just thank her for the note."

I thought about Madame Primrose that night. Did she get to see her grandson's dead body, or was he buried somewhere far from home? Did she feel there was no closure, just a dull aching hole in the pit of her soul that would never heal?

Because that's how I felt.

❧

Monday, November 11, 1918

The Haviland church bells rang out at 11:00. Mrs. Westcott took a note from Miss Biddle. I thought I would throw up in my pencil case if she called my name again.

"The war is over!" said Mrs. Westcott. "Thank the lord! Our boys will be coming home soon!"

Everyone cheered. Some cried. I wished Christie never signed up. Maybe, if they were still alive, Jimmy Joe and Packy might be home soon. At least I had that.

Classes ended early so a hastily arranged patriotic assembly could take place in Ormsby Hall, followed by a prayer service. Dr. Wisdom read aloud to the student body from David Lloyd George's speech in the House of Commons. I found it hard to concentrate on the words - I was wondering what Christie had died for.

❧

Sunday, November 24, 1918

Henry drove Maisie and Mulligan around Lake Gleneida. A thin layer of ice covered the black water, except in coves where ducks and swans swam like it was the middle of summer. I was wrapped in a horse blanket, snuggling Sullivan, who sniffed and licked my face incessantly.

"How'd you get Maisie and Mulligan out from under Da's nose?" I asked. The black branches of pine trees, like charcoal drawings, were etched against the smoky afternoon sun.

"Haven't seen your Daaround for weeks. No one has. I'm just exercising the horses. I think Mr. Salmon has taken over the feeding and the milking."

"Oh poor Bridie, now that she's with calf and all!"

"Don't worry, Jay, I'm keeping an eye on everything for you."

"Thank you. Maybe I should come up and check on things next Saturday. The dorm's empty on weekends now, what with everybody being pulled out of school, 'cause of the flu." Sullivan jumped from my arms and raced alongside the rig, carrying a fallen evergreen branch in his mouth.

"Doc Birdsall says there hasn't been a case in these parts all month."

"That's good news. Has Doc been able to find out anything about Eileen?"

Henry shook his head.

"I didn't think so. Oh, I forgot to tell you. Mam wrote that she heard from Jimmy Joe. Packy's alive! He's in a hospital in France, but she doesn't know how badly he's hurt. That's all the telegram said."

"Glad to hear it. It'll be good to have Packy home. Did you hear Artie Hubbard enlisted? He shipped out last week."

"What a coward. Everyone else is coming home, and he takes off. He probably wanted to get away from Da."

We stopped so Sullivan could jump back up in the rig. He had a dead bird clamped between his jowls.

"Get that thing out of here!" I kicked the poor bird into the road.

"Doc has been in contact with places he knows of in the Bronx, and now he's looking in Connecticut and Manhattan. Do you have any idea where your Da would find a place to send Eileen?"

A flock of geese flew in a lopsided V formation overhead. They called to encourage a straggler until he caught up to his place in the V.

"When he came over from Ireland, I know he moved in with his cousins on the west side of Manhattan."

"I'll tell Doc. Oh, and I have to tell you something else. I was making a bank deposit for Pa, and I saw Felix and Ernie sitting in that saloon on Main Street. They told me your Da let them go."

"That means things must be really bad. Da got them dirt cheap because they're so old."

"I shouldn't have told you that. You'll just worry. Let's change the subject. What's been going on in that snobby school of yours?"

"No one's been eating in the dining hall anymore, because we're all squished together in there, and girls are saying that's how the flu is spread. There's a rumor that the school's going to shut down if anyone gets sick, even though there hasn't been a single case since October ended. Everyone stays away from me, except Florence, because word's got around that I'm contaminated."

"Enough about the flu. Tell me again why you won't spend Thanksgiving at my house this year? My ma said it's okay, and you'd get to spend time with Sullivan…and me." He pulled me in closer to him. His chest felt like a crackling fire does after being out in the cold.

"Your mother didn't like me before everything happened, Henry. I know you're trying to be nice, but I'd ruin her status at her whist club if the members found out I was at your Thanksgiving dinner, what with Eileen pregnant, and Da spending a night in jail."

"I never get to see you anymore. Feels like we're not even a couple anymore." He took his arm from around my shoulders and sat up straight. "Are you going to eat turkey all alone in your room Thursday?"

"Ruth asked me to join her at the Lakeside Inn for Thanksgiving. She wants me to work on some banners. The Women's Party is going to propose an amendment to the constitution allowing women to vote in the next presidential election. Isn't that exciting?"

"Sounds like a great time, you and some old lady eating in a damn restaurant on Thanksgiving." His eyes darkened, and I saw that morose look of Mr. Harkins on his face. This made what I had to tell him next even harder.

"Ruth has to move a lot of her files to her new office in Albany to get ready for Al Smith's inauguration on New Year's Day."

"What does that have to do with you?"

"Well, I've been thinking that if I help Ruth, maybe she could help me find Eileen. I mean I'd be down in the city, and she's got to know plenty of people."

"I suppose so." Henry eyed me suspiciously. "What are you getting at?"

"I don't want to go home for the Christmas break."

"Oh, Jay, no Christmas either?" Henry stopped the rig. "Are you trying to tell me something? Because if you don't want to be with me, just say it! Go down to the city and work on Christmas? Are you crazy?"

"No, Henry, I'd love to spend Christmas with you, but I need to find Eileen. I mean, Mam's taken work making millinery flowers, so she won't have much time off anyway. I'll visit her at Aunt Bridie's, but I don't want to go home, especially with no Christie or Eileen."

"Listen, I got to be getting these horses back before dark. They're getting cold."

"Bye, Henry."

Sullivan whimpered as the rig pulled away from the dormitory, leaving me alone with the navy-blue sky after the sun set. I stood in the cold watching the first star forming. I made a wish. "Please, let Henry wait for me as I try to make my way without a family to speak of. I've got to find Eileen. Please make Henry understand."

Chapter 11

Tuesday, December 10, 1918

I was supposed to be measuring moss growth in science. Instead, I sat mesmerized by the Nor'easter swirling outside the window. Vanilla frosted snow was spread evenly on each step of the double staircase. Bare black tree branches, glistening with ice, swayed gently against a thickening coat of ice on Lake Gleneida. Everything looked soft and dazzling in brilliant white. As clanking radiators hissed steam, the snow was creating sparkling spirals and spheres, transforming Haviland into a Winter Palace. The world became quiet, while billions of snowflakes danced in the biting wind.

"Miss McKenna. Stop by during lunch, would you?"

By the time I knocked on Miss Chichester's door, I had imagined every punishment for my daydreaming, short of Chinese water torture.

"Ah, Miss McKenna, come in."

She took two painted china teacups and a canister of Earl Grey tea out of a cabinet. She lit a gas burner under a stand on which she placed a glass beaker filled with water. "I had to promise my mother before I left South Deerfield that I would still serve a proper tea every afternoon. Sit down, Miss McKenna."

I didn't know where to place my book satchel, so I tried in vain to balance it on my lap. I ended up sitting on top of most of my skirt, so it was pulled too tight across my lap.

"Tea, Miss McKenna?"

"No thank you." I was positive I would scald myself if I tried to hold a cup of hot tea in this position.

"Well then." She was perched gracefully on her stool. I half expected her to raise her pinky as she brought the teacup to her lips.

"I was wondering if you would work with Nathalia in this lab a few mornings each week."

"You're joking, right?" I had to steady myself on the stool for fear of toppling over.

"I am not. I think it would give her time to complete her math homework and science lab reports, at least until after the Christmas Concert is over."

"You want me to tutor Nathalia?"

"Well, yes. I do." She offered me a thin cucumber sandwich with the crusts cut off. "You see, it appears she had a tutorial arrangement in place that has not worked out."

"Begging your pardon, Miss Chichester, but couldn't you find someone else? I got suspended the last time I tried 'helping' Nathalia finish her English essay."

"But Nathalia requested you. She's convinced Mrs. Westcott and I that there will be no more shenanigans involving you doing her work for her. And she does seem to work well with tutors, as her recent lab sections have proven." She took a ladylike bite of a sandwich. "Tutoring would look very good on your record, Miss McKenna, You want your scholarship to stay in place for next year, I'm assuming?"

Defeated, I asked, "When would I have to start working with Nathalia?"

"We could start out with, say, once a week. Let's say, Friday mornings? Could you be here by 7:45 a.m.?"

Friday, December 13, 1918

Friday the thirteenth found me listening to the ticking clock in Miss Chichester's classroom. It was a slow, methodic tick, produced at one second intervals. I multiplied to find that I had endured 2,800 of these ticks by the time Nathalia showed up for our tutoring session.

"We haven't much time before class starts. Let's see what you have." I spread my completed lab sections out on the desk. Nathalia produced some papers from her book satchel.

"These are just the notes I slipped under your door the other day. You were supposed to analyze the moss growth."

"I'm dead tired. Let's just do it now and get it over with."

"I'm not doing your work for you."

"Then what am I doing here? Miss Chichester said you were going to help me."

"I'll help you as much as I can. Just try and do the analysis, tonight, okay? Here, I'll go over the steps with you again."

Of course, this was a complete waste of my time. By Sunday night, I had heard nothing from Nathalia so, once again, I went to her room. The door was answered by Mrs. Keeler, the school nurse.

"Miss Ormsby is weak and needs her rest. She cannot be disturbed."

Back in my room, I analyzed the moss growth myself, and wrote up her results and conclusion. It took me until midnight to finish. Miss Chichester accepted both of our sections without question. I received a 95, my highest grade yet. Nathalia received the same.

"Well done, ladies. You're a truly successful partnership."

Nathalia beamed. I felt hollow.

❖

Wednesday, December 18, 1918

Nathalia sat next to me for the December Writing Celebration.

"May I have my essay, please?"

"You know I don't have your essay."

"But you're supposed to be helping me."

"I did help you. We planned it all out together. I can't do any more of your work. I'll get expelled, for sure."

"You didn't write the October essay. I typed that one myself. Why didn't you tell me earlier you weren't going to help me on this one?"

"And what happens if I don't? Am I going to trip over another pile of whiskey bottles? Or am I going to find an influenza sign nailed to my door? Huh, Nathalia?"

I was shocked to see tears gathering at the edges of her eyes.

"You think I did those things? Why is everyone accusing me? I didn't play either of those pranks. You actually think I would do something that mean?"

Nathalia approached Mrs. Westcott, holding her stomach. I didn't see her for the rest of the day.

❧

Friday, December 20, 1918

Report cards were given out during the last few minutes of school before Christmas vacation. I wanted to read mine in private, so I shoved it in my satchel and hurried back to my dorm room.

There was a knock on my door. It was Ruth.

"Want some help bringing your things out to the car?" she asked.

"Sure, thanks!" I gathered my valise and satchel. Ruth grabbed my laundry bag and led me out toward the Saxon Six Roadster parked behind the dorm.

"Merry Christmas, Jay!" called Lydia from behind her desk.

"Merry Christmas!" I returned as we went outside. "Oh!"

There was Henry with Maisie and Mulligan tied up to the hitching post. The horses' nostrils were blowing clouds of white, steamy breath in the cold air. Sullivan leapt from the rig, racing to me. He jumped up into my arms, licking my face. I nestled my nose into his velvety soft ears, basking in his still puppy scent. My eyes filled with tears. "My baby, I missed you so much!"

Henry came to me, turning his flannel coat collar up against the damp wind blowing off Lake Glencida and looked up at the grey sky. "It's going to snow."

"You never told him?" Ruth whispered from the side of her mouth.

"Henry, I …"

"Come on, stop stalling. Where's your report card?" He grabbed my satchel and rifled through it. "Show me how many A's you got."

"Ruth, I wonder if I could have a minute to …"

" I'll wait in the car." She took my laundry bag.

"Well, go on, open it." He blew on his fingers to warm them.

"All right." I put Sullivan down and slid the sealed envelope open with my fingertip and read the even, cursive penmanship of Dr. Wisdom:

Algebra: 96
English: 84

Social Studies: 88
Science: 94
French: 74
Bible Study: 89
Physical Education: 83

Attendance and Punctuality: Fair. Student arrived tardy to French class on 10/17/18.

Deportment: Poor: Student has been placed on probation for habitual offenses of Haviland Honor Code. Student received a school suspension on 10/25/18 for committing forgery.

"Congratulations, Genius. Too bad about all this stuff at the bottom. These are the kind of messes Christie used to get in." He stopped and touched his gloved hand to his forehead. "Oh God, I'm sorry. That was a dumb thing to say."

"It's okay. I guess it's the McKenna coming out in me. Anyway, all Mam's going to concentrate on is the cursed French grade."

"I wasn't thinking, I swear. I was hoping you'd change your mind about coming home."

"I miss you so much, Henry, but I can't go home to Da." My tears felt like hot razors slicing down my freezing face. "I can't keep you here too long, Henry. Poor Maisie and Mulligan can't stay out here much longer in this cold."

Henry looked away, kicking the hard, frozen stones on the driveway. "I better get the horses back, then." His blue eyes blazed with hurt. "Should I hold onto Sullivan?"

I kissed and snuggled my dog before turning him over. "Don't be mad. Please. Try to understand. I don't want to hurt you, but I have to find Eileen."

"I'm trying." He started back. "Wait a minute."

He ran over to the wagon so Sullivan could jump up onto the seat. He brought back a small package wrapped in brown paper tied with red and green twine. "I wanted to give this to you on Christmas Eve, but…open it now, Jay, please, I want to see if you like it."

I took off my mittens and carefully unwrapped the gift as best as I could with fingers quickly growing stiff from the cold. It was a small book that fit in the palm of my hand. Its title read, *The Golden Treasury Selected from the Best Songs and Lyrical Poems in the English Language*. I held it up to my face and smelled the newness of the leather cover and rich, heavy paper.

"I love it. Thank you."

"Come around here behind the rig. Evangeline is gawking at us through the window."

Henry's lips against mine tasted cold and hot at the same time.

"Will you write me?" Henry took my hand in his.

"Of course I will."

"I'll see you on New Year's then?"

"Goodbye, Henry."

"Goodbye, Jay. Take care of yourself." He tipped his cap at me, and snapped the reins to guide Maisie and Mulligan home. I knew then and there that I would love Henry Harkins until the day I died.

It had started snowing, and by the time we reached the city, it was coming down so heavy, it had knocked out the electricity at Ruth's brownstone on 42nd street off 5th Avenue.

"I can't thank you enough for taking over the driving in this beastly weather, Jay." Ruth struck a match to light the stack of kindling in the hearth. "You, just on the verge of your fifteenth birthday, and already you're better behind the wheel than I am!"

"I wouldn't say that. I almost went off the road a few times when it started getting slick, and we lost time when I had to change a tire and refill the gas tank."

You'll never cease to amaze me, Jay McKenna! You know your way around an automobile as well as any mechanic. Let me show you where you'll be staying so you can change into dry clothes. You look like a snowman!"

"Wait until I tell Eileen I drove a Saxon Six Roadster!" I tore off my snow crusted Haviland coat and hung it over the fireplace grate to dry.

Ruth's pugs shook the snow off their fur and settled down on the hearth rug.

After starting a fire in the hearth of the room where I would be sleeping, I unpacked and changed from my wet uniform into my warmest sweater and wool skirt. I named the lavish guest room, 'the tassel suite,' because of the gold tassels hanging from the drapes, the tasseled perfume atomizer, and the cloche hat with a tassel hanging from the brim. Good God, I even had my own fainting couch! I feigned a swoon, hoping to look like Lillian Gish, but got up quickly when I heard one of the couch legs almost give way. Through the tall windows, I watched the snow cleanse the soot off the streets below. If I looked far to my right, up to the corner of 42nd and 5th, I could see the white steps leading up to the New York Public Library. On our way here, I had seen the two marble lions standing guard outside the main entrance. They wore Christmas wreaths around their necks. Slowly, quietly, dusk darkened the skies to charcoal grey.

The welcoming whistle of a tea kettle drew me out into the kitchen. Ruth took a dishtowel and wrapped it around the handle of the kettle as she lifted it off the flame.

"First we'll have glezel tei to warm up." She plopped a few sugar cubes in two tall glasses of hot tea. "I've been hoarding these like a miser since the war. Drink the tea through the sugar cubes, like this."

"It's good," I sipped the hot drink while perched on a window seat. "I'd like to make some supper as a way of repaying you for letting me stay here. I'm not much of a cook, but I'll try." Mam would have killed to cook on Ruth's very modern Garland stove.

"I'm sure you're better than me." Ruth said. "I don't know what Kitty left me in the icebox for dinner, but go ahead and see what you can come up with."

In the kitchen, I was able to scrounge up a few potatoes, parsnips, and an onion in the larder, as well as a leftover beef brisket in the ice box. I had helped Mam enough times to know that if I threw everything in a cast iron pot with some water, covered it, and turned up the flame to let everything boil, something delicious would result.

"The stew should be ready in under an hour. Which room would you like me to organize?"

"Most of my files have been moved up to Albany, but I had one file cabinet brought to this house last week because it contains information that will be valuable to the Women's Party. I'm not the most organized person in the world. That's where you come in, Jay."

After turning down the flame under the stew, I joined Ruth to investigate the job I was to undertake this week.

"The Women's Party has some big plans, and I've the resources to help. I brought folders of contacts home from Al's office earlier in the week, but so many of them are outdated. I was wondering if you could help organize an office for me in the second spare bedroom here, Jay." She summoned me out into the hallway. "Let me show you what I'm talking about."

We brought kerosene lamps into the cold, dark room next to mine. My lamp lit up the fire trap crowded with messy piles of folders, newspapers, and ledger books. I thought I made out a dust covered roll top desk, a file cabinet, and a cord I assumed led to a telephone somewhere.

"Whoa, this looks worse than I remembered!" Ruth coughed and swept the dusty air out of her face. "Kitty won't come in here because she saw a mouse, and I'm no good at filing. If I'm able to have the necessary resources at hand, right in this house, our Women's Party can really start making things happen."

"How far back do you want me to go before I start tossing documents?"

"I'd say ten years. That way I won't have files bulging with useless information. If you can figure out some kind of organization system for me, I'd really appreciate it."

"I'll do my best."

"Wonderful. This should keep you busy until you visit your mother for Christmas. I'll be back and forth to Albany all week before Al takes office on the first of January. Will you be okay by yourself with the dogs while I'm gone?"

"I'll be fine. And thank you. I appreciate this."

"Don't thank me until and unless you survive this mess!"

I knew somewhere, buried beneath the piles of rubbish, was a clue as to where I would find Eileen. I wasn't leaving the city without her.

Around 7:00, I carefully lifted the heavy lid off the pot of bubbling stew. I inhaled the familiar aroma of beef mingling with potatoes, and moved the pot to a cooler spot on the stove.

Ruth ladled the stew into bowls, and invited me to the dinner table.

"What do you want from your new governor, Jay?"

"Gosh, I don't know. I'm just trying to survive my sophomore year at Haviland."

"You're the perfect person to tell me how Al can best serve the upcoming of generation of women. The war has changed everything, Jay. Women are poised to take on positions of power in business, law, medicine, education; the sky's the limit. What can the government do to help girls reach their full potential?"

When we returned to the parlor, Ruth sat in front of the now roaring fire and picked up her knitting. It was a soft pink baby blanket. "I like to bring these to the foundling homes when I make inspection visits." The clicking of the knitting needles soothed my nerves as I thought about Eileen. I was certain I'd come to the person who would help me rescue her.

We talked well into the night about Al Smith's work to improve working conditions for women. Quick as lightning, Ruth turned the pretty yarn around, another row finished. I told Ruth about poor Mrs. Bumford, forced to work with a broken wrist. We discussed the president's long overdue support for federal suffrage now that the war was over. I started yawning when the beautiful blanket reached all the way down to Ruth's ankles. This extraordinary woman had opened my eyes to a world beyond Brewster, and she suggested an idea for a life changing adventure for yours truly.

❖

Tuesday, December 24, 1918
I got to work transforming the huge mess in the spare bedroom into some semblance of an office with a desk, a typewriter, chair, and a telephone. I divided the stacks of Ruth's folders into neat piles, and coded them according to subject, discarding anything older than 1909. Mam telephoned from Aunt Bridie's apartment to say she had to work through Christmas to fill a large order for millinery flowers, but would be able to see me later in the week.

I awoke Wednesday morning to the miserable realization that I was about to spend my fifteenth birthday utterly alone. This was to be my first Christmas birthday without Christie, Eileen, Sullivan, cake, or presents. Alice and Lucy snuggled their warm bodies against my shoulders, and I stroked their soft ears for an hour, crying with the loneliness and unfairness of it all.

After I tired of feeling sorry for myself, I announced to the pugs, "We've a few days alone to find out where Da took Eileen. We've got to keep digging."

They leapt out of bed and scratched on the door, waiting to be let out. I attached their leashes and led them down the steps of Ruth's brownstone onto 42nd Street. When I reached 5th Avenue, I turned left and walked them up the magnificent expanse of steps to the pink marble lions outside the library's main entrance. How I wished to go inside, but I was sure dogs were not permitted into such an esteemed institution. Instead, I wandered through Bryant Park, watching doughboys home from the war stealing kisses from sweethearts, and women in fur collared coats on the elbows of men clutching parcels of gifts. Back out on Fifth Avenue, everyone seemed in a terrible hurry to catch the trains at Grand Central to visit loved ones. I pressed my nose against windows filled with the grandest displays of rocking horses, toy trains, and porcelain dolls. What would Eileen say when I told her of my cosmopolitan adventures?

I knew one thing. I liked this. It was exciting walking these dogs by myself through Manhattan, and I *would* get inside that library someday.

Once I was fortified by a bag of steaming chestnuts from a street cart, I returned the pugs to their spot in front of Ruth's fireplace. I pored over documents in the file cabinet. I found information on adoption agencies, resources for orphaned children, poor mothers, widows with children, immigrant mothers, but nothing about unwed mothers to be. As I scanned pages of pending legislation on the fair and equal treatment of women in the workplace, I tried to decipher the difficult legal language, hoping to find a clue anywhere that could help me. It was while reading of Ruth and Al Smith's work with the Ladies Garment Workers that I lost myself in a world of which I very much wanted to be a part.

❧

Friday, December 27, 1918

The office was just about ready. The desk gleamed from the precious linseed oil I had rubbed laboriously into the dry wood, and the swivel chair no longer squeaked after I had greased its gears. I crouched down to organize the last few files in the bottom drawer of the cabinet. An old folder was shredding a bit on the top, obscuring the title. Most of its contents were outdated. Just as I was ready to toss it, I came upon a wrinkled sheet of paper with some addresses scribbled on it in faded ink. Looking closer, I made out, "Saint Camillus Convent, West Side. Most Precious Blood Convent: Takes in young women in trouble, West 90th, Sacred Heart Convent, Lexington and 72nd."

My heartbeat quickened. Da was from the West Side, and these were all Catholic convents. I took the paper and slipped it into my pocket. Standing up, my legs aching from kneeling on the floor for so long, I started for the telephone.

"Stop! Thief!"

A girl in a maid's uniform was coming at me, but it wasn't Kitty.

"Caught you red handed, sneaking something of Miss Ruth's in yer pocket! Give it here, now!" She grabbed my arm. "Annie!" Another Irish girl in a starched white apron appeared in the doorway. "Get the judge who lives down the way! Tell him there's been a theft!"

The dogs came running. Alice jumped and nipped at the first maid's legs, yelping and growling. Lucy ran around her in circles, howling.

"No, you don't understand, I'm working for Miss Lefkowitz! Let me go!" I tried to free my hand from her grip. "Let me explain, please!"

"I'll have none of yer malarkey. We'll see what the good judge has to say about you sneaking into Miss Ruth's house and going through her belongings. I knew you were a thief the minute I set eyes on you!"

She blocked the door until Annie returned with the judge. Tomato sauce stained the broad expanse of his undershirt, and his braces hung down on either side of his trousers.

"What's the meaning of this, interrupting a man during his luncheon?"

Alice jumped up so high she was able to nip at the judge's blue veined nose."Get this animal off me, now!"

"She's a thief, I tell you!"said the first maid. "Just go ahead and take a look at what she's put in her pocket!" Lucy yelped and snapped at her hands.

The portly judge approached me, scowling. One continuous black eyebrow was slashed across his forehead. "Who are you, and how'd you get into Miss Lefkowitz's private quarters, young lady?"

"I'm working for Miss Lefkowitz, honest! My name's Jay McKenna. She asked me to set up an office and organize her files." I picked up the candlestick phone receiver. "Here, call her office in Albany if you don't believe me."

"Mein Gott! What's the meaning of all this? Leave Jay alone, now!"

Ruth approached the judge. "What are you doing in my home? And wearing barely more than your drawers, at that!"

"Your maid came barging into my home to report a robbery! She's accusing this girl of stealing from you."

"Ruth, I didn't steal anything, honest!" I took the paper from my pocket and handed it to her. "I was cleaning out the files and came across these addresses. I think my sister Eileen may be at one of these places. My Da took her away when he found out she was … in trouble, you see, and I'm just trying to find her!"

"Everybody calm down. Where's Kitty, and who are you two?"

"She took today off to visit kinfolk in Brooklyn. I'm Katie, and this here is Annie. We're filling in."

"I left Kitty a note on the kitchen table explaining that Jay would be staying here for the week."

"I'm sorry, Miss. I hadn't gotten to the kitchen yet. I always start in the laundry. If you'll excuse me, I'll get on with the washing." Katie curtsied and left. Annie followed.

"I apologize for the confusion, Judge Drew. It's all been a misunderstanding."

"What are all these files for, and why do you need a home office?" The judge picked up an appointment book from the desk. "You've had an awful lot of suspicious types over your house lately, a bunch of women known for making trouble around the city."

"Good day, Judge Drew." Ruth took the book from him. "Al will show you out."

"Al? Now you're receiving strange men in this house? Who's Al?"

"Where'd you put the sandwiches, Ruth? I'm starving after that long train ride from Albany! And I'd die for a cold beer!"

Chapter 12

And there he was, chomping on a cigar, wearing his derby. Governor-elect Alfred E. Smith was standing in the doorway.

The judge's eyes bulged out of his head. "Uh, excuse me, uh, sir, uh I mean Governor. Oh no, you're not that yet." He tried to yank his braces up over his shoulders. "I mean, uh, pleased to meet you, Mr. Smith! I didn't vote for you, but I wish you all the best. Well, I better be going now."

"Nervous sort of fellow. Well, what can you expect from a Republican?" Mr. Smith ducked his head under the archway. "Everything okay around here? Seriously, I'm starved."

"Katie, Annie," Ruth called. "Unwrap the pastrami sandwiches I brought up in the delicatessen bag, please, and pour Al a glass of beer. I'd like a glezel tei."

"A what, Ma'am?"

"Just make hot tea, but pour it in a glass and set out a bowl of sugar cubes. Make one for Jay, too."

"Now, why don't you tell me everything?" She took off her sable coat. "I'm sure I can help you find your sister."

I poured out the whole miserable story about Da taking Eileen away.

"And you think he might have brought her to one of these places?" She read the addresses on the paper.

"I'm thinking she's in some place like one of these in the city. Doc Birdsall checked every place from Brewster down to the Bronx, and he can't find her anywhere."

"Well, I've just got to make some phone calls." She put on her wire framed glasses and gave the telephone operator the first number. "I wish you had come to me sooner, Jay. I've been doing this my whole life. Go out and have a sandwich with Al. Tell him I'll be a few minutes."

I joined Mr. Smith at the kitchen table. The pastrami tasted salty. My eyes watered from all the horseradish in the deli mustard.

"You can't get good rye bread like this outside the city!" Mr. Smith finished half a sandwich in three enormous bites. "Ruth brings it up to Albany for me. That's some good pickle, too, isn't it, kid?"

"It's very good." I strained my ears to listen in on Ruth's conversation.

"Sit tight, kid. Ruth's going to get your sister home to you. If anyone can do it, she can." A smear of mustard stained his chin.

"I hope so. Are you looking forward to being governor?"

"I've got a lot to learn, I'll tell you that much. I'm going to read every piece of legislation I can get my hands on. What about you? What do you want to do?"

"I want to do what Ruth does, help women get decent wages, working conditions, housing, and health care."

"Stick close to her, kid." He jerked his thumb toward Ruth in the office. "Make her teach you everything she knows. She got me elected, you know."

Finally, Ruth appeared in the kitchen. "You were close, Jay. It wasn't any of the three names I had written down, but they referred me to St. Rose of Lima's on Thirtieth, between Park and Madison."

"You found her?"

"Yes, she's there. Get me a pencil so I can write the address down. We'll drive over and get her ..."

But I couldn't wait. I yanked my school coat from the closet so hard it snapped the hanger in half, and rushed outside into the biting air. After slipping on the ice coated stairs, I swore and righted myself. Madison Avenue. I remembered passing Madison on our way here, but which way was it? Everyone walking up and down Forty Second Street looked cold and in a rush. I dared not ask the cop swinging his night stick, because he looked like Da with his ruddy face. I thought I heard Ruth shouting my name in the distance, but I was hell bent on getting Eileen out of whatever rat hole Da had brought her to.

Impulsively, I ran toward Grand Central Station. I tried to look above the throngs of people holding scarves against their wind chapped faces, their soaked boots crunching along the snow and ice crusted sidewalk. Madison! I made out the letters of Madison Avenue up ahead! Okay, which way was 30th street?

Turning right again, I attempted to cross the busy street and got splashed with dirty slush from a trolley car. With my now soaked stockings bagging at the knees, I rushed down the cavernous side street until I came upon the next sign, which read 41st street and Madison. I was going in the right direction! I plunged ahead, adopting the cold grimace of my fellow travelers. I defied anyone to cut ahead of me when I was waiting to step down from the curb into traffic.

I turned the corner at Madison and headed up toward what I hoped was Park Avenue. Not seeing anything that looked like a church, I looked down on either side of the street, as wrought iron railings and concrete steps carried people off the street into shops and restaurants. Panicking, I saw the crossway up ahead. Where was this place?

I spotted an ominous black door at the foot of another set of railings. Cautiously, I made my way down the icy steps and rapped the brass knocker on the door. Nothing. I rapped again, harder this time. The door creaked open and a kind face greeted me.

"Welcome to St. Rose of Lima's Convent. Don't worry. You're safe here." The nun looked to be about my age, her chest pressed flat beneath a huge rounded stiff collar. A few errant wisps of black hair were visible from either side of her face, which was surrounded by a starched wimple.

"I've come for my sister, Eileen McKenna. Where is she?" Not waiting for an answer, I shouted "Eileen! It's Jay!"

"What is the meaning of this?" A towering nun draped in voluminous black robes floated into the hallway, which smelled like dirty diapers. "Sister Albertine, I've spoken to you before about admitting strangers in off the street!" The Mother Superior figure glared at me with small brown eyes behind a pushed in nose like Sullivan's. No hair showed from either side of her wimple.

"If you're in trouble, you can't just wander in here. You need to be referred by your parish. Leave now, or I'll call the authorities." She grabbed my elbow and ushered me toward the door.

I pulled away from her. "You've got my sister locked up in here, and I'm not leaving until she comes with me." I tried to heed Mam's warning about curbing my temper.

"If you promise to calm down and tell me your sister's name, I can look her up in our record book to see if she's even here."

I sat down on a bench, even though I hadn't been offered a seat. "Thank you. Her name is Eileen McKenna, and I assure you, she hasn't been referred by our parish. My father kidnapped her against my mother's wishes. Monsignor O'Brien has been looking for her ever since."

I waited on that hard bench in the dark hallway so long that I started shivering. My breath was visible in front of me. There was no steam coming from the radiator. My feet felt miserably cold and wet, and I stunk of wet wool.

Sister Albertine smiled at me, wringing her hands beneath the folds of her habit.

"I'd offer you something to warm up, but I'm not allowed in the kitchen without Mother Superior's permission."

"Why do you stay here working under these conditions? Can't you get a transfer or something?"

"I want to help the mothers and their babies. They so need a friendly face."

After an interminably long time, The Mother Superior returned. Alone. My heart sank.

"You were wrong, Miss McKenna. Your sister was indeed referred to us by a parish representative. In addition, her father signed papers giving the convent custody of your sister and the baby when it arrives. Now if you'll please leave us in peace to do God's good work."

"I don't believe you." I promised to say two Hail Mary's for penance. "May I please see the paper?"

I read the familiar, even signature "Bernadette McCree." Nosy old Gran McCree, the rectory secretary at St. Luke's! She was in on this whole thing with Da! "Leave it to that busybody."

"So it turns out you've had a wasted trip." The Mother Superior gripped my elbow again, harder this time, but a rush of cold air from the doorway and a familiar voice stopped her.

"Eileen's mother was never notified of this arrangement, so your custody claim will never stand up in family court. You know that, I'm sure."

"Ruth! They won't let me take Eileen!"

"You led us on a wild goose chase, kid!" Al Smith came in through the door, blowing air into his bare hands. "It's freezing out there! Are you trying to catch pneumonia?" He sniffed the air. "Holy Mother of God! What's that rotten stench? Let go of her, now, Sister, and get the fires going! You could hang meat in here! What kind of two-bit operation are you running, anyway?"

Ruth stepped forward. "I'm from Governor-elect Smith's Department of Social Services and Family Welfare, and am representing the McKenna family. Release Jay's sister to her now, or I'll have this place shut down by the Board of Health within the hour!"

"I'd do what she says if I were you, Sister! Miss Lefkowitz, here, is my chief advisor, and she's damn, uh, pardon me, darn good!" Governor-elect Smith swung open all the doors on both sides of the hallway. He reminded me of Christie when he brought me to the dorm on the first day of school.

"Better yet, give me a phone so they can pay you a visit now. This pigsty looks long overdue for an inspection. I can barely see my hand in front of my face it's so dark in here. I've counted about five health code violations in the few minutes I've been here. And you're keep babies and young mothers in these filthy conditions? You ought to be ashamed of yourself, Sister!"

Mother Superior's cheeks were mottled red with anger. She shoved a paper in Ruth's face. "Here's our authorization to care for the mother to be, signed by Gerald McKenna and the clergy secretary of St. Luke's Catholic Church, granting our facility custody of the baby when it arrives."

"So you can sell Eileen's baby to the highest bidder, more than likely." Ruth was nose to nose with the Mother Superior. "Again, this girl was taken without her mother's consent. I'm sorry to have to drag your convent into the twentieth century, Sister, uh?"

"It's Sister Mary Benedicta. Mother Superior to the likes of you!"

"Sister Benedicta, as Eileen is a minor, Mrs. McKenna has parental rights, which you've clearly violated. I've seen many cases like this argued in court, and the judge always sides with the mother. I can reach Mrs. McKenna by telephone and have her here in person to pick up Eileen. Are you sure the church is willing to go to the legal expense you will undoubtedly incur when you are certain to lose?"

"Are you willing to go through the time and expense of advocating for these shanty Irish whose immoral behavior lands them in this sort of trouble? The convent is full of them." said Sister Benedicta.

I opened my mouth to speak, but Ruth stopped me with her raised hand. "Ignore her, Jay. It's not worth your getting upset."

"Excuse me, Mother Superior, but I'd best check in on the little ones. Nice meeting you all." Sister Albertine disappeared down the hallway.

"I'll be writing to the Archdiocese about this travesty of Justice, Mr. Smith. You and your crooked political cronies at Tammany Hall bullied your way into Albany, but you can't bully me!"

"The Archbishop and I used to work together in the fish markets when were just boys. When you write, tell Father John that Al sends his regards."

Sister Albertine returned with Eileen. I ran to her.

"What are you doing?" demanded Sister Benedicta.

Sister Albertine gave Eileen a little push. "Run, Eileen! Your sister is here to take you home. Go!"

Sister Benedicta made a move to grab Eileen, but Mr. Smith blocked her way. "Ruth, grab a bus to get the girls home. I'm staying here and calling police headquarters to get a search warrant. Jay, take your sister and go now."

We ran toward the door to the sounds of Sister Benedicta screaming at Sister Albertine. I wanted to go back and take the young nun with us, but I had to get out of there - and fast.

I tore off my coat and wrapped it around a shivering Eileen standing between Ruth and I on a crowded bus. She sobbed into my shoulder. "Thank you so much for finding me, Jay. I thought I was going to die in there."

"Did the nuns mistreat you?"

"Mother Superior was awful, but Sister Albertine and the other young sisters had it just as bad as us, what with the cold and never enough food to go around. I feel sorry for them."

"What's going to happen to poor Sister Albertine?" I couldn't believe her bravery.

"Al's not going to leave until the mothers and babies are placed somewhere safe. He'll make sure Sister Albertine and the other sisters are taken care of. That's what we do. I'll join him once I get you two back to your mother."

"But what about the last few files in the cabinet? I can't leave without finishing the job."

"Jay, you could eat off the floor in that office now. Do you remember what it looked like when we first came here? You're a miracle worker! I can handle a few files on my own."

We stopped at Ruth's house so I could get my things. Ruth served Eileen tea and challah bread smeared with butter. She devoured slice after slice of the thick bread. Without makeup, she looked about twelve years old save for her swollen belly beneath a filthy grey smock. Her usually fluffy hair hung lank over her shoulders, and she was so pale and thin, I thought she would break.

❊

I looked at the address I had written down: 591 Amsterdam Avenue. Yes, this was the right building. I recognized it from the few times we had visited Aunt Bridie on holidays.

"Are you okay to climb the stairs?"

"I'd climb ten flights to see Mam. Let's go."

The dark ground floor of the building still had those small black and white tiles on the floor that I used to hop across when I was little. As we climbed the stairs to the fourth floor, we were greeted by the familiar smell of boiled cabbage.

"Glory be to God! It's a miracle! Nonie, get out here!" Aunt Bridie hugged us both so tightly she almost knocked the wind out of me. Mam wept, and ushered us inside to the kitchen table, where the kettle was put on straight away.

"There were very strict rules about bedtime and talking, and we all had chores to do. I was always stuck in the kitchen, scrubbing pans. Don't let Da take me back there Mam, please?"

"You're not going anywhere. Try to eat something now." Mam nudged a bowl of lamb stew toward Eileen. "I'll bring out the tub and fill it clear up to the top with hot water so you can have a good, long soak. There'll be no water conservation in this kitchen today!"

Mam found me reading *The New York Times* on the sofa after she settled Eileen in for her bath in the kitchen. She brought me some small wrapped packages from under the little tree that stood in the corner. "I'm thinking you didn't have much of a birthday or Christmas. There's nothing much, just hair ribbons and some penny candy. I didn't want you to think I'd forgotten."

"Thanks." I unwrapped a butterscotch and popped it in my mouth.

"No, thank you, Josephine." She smoothed back a frizzy curl from my eyes. "I'll never forget what you've done for us. We wouldn't have Eileen home for Christmas without you."

Later on that night, I tried to get comfortable in the bed Aunt Bridie had made for me by pushing two sofa chairs together. Eileen was hugging a pillow on the couch.

"I thought he loved me."

I leaned over on my elbow. "I know you did."

"He told me he loved me. That's the only reason I let him, well…" Her voice broke. "I don't want you to think I'm some kind of…"

"I don't think that."

"But everybody else will. I'm so scared." She ran her hand over her swollen belly. "I heard it really hurts, when, you know, you have to push it out of you."

"I heard that too, but Mam will be there with you, and so will I. And who cares what anyone else thinks?"

"Thanks, Jay."

I swung my legs over the armrest of my too small bed and tried to sleep.

I woke sometime in the middle of the night to someone calling my name. Through the window, a half moon appeared from behind a cloud, bright enough to shine through the ice patterns swirling among the panes. Someone was tapping on the window. I climbed over the armrests and picked up a heavy vase. In the moonlight, I made out a dark figure standing outside the window on the fire escape, jiggling the latch from the outside.

Before I had a chance to scream, the figure successfully unlatched the window from the outside and threw it open. I hid behind the sofa.

"Didn't you hear me calling? The building was all locked up, so I had to climb up the fire escape! I was about to freeze to death out there!" The figure climbed inside.

I slowly rose to see my eldest brother standing in Aunt Bridie's parlor. With the moonlight illuminating his blue Marine dress coat, he looked like a Christmas gift sent down from heaven by Christie.

"Jimmy Joe!" I ran and buried my head in his chest, which smelled like lemon drops, tobacco, and faraway places. His right eye was patched, and his face was burned down one side, but he was still my brother.

Ma came running out of the bedroom. "What in the name of suffering Christ is going on out here? Oh, Jesus!"

Aunt Bridie actually poured me a small glass of brandy once we were all gathered at the kitchen table, as there was no more thought of sleeping. I drank it down quick before Mam could see me. Eileen had wisely wrapped herself in a big quilt.

"Packy's company went missing during the Meuse Argonne Offensive, at the end of September, or maybe the beginning of October, I forget. I was with the same division as Packy, the 77th, but in a different company. Turns out, they brought Packy to the same base hospital where I was being treated for burns. He was hit by a German shell, but since he was missing for awhile, the doctors couldn't save his leg 'cause of gangrene. Leg or no leg, he'll get home eventually."

Mam grew quiet.

"He's still the same old Packy, Mam." Jimmy smiled. "When I got out, I visited him at the hospital where they moved him after his surgery. He's got his eye on one of the American nurses there. She's sure to give him a run for his money!" He laughed that deep laugh I'd missed for ages.

"What do you mean by give him a run for his money?" Mam had that mother tiger look in her eyes.

"Charlotte's one of those girls with all sorts of modern notions. You know, the college type who doesn't let a fella get a word in edgewise."

Aunt Bridie refilled our glasses. "And how are you doing?"

Jimmy Joe touched the patch covering his eye. "A bomb exploded near me at Argonne. It just about burned half my face off, but I'm still as handsome as hell, right?"

"How'd you know to come here, and not home?" I studied his face. The right side of his nose kind of melted into his cheek, and his right ear was singed, as well as his neck. Somehow, he was indeed still good looking, kind of rugged now, like a pirate. His right hand kept shaking, though.

"Doc Birdsall and Monsignor O'Brien have been sending letters." Jimmy Joe downed the shot of whiskey Aunt Bridie had set down. The shaking eased. "They were all forwarded to me in the hospital. No one's seen Da, and the farm's all run down. Mr. Salmon took over the cows and the milk delivery route. Doc wrote that Harkin's boy, not the idiot, the younger one, has been stopping by with feed and straw for the livestock, and has been mucking out the barn. Doc says he always brings Sullivan with him. Can you imagine that? " He took a long drag on a cigar he produced from his shirt pocket, blowing the smoke in rings. Christie used to do that. "Maybe Da left town."

I hadn't even written to Henry to thank him. What was wrong with me?

"Well, Good riddance to bad rubbish, that's what I think," Aunt Bridie said.

"I was thinking, on the ship home, that I'd like to try and make a go of diversifying the farm, Mam. We can't just rely on dairy farming, anymore. I was thinking apples, and maybe potatoes." He laid down his cigar in an ashtray. "I figure there'll be plenty of guys willing to work for cheap, and when Packy gets home, he can handle the business end, even if he can't do farm work anymore. He's always been good with numbers."

"The bank's going to take the farm, Jimmy Joe. You've got your railroad job waiting for you."

"Let me talk to the guys down at the bank and try to work something out."

"You sure you want to take it on?"

"The only thing that kept me sane over there, when all I could hear were my buddies screaming in the beds next to me as the doctors ripped the shrapnel out of their backs, was the thought of putting my hands in the dirt, and bringing something to life."

"Okay son, if you're willing to do the work. It's going to be a long road back, what with all the bills and shortages from the war, but we'll go home if that's what you want."

❄

Monday, January 6, 1919

Henry's eyes reflected the brilliant sapphire of the January morning sky on this first day back to school. There was no sign of Da on the farm when we arrived back from the city, so I felt safe staying there for the remainder of my vacation.

"You're awful quiet." His breath came in curls of white smoke. "I figured you'd be bursting with all the good news. Everything all right?"

He was driving a low cutter. Maisie and Mulligan pulled the sled. Bundled up under three horse blankets, with Sullivan between us, we coasted over the frozen landscape of snow covered firs, glistening in the early sun. Out on Lake Gleneida, men were pushing long saws back and forth to cut blocks of ice.

"Florence wrote me after Christmas. I guess mid-terms start at the beginning of February."

"You'll do fine."

"Evangeline said they're brutal. You have to remember lessons presented way back in September. A lot of girls fail them."

"I know what mid-terms are, Jay. We had them at the village school, remember?"

"Florence wants us to join a study group to prepare for them."

"That sound like a good idea." He looked at me quizzically. "What are you getting at?"

"Well, the thing is, mid-term study groups meet on Saturdays and Sundays, when we don't have class, to review the material we've forgotten."

"I see. So you're trying to tell me you won't be coming home on weekends any time soon." He gave the reins a little snap and looked ahead. "Do you know how long?"

"Until mid-terms are over, I'm thinking after that first week of February. Then things can get back to normal again."

"You mean I can then resume my services as your chauffeur?" His jaw had a hard edge to it.

"You're not my chauffer, Henry. Come on."

"I'm not? Well what am I then? Let me think. I drive you to and from school for a few months and watch your dog for you. Then you spend Christmas vacation hanging out with the governor, but you don't call or write, even though Ruth has a telephone. Now you're telling me not to come for you at school for about a month."

"I was trying to find Eileen, for heaven's sake!"

"I thought maybe you were my girl, Jay, but I feel more like your hired hand, because while Clarence and George were out chasing skirts the past few months, I was cleaning cow piss out of your barn, waiting to hear from you. Everybody's calling me a sap." He swatted Mulligan way too hard on the rump. "Damn it, Jay, what am I supposed to think?"

"That's not fair, Henry, and you know it."

Henry stayed silent for the rest of the ride. I didn't know if his ears were so red from the cold or from anger. I waited until we reached the dorm before I spoke.

"I, uh, I was going to ask you if you'd take me to the Valentine's Dance after mid-terms are over."

"Valentine's Day? What's that, like six weeks away?"

"Yes. Friday, the 14th of February, in the Haviland gymnasium. You can bring Clarence and George and the guys if you want."

"I'll have to see."

A bald eagle soared over the lake. After a few silent moments, Henry snapped the reins of the cutter and drove away.

Henry was right. How was I going to make things better between us when I was going to be stuck at school for a whole month?

No one greeted me at the reception desk. "Where's Lydia, and what's that awful smell?" I plunked my things down on my bed and hid the book Henry gave me for Christmas, safe from prying eyes. I held my nose as I looked for the source of the ungodly stink in the room.

"Guess you're the last one to know the gossip around here." Evangeline said. "While you were out smooching with lover boy, Betty Cornish, the new residence assistant, came around and introduced herself to everybody."

"A new resident assistant? What happened to Lydia?"

"Well, apparently there's been some kind of huge scandal involving Lydia that has to do with violating the honor code. She's been forced to step down. It's positively all over the school."

"That ridiculous honor code again! There must be some kind of mistake. Do you know what she's been accused of?" I opened a window to let some fresh air into the room.

"Not yet. But I aim to find out, and soon. I'll bet I'll know by the end of the school day."

"I've no doubt about that." I put clean linens on my bed and then tucked Henry's book inside my pillow case, hoping he would forgive me. Another surge of acrid air hit me like a brick wall.

"Where is that stench coming from? And what is that?" A small pouch hung from a string around Evangeline's neck.

"When Mother got word that your brother died of the Spanish flu, she insisted Mary Agnes and I wear bags of camphor to ward off the disease." She produced wilted vegetables from the pockets of her cardigan. "I've got to eat these onions all day and carry this potato to protect myself."

❧

Thursday, January 9, 1919
Florence filled me in on the Lydia mystery when we were doing homework in her room.

"From what I've heard, Lydia lied on her application to become a resident assistant. That's all I know, except for some rumors that the lie was to cover up a crime."

"Something doesn't sound right. Lydia's not that kind of person."

"Maybe you should ring the governor and ask him about it."

I whacked her with a pillow. She whacked me back.

"What's all this stuff?" I picked up a magazine from a pile on her bed. Florence took it back from me.

"Weren't you raised better than to go nosing around in other people's business? Oh I forgot, you were raised in a barn."

"I was just curious. Jeez!"

"Calm down, Hayseed. They're just a bunch of back issues of *Sage and Lavender*. Mrs. Westcott thinks I should submit my December essay to the magazine."

I picked up another copy. The cover had hand drawn silhouettes of students' faces, as well as pictures of paintbrushes, paint pallets, and fountain pens. On the lower left hand corner of the cover was the date June, 1918. This was last year's issue. I opened it and read a poem about each member of the graduating class. There was then an account of a ride to Danbury for the senior girls' graduation picture, whereby they scared the driver of their coach when they shouted the Haviland school cheer. I didn't even know Haviland had a cheer.

When I turned the page, a sheet of paper torn from a notebook fell out. Across the top of a poem, someone had written "Not suitable for publication."

"Florence, look at this." We mouthed the words together as we read.

> *If Only, My Love.*
> If only our two hearts, my darling,
> Could join as one,
> Truly, freely, purely,
> Our love would sing sweet music,
> As you my dearest one,
> Could walk with me, hand in hand,
> Precious, devoted, honest.
> No more discord, secrets, or shame,
> Oh how I long for harmony!
> If only our two hearts, my love,
> Could join as one.
> By Violet Crane, Class of '21

Florence took the paper from me and read the poem again. "She was in love with someone."

"It's more than that. She used the term, "If only," in her title, as well as to begin and end her poem. Why couldn't she be with the person she was writing about?"

"No secrets, no shame? Forbidden love?"

"Maybe it was someone her family disapproved of." I thought of Eileen.

"The Cranes are pretty snooty. Maybe she was in love with one of the help. There's a groundskeeper who's not half bad looking - for a white guy."

When we stopped laughing, we composed ourselves and read the poem again to search for clues.

"What about the word, "shame?" What was she ashamed of?"

"Maybe it wasn't Violet who was ashamed. Maybe it was him."

"Why would someone be ashamed of loving Violet? She was pretty, and smart, and ..."

"Maybe he wasn't free to love her."

"A fourteen year old girl carrying on with a married man? Are you crazy?"

"No, are you crazy? Now shut up and let me talk. She wrote about some kind of secret or forbidden love. She used the word, "discord," which means some kind of disagreement or conflict. There's this one line that reads "No more discord, secrets, or shame." What kind of love must be kept secret?"

"An affair between a teenage girl and a married man."

"Maybe we're over thinking this. There's a possibility she just made the poem up. Violet was a good writer."

"I don't know. I think Violet wants us to find out what happened to her."

"You mean like, she sent us this poem as a sign?"

"Yeah, I think she did. You know, now that I think about it, the pilot of the plane told us a lot. I think I know why Violet's father wanted the investigators to talk to Dr. Wisdom."

"What did the pilot say?"

"He said Violet asked him where Haviland was, and how high they were flying. Then, after he told her they were over the school, he looked back, and the door to the cabin was open, and she was gone. I guess the wind carried her to our property. She looked like a doll falling, I remember."

"When you put it that way, it sounds like when Violet knew she was flying over Haviland … she jumped."

"I've been thinking that, too."

"I just remembered something Mama told me over vacation. Dr. Crane, Violet's father, wants the investigators to question students here."

"You mean us?"

"I don't know, maybe. Mama said that when Dr. Crane came up for Christmas, she heard him say he was setting up a meeting with Dr. Wisdom."

"Do you think he suspects someone here?"

"She did fall, or maybe jump, the day before school was about to start. Maybe she had a problem with a teacher or another student."

"Yeah, but to kill yourself to solve a problem at school?"

"It's just that if Violet did jump when the pilot said they were flying over Haviland, maybe her death *is* connected to this school. Maybe she wanted to send a message to someone. I mean up until now, there's been no answers, no clues. But after hearing what you've said, well, jeez, it sounds like she chose the spot where she wanted to jump. There had to be a reason."

"I'm not even sure if I want to know the reason. I've got enough problems of my own at this school with Nathalia. I can't take on a suicide investigation."

By the way Florence clutched the goose-bumped flesh on her upper arms, I knew she, like I, felt another presence in this room. I picked up the poem. "Violet wants us to find out what drove her to jump out of that plane, doesn't she?"

"I think maybe she does."

"What do we do now? I'm the last person who needs to start stirring up trouble in this school with questions."

"Nothing yet. I'll tell Mama what the pilot said, and I'll ask her to find out about Dr. Crane's meeting with Dr. Wisdom. That will guide what, if anything, we should do next."

❄

Saturday, January 11, 1919

Florence and I attended the first, grueling, study session. There were about twenty girls crammed around a long table in the library. Several of them, including the librarian, were wearing those frightening white masks, even though far fewer cases of Spanish flu had been reported since the new year.

After an hour, Evangeline stood up. "How many more ancient history dates can they expect us to remember?"

I walked to the window to stretch my legs. "Is it ever going to stop snowing? I'd give anything to see a blade of grass. What if it snows on Valentine's Day and the dance has to be cancelled?" I said.

"Oh, no! Clarence promised he's coming with the whole baseball team! You are not going to believe how beautiful my dress is going to be. Mother ordered the most expensive gown in the entire Perry, Dane, and Company catalog. Oh wait until you see it!"

"I can't take her anymore." I nudged Florence. "Let's get out of here."

Everything was quiet outdoors. We followed deer and rabbit tracks to the brook, where a narrow stream of water between the ice rushed over the stones.

A majestic eight-point buck was staring at us. The poor creature had to be starving from the cold to come so close.

"I don't even know if Henry's coming to the dance. I haven't heard from him since he dropped me off."

"You're going to lose that man if you don't make time for him. Plenty of girls are just waiting to steal a fine catch like him."

"You know I can't get away with all this studying, and Nathalia's starting with the excuses again. I don't get it. How was she capable of writing that perfect essay in October?"

A noise spooked the buck. His white tail popped up as he sprinted away.

"She wasn't." Lydia, bundled up in a red beret and scarf, was walking toward us.

"What are you doing here?"

"I needed a break from the study group, same as you."

"What did you just mean, when you said she wasn't?"

"Mind if I join you?" She made her way across the snow covered stones in the brook. "Nathalia didn't write that essay in October. I did."

"You?"

"I'm sorry, Jay. I should've had the courage to tell you long ago. I had no choice."

"I don't understand."

"Last year, I was Nathalia's English tutor. I didn't want to do it, but the business office told my mother they would reduce my tuition if I took the position."

"I understand that, but why did you write her essay this year?"

"I tutored Nathalia in English, French, social studies, and bible study. I loathed every minute of it because it seemed, as time wore on, I was doing her work for her."

"Exactly!"

"When I refused to write any more papers for her, I came to the reception desk one morning and found a manila envelope addressed to me. Inside was a copy of the arrest warrant my stepfather got the summer before."

Just like the whiskey bottles.

"Nathalia somehow gets information on students here. She uses it to force people to do her work."

"What happened to your stepfather?" Florence asked.

"I guess it doesn't really matter anymore, now that it's all out in the open. You see, my real father died of consumption when I was four. He left everything to my mother. She got remarried to a fortune hunter who gambled away most of her money. The rest he spent on other women. Our house went into foreclosure. Then there was a scandal involving him and a girl not much older than me. That's where the arrest warrant comes from."

"I'm sorry."

"I was terrified of people finding out. When Nathalia begged me to write another paper for her, I agreed."

"But didn't the teachers know your handwriting?" Florence asked.

"I typed it."

"That's what you were always hiding at the reception desk. That's why you always looked so upset."

"I refused to do any more of Nathalia's work when we arrived back at school this year, but she came begging me to do her summer reading report. She has a way of putting things that makes me feel sorry for her."

"I know."

"I refused again when she asked me to write her September essay, but I gave in and wrote the October writing sample and her part of your lab, Jay. I felt so sorry for you, getting suspended for trying to type it yourself. After October, I stayed strong and didn't give in to her."

"That's when Miss Chichester asked me to tutor her."

When I refused to do any more of her work, Nathalia stopped showing up for tutoring. Then I received an anonymous note on the reception desk. It said someone had evidence that I had violated the honor code, and I was about to be exposed. I figured it was her way at getting back at me. I ignored it."

She took a handkerchief to wipe her eyes. "Right before Christmas break, I was called into Dr. Wisdom's office. Someone had forwarded her a copy of the arrest warrant along with the sheriff's report. These came with a letter accusing me of lying on my application for R.A. Dr. Wisdom showed me that when the application asked if I came from a good family of strong moral values, I had answered, "Yes." A copy of the application was sent to her, with my answer circled in red."

"How does Nathalia find all of this?"

"Who knows? Dr. Wisdom said the school couldn't afford this type of scandal. I had to resign. There's no money to pay next year's tuition, so I'll be leaving school at the end of June."

"This isn't fair. I think we should go to Dr. Wisdom and tell her what's going on."

"There have to be more students affected by this than just you and Jay," Florence said. "Lydia, you said you tutored Nathalia in English, French, social studies, and bible study didn't you? Well, what about science and math? Who tutored her in those subjects?"

"Violet Crane."

Chapter 13

Friday, January 17, 1919

"Just read this section of my notes at the bottom of the page. You'll find the answer there." I checked the clock to see how many more minutes of tutoring torture I'd yet to endure.

"Read it to me, please." Nathalia pushed the notebook back to me. "My eyes are tired."

"It's right here in front of you."

"Can I just tell it to you instead? I know the moss grew 4/16 of an inch this week. I know that fraction can be reduced to ¼. I observed that moss sample A is growing the fastest, and I think it is because it is receiving the most direct sunlight. My hypothesis is that I think its soil might hold more water than the other samples."

Miss Chichester looked up from correcting her lab reports.

"Very good, Nathalia!" I said. "Well done! See, you know all this. Now just write that down. That's your analysis. You just said it. Write it down now so you don't forget."

"I will later, Jay. I'm so very tired." She pouted like a small child. "Can we stop now?"

"Miss Ormsby, Miss McKenna, come up here." Miss Chichester was holding our lab report in her hands.

"Am I correct in assuming that these are your signatures, ladies?"

"Oh, yes!" Nathalia said.

"I see. And if I were to quiz you separately on the results that you achieved on this lab, both of you would earn the scores reflected on this report?"

Neither of us said anything.

"You're both aware that there is a forgery policy here which will result in your expulsion if I can prove that one of you completed this lab and signed the other one's name?"

I started to see black dots in front of my eyes. Miss Chichester's voice sounded far away.

"Allow me to get straight to the point. I've reason to believe this report is a forgery. I see my trust in you has been misplaced. I believe my instructions for you, Miss McKenna, were to help Miss Ormsby during your tutoring sessions, not to do her work for her."

She tossed the report in her wastepaper basket. "I want to see you both after school today. You will sit at opposite sides of the room with your notes and rewrite your respective sections of this lab report in front of me. We'll get to the bottom of this, ladies."

"I've choir practice today, Miss Chichester. I'm sorry, but I won't be able to make it."

"You will be here, Miss Ormsby. You're both dismissed."

"I'm going to Reverend Courage about this right now!"

❈

Nathalia approached our table during lunch. "May I talk to you in private, Jay?"

Everyone in the dining hall was staring.

She took me into the lavatory, of all places. "I need the notes."

"I can't. I did your work, and now we're in trouble." I held on to the sink so that if I passed out I wouldn't crack my head on the tiled floor.

I saw a flash of something, anger, desperation maybe, in Nathalia's eyes. "Please. I need them."

"I'm sorry, I can't." I ran out of the lavatory and through the door to the courtyard, breathing in the freezing air until my lungs hurt. I couldn't get the look of Nathalia's piercing eyes out of my head.

"Get inside before you catch your death!" Mr. Gallagher was shoveling a path in the snow.

I showed up after school outside science class. The door was slightly opened. Mrs. Westcott and Miss Chichester were conversing in hushed tones. I stepped away from the door when I heard my name.

"I'm telling you Lila, it was Nathalia Ormsby asking Josephine McKenna for her science notes. My eyesight isn't so good anymore, but I still have my hearing."

"But Mae, whatever were you doing in the girls' lavatory?"

"Lila, you're still young. At my age, to wait for hours until lunch break to use the women's facilities is quite a feat. They're located clear at the other end of the building. It's easier just to use the girls' lavatory." I heard a spoon stirring around the inside of a teacup. "I'm telling you, Nathalia was clearly pressuring Miss McKenna to copy her notes for her."

"That settles it, then. I'm going straight to Dr. Wisdom, and you're coming with me as a witness."

I backed away as I heard Miss Chichester's heels clicking toward the door.

"I've suspected this all along, and now I've proof!"

"No, Lila, you mustn't! We've already been warned by her parents not pressure Nathalia with regard to schoolwork. You don't want to lose your position, do you? Don't act in haste."

"It's unfair that one student is given special treatment simply because her parents give money to the school!"

"Times are bad, Lila. Money's tight with the war just over. Enrollment is down. No request of Mrs. Ormsby on behalf of her daughter will be denied as long as this school is wanting. There are rumors that the scholarship program may be threatened. That would be a shame for Miss McKenna, wouldn't it?"

I realized at that moment that I wanted to stay at Haviland. Despite Nathalia, despite Evangeline, I wanted to someday graduate and work for Ruth.

I waited until Mrs. Westcott left the classroom before I dare enter. Taking my seat, I began my lab report sections based on my notes. Nathalia arrived about a half hour later. I worked until Miss Chichester called time at 6:00. I approached her desk and handed in my report. Nathalia followed me.

"This is incomplete. I've Miss McKenna's work and conclusions, but not yours, Miss Ormsby."

Nathalia said nothing. I looked away.

"Miss Ormsby, your choice not to contribute your sections has resulted in your receiving a zero for this lab report. Miss McKenna, I am deducting 25 points for your part in the original forged report. You will receive a grade of 75. I am speaking to Dr. Wisdom of this incident, and notes will be put in both of your record folders. Miss Ormsby, you are dismissed. Miss McKenna, please stay."

She motioned me to sit. "Miss McKenna, why didn't you bring to my attention that Miss Ormsby was not completing her share of the lab work?"

"I, uh, I wanted to, but I ..." The words came out a jumbled mess.

"Is there something you wish to tell me, Miss McKenna?"

"I believe, I think, Miss Chichester, that it's possible Nathalia may have a problem with reading."

"Go on. Why do you believe reading is a problem?"

"Well, I noticed during our tutoring session this morning that while Nathalia avoided reading from the notes or the textbook, she was able to tell me exactly what she observed about the moss growth. I think she may possibly have a problem reading and writing, because she knows the material. She just avoids taking notes."

"Interesting. I'll look into this. You may go."

I was doomed. I had a feeling that flash in Nathalia's eyes today in the lavatory was only the beginning.

❧

Wednesday, January 22, 1919

I didn't have long to wait. The following week, Helen Starr approached me.

"Nathalia wants to see you in her dorm room after school. Be there at 3:15."

I knocked on Nathalia's door at the appointed time. Her eyes were puffy from crying. She blew her nose, rather loudly. "What did you say to Miss Chichester?"

"I didn't say anything to her."

She picked up a letter and shoved it in my face. Her hand was shaking "Read this to me!" She was near hysteria. "Read it to me, now!"

I did as she told me.

154

"Why do I have an appointment in the main office to take, 'a battery of academic assessments'? What did you tell her?"

"I said nothing."

"Just go. Do not tell anyone what I've told you. I mean it Jay, not a soul."

I swore I would take her secret to my grave. I figured it wouldn't be a very long wait.

❈

Tuesday, February 4, 1919

I woke early the day before the dreaded French midterm, hoping to grab an early breakfast so I could cram in as much studying as I could that day. The grey dawn matched my mood. Dressing in the dark, I walked in the sleet and snow over to the dining hall.

I heard someone shouting from the kitchen entrance. Mrs. Bumford grabbed me. "Miss McKenna, you'd better come quick."

I ran toward the cash register, where I saw students crowding around to read a bunch of papers stuck to the wall.

"What's all that glued up on the wall?" I asked.

"Some scoundrel defaced school property, and I saw your last name on the papers!"

"Jay! Come here!" Florence was jumping up, tearing down papers stuck to the low ceiling above the cash register. "She's at it again!"

Above the food line, a row of invoices were stuck to the wall. The strong smell of mucilage hung heavy in the air. A dining hall worker who spoke Italian was ripping the invoices down, making a sticky pile on the floor next to a dripping glue brush and pot.

I picked them up. Upon closer inspection, I could make out the letterheads for Brewster Feed and Farm Supplies, The Putnam County Savings Bank, and Lobdell Dry Goods.

"What's all this about?" I peered closer. The first one read "$11.00 past due. Cash only." It was the Lobdell's bill for my school supplies! I squinted to read an overdue feed bill from Henry's father, a letter from the bank threatening foreclosure on our farm, and a notice demanding that Da appear in tax court.

"Run into the kitchen and get me a bucket of water. I'll scrape the glue and bits of paper off the wall," said Mrs. Bumford.

"No, No." The Italian woman tapped her chest. "I do."

"Thanks. I'll get a ladder to get the ones way high up there."

"No, Mrs. Bumford. You're wrist is just after healing. I'll get the ladder."

Florence and I scratched off the last of the bills with knives and our fingers. I peeled dried glue from my hands.

"When I showed up for work, I saw some girl running out the back exit," Mrs. Bumford said. "I called to her to stop, but she tore out of here before I could turn on the light switch. It was dark, so I didn't get a good look at her. I'm sorry. I don't know why somebody would do such a thing."

"I do. She had light blonde hair, right?"

"No, Miss Jay. I didn't get a good look at her face, but she was definitely a dark haired girl."

❦

Friday, February 7, 1919

"Dark hair?" Evangeline echoed. "Maybe it was Mercy." While everybody was celebrating the end of midterms, I was panicking. I still hadn't heard from Henry, and the dance was a week away.

Desperate, I actually offered to ride with Evangeline up to her house to pick up her dress for the dance, hoping to see Henry.

"I'm going to save every dance for Clarence. Oh, Jay, I have to pinch myself when I think of how lovely I'm going to look in my red chiffon taffeta!"

When we were approaching Brewster, I asked "Do you mind if we drive through the village?"

"Yes, I do indeed mind. I want to see my dress." Evangeline bore left down Railroad Avenue toward Prospect Street. Before we made the right turn, I noticed someone tall standing in front of the fire house. My heart quickened. Was that Henry? He started waving at me.

"Evangeline, let me off here, please!"

"Lover boy will have to wait, Jay. I don't want to keep Mother waiting. We'll stop on the way back."

I sunk back into my seat, dejected.

"Oh, it looks like something spun by angels!" Evangeline twirled around in a loud red dress at least two sizes too small for her. I waited with Mary Agnes in the parlor while Evangeline changed. When she came back downstairs, she wrapped the dress back up, grabbed the stack of boxes on the kitchen table, and shoved them toward Mary Agnes.

"Put these all in the car, and be careful not to crush anything. Go on now, while I say goodbye to Mother and see if Clarence is home."

❊

As we headed back toward school, Evangeline whispered to me, "I've never ever told anyone this, so you have to keep my secret. At night, I practice kissing Clarence by kissing my mirror. I want to be prepared!"

"Stop the car!" I ran into the firehouse and asked if anyone had seen Henry.

"He was just here, Jay," Mr. Harkins looked around. "Where'd that boy get off to?"

"Would you please tell him I stopped by, and tell him the Valentine's Dance is on Friday?"

"A Valentine's Dance! How romantic!" the firemen shouted.

"Yeah, I'll let him know."

I trudged back to the car, wanting to murder Evangeline.

❊

Friday, February 14, 1919

The melody of, "Till We Meet Again," echoed from the Will Wells Orchestra playing in the gym.

"Look how pretty everything looks." Pink and white carnations set in vases graced round tables covered in red cloth. Everywhere you looked, hearts of all sizes were affixed to the walls which were draped in sheer fabric. Some even hung from the ceiling. Florence and I stood at a table bearing place cards with names written in fancy penmanship. "I don't see my name. I'll go ask Evangeline. She's on the welcoming committee."

Evangeline, enveloped like a meringue in layers of red taffeta, scanned her list. "You're listed under students on probation, Jay. That means you're not permitted to attend school dances. I'm going to have to ask you to leave."

"No, no, that was from way back in October when I got suspended! There's got to be some mistake."

"Read it and weep. There was a note placed in your folder on January 17 for cheating, again! It's all right here, Josephine McKenna: On probation for violating the Haviland Hon ..."

" I know what it is, Evangeline!" I cringed as people started to stare. "Why don't you read it a little louder so everyone can hear?"

Florence sidled up to Evangeline. "My, don't you look pretty in that red dress."

"Why thank you, Florence. It's brand new."

"Now how about you just draw an itty bitty line though that nonsense next to Jay's name and let us all in? Won't you do that one little thing?"

"Well, I, uh, there's Dr. Wisdom," said Evangeline. "Let's see what she has to say about it."

"Forget it. I'm supposed to meet up with Ruth after the dance. I'll just call her to come and get me now." Something caught the corner of my eye. Leaning against a pole at the other side of the gym, talking to Clarence and George, was Henry.

"Oh, no! I'll wait outside. Florence, please go tell Henry I can't come in. That's him, right over there."

"Jay!" His black hair was parted in the middle and slicked back like a matinee idol. He wore a bow tie with a white dress shirt, and his shoes were polished to a high shine.

"Hi, Henry."

"What's going on? Your friend just told me you're not allowed in the dance!"

"I didn't know, honestly, or I would have told you not to come. I got suspended in October for writing Nathalia's essay for her, and I was caught cheating again in January, but I had no idea I was on probation. I'm so sorry."

"Great, just great." He ruined his hair by running his fingers through it. "Now what am I supposed to do? I spent fifty cents on a haircut, and now I'm stuck at this dumb dance! Why are you always getting in trouble here?"

"It's not my fault, Henry! Oh, just forget it. Go inside and have a good time. I'll go back to the dorm."

"No. I came to see you." He put his suit jacket around my shoulders. "You're going to freeze to death out here. Don't you even want to come inside for a few minutes, just to talk to me?"

"Of course I do, but that witch Evangeline will just kick me out."

"Come back inside the entranceway. Just hide over here behind the doors. She can't see us here."

"I feel so foolish now, not even being able to dance with you. I'm glad you came, though, really."

"Wasn't sure if you still wanted me to."

"I asked you to this dance, remember?"

"That was a month and a half ago, Jay. You promised me you were going to write and tell me when I could pick you up again after midterms were over." His chiseled face again bore that slight resemblance to his father's scowl. "I thought you had forgotten about me. And then, when you drove right past me the other day, I didn't know what to think."

"Henry, I came back after Evangeline picked up a dress at her house. Didn't your father give you my message?"

"Yeah, he said you stopped by after I left. I was so excited to tell you in person that I officially joined the fire department. I guess it doesn't matter."

"It does matter. It's wonderful news." I touched his sleeve. "Things got so crazy with midterms, and then this whole big thing with Nathalia, it was awful."

"I figured once you didn't need me to drive you to school or watch your dog, you weren't interested in me anymore. Listen, just forget it. I don't want to argue, okay?"

Just as I was about to apologize again, Wally Bennett ran over to us and grabbed Henry. A fresh wave of grief flooded over me. Wally had been chosen by the team to replace Christie as team captain and pitcher

"You got to get in here and see this!"

I poked my head inside so I could see what was going on.

George and the rest of the baseball team were teasing Clarence. Several girls were gathered around a chair at the table, giggling and whispering. Not again, I silently prayed. Keeping my head down, I snuck inside to get a better look.

From a big white box, Clarence was pulling out what looked like a large, full corset of some sort. I recognized the catalog name of Perry, Dame, and Company, stamped on the brown paper. Clarence's prominent ears turned purple. I nudged my way through the crowd until I was close enough to see George grab the corset and read the attached tag to the crowd. "Reducing Corset, especially designed for stout figures!"

"What in the world is this?" Clarence cried out above the howls from his teammates. The boys grabbed at the ridiculous garments Clarence was trying to stuff back into the box.

"Try them on, Clarence." shouted Wally. "They're just your size! Who's it from?"

"Guys, look!" Clarence held up the gift box sitting at his place. "The box has my name on it, I swear, guys, I had no idea what was in it! See for yourselves if you don't believe me."

Sure enough, the box was clearly marked with his name. He pulled out a letter after stuffing a ruffled petticoat back into the box, only to have Wally grab it back again and start prancing around in a ridiculous imitation of a girl. Clarence read the sheet of monogrammed stationery, covered with girlish writing.

I was now close enough to him to make out the names. "Mrs. Clarence McLeod," "Mrs. Evangeline McLeod," and a scrawled heart enclosing the names "Clarence and Evangeline forever." There were puckered lip imprints in red lipstick on the paper. George made smooching sounds and pretended to be Evangeline trying to kiss Clarence. This sent the boys into another round of hoots and hollers.

"Jay!" Florence signaled me to join her behind a table. "Stay behind me so the teachers can't see you!"

"Who could have gotten hold of Evangeline's catalog order? She told me I was the only person she had told about pretending to kiss Clarence just the other night."

"Which one of you jerks did this? This is some kind of sick gag or something!" Clarence tried to hide the letter by shoving it underneath an oversized pair of lacy drawers in the box. He made an attempt to toss the box under the table, but Wally grabbed it from him, throwing all the underwear up in the air. Everybody started tossing the garments around. George was wearing the huge reducing corset on his head.

"Get down!" Florence pushed me under the table. "Evangeline's coming this way!"

Evangeline barreled her way through the crowd along with Dr. Wisdom and Mrs. Westcott.

"No Evangeline! Don't go over there!" I tried to block her way.

"Dr. Wisdom, she refuses to obey the rules. You are forbidden to be here, Jay. Look at the ruckus she is causing with the boys! Please remove her!"

"What is the meaning of all this horseplay?" asked Dr. Wisdom.

"Okay, Evangeline!" I shouted as I was led away by Helen and Mercy. "Go right ahead! Don't say I didn't warn you!"

She started frantically trying to grab her underwear. Every time she reached for an undergarment, a boy would throw it to someone else, causing her to run after it again. She shoved the letters with the kiss imprints down the bodice of her dress.

Outside again, I peered through a window to witness Mary Agnes making her way back through the crowd. I had to hand it to her, running off to find whoever did this, with the way Evangeline treated her.

Evangeline came lumbering through the gymnasium door with her corset and underthings under each arm. Her flushed face was streaked with sweat and tears.

"What did I ever do to anyone?" She threw everything behind the seat of her father's roadster. "I can never show my face again." Convulsing in sobs, she put the car in reverse.

I walked over to the car.

"Get out of my way. I just want to go home." She raced down the school entrance way, skidding a bit on the icy driveway.

I snuck back inside and carefully snaked my way through the dancers, staying low. Through the partially open locker room door, I saw Nathalia yelling at Mary Agnes. I couldn't make out any of the words due to the volume of the band.

I waited until I saw Nathalia leave before approaching Mary Agnes. "Don't take her on. It's not worth it. We all know she did it. Evangeline went home."

She stuttered "I ... I need to..." and walked past me into the crowd. I had enough problems of my own without trying to figure out what was going on with her. On my way back, I passed Florence.

"Do you know where Henry is?"

"I haven't seen him."

"When you do, just tell him I'm waiting in the back so Helen and Mercy don't see me."

"Wait, Jay, I'm coming with you. I don't know any of those boys. I feel funny sitting at the table without you."

"He's not here." I scanned the entire gymnasium. "He wouldn't just leave, would he?"

"Maybe he went outside looking for you." Florence grabbed her coat. We made our way through the crowd of boys smoking by the door and ventured into the frigid night air. A pair of headlights suddenly lit up the entranceway of the school.

"That looks like Ruth's car. What in the world is she doing here already?" I took a closer look at the white roadster. "Wait a minute, that's not her driving."

I approached the car. The sound of tires screeching on the ice forced me to back up.

"Watch out, Jay!" Florence screamed. She grabbed me out of the way as the car lurched forward. When it backed up, I saw Henry in the passenger seat, yelling at the driver, whom I couldn't see behind the steering wheel.

"What is Henry doing in Ruth's car?" The driver put the car in forward gear and tore down the school's entryway. The alarming sound of grinding gears and rapid engine acceleration caused the dance guests to empty out of the gym.

We all chased after the car. The roadster swerved on ice and scraped the side of a towering oak tree, leaving a scratch that ran the full length of the passenger side. Somebody was going to get killed.

"What in Sam Hill is going on out here?" Mr. Gallagher's ring of keys jangled as he raced off after the runaway vehicle. Florence and I slid down the icy roads behind the roadster as it sped down Seminary Hill.

I couldn't believe my eyes. People rushed out of their homes and joined the mob. An old lady had grabbed a shot gun. "I'm going to shoot out the tires!" she yelled. "Confounded kids, joy riding on my property!"

Someone shouted "They're heading toward the lake!"

Main Street hugged the shores of Lake Gleneida. I screamed as the beautiful automobile raced toward the lake's edge. The roadster was airborne for a few seconds before crashing head first through the ice.

"Henry!" I screamed, running on to the frozen lake. Clarence and George caught up to me on the ice. Slipping and sliding, we edged our way to the car, already starting to sink. I lay down on the ice. "Hold my ankles, tight, so I don't fall in!" I yelled to Clarence. "I'll try to pull them out!"

"Get out of the way!" Clarence shoved me to the side. "I'm going in!" He dove into the icy water.

George lay down on the ice beside me. "Grab my legs!" he yelled to Wally.

I felt someone pulling at my feet.

"We got you!" yelled Florence, squeezing one of my ankles. Lydia held the other one. Wally and the baseball team made a chain behind George.

"Pull!" George yelled. I reached toward the car, as far as I could until I was able to grab hold of Henry's hair. He was slumped against the windshield.

"Pull, Jay, pull!" Florence screamed. With all my strength, I pulled first at his hair, then his shoulders. Together, George and I dragged Henry's limp body from the car onto the ice.

"Help!" cried Clarence from the other side of the car. "She's choking me! I can't breathe!" His head went under. I jumped into the glacial water, and tried to swim to him. The shock of the icy plunge sucked all the air out of my lungs. I struggled to breathe. George dove in after me. Henry's suit jacket was weighing me down.

"George, pull my jacket off! My arm's caught!"

George yanked the wet jacket from my arms. I was now able to make my way over to Clarence.

"Get her off of me!" George struggled with the girl dragging Clarence down. I succeeded in getting her arms unlocked from his neck. In the dark, I couldn't make out her face.

"Over here, Jay!" Florence and Lydia were waiting at the edge of the hole in the ice.

"Push them out!" George yelled.

With my arm under Clarence's head, I dragged him to the edge of the hole. George and I heaved his arms up and out on the ice into Florence's hands. She and Lydia yanked him onto the ice.

The girl lost consciousness as I tried to push her up. George grabbed one of her shoulders, and I grabbed the other. Her blonde hair was plastered to the sides of her bone white face. Just then, the moon came out from behind a cloud. I looked at her. It was Nathalia.

"Just get her arms up here!" yelled Florence.

My strength was giving out in the numbing water. With one last heave, we pushed her up. Florence grabbed her.

I fell back into the lake from the effort, swallowing water. I looked to my left. George was going under.

"Come on!" I screamed. "Get up on the ice!" With a surge of adrenaline, I pulled him up to Florence first, then grabbed hold of both her hands and let her drag me out of the water. Someone threw a blanket around my shoulders. I heard the clang of the fire pumper bell. With my teeth chattering, I got up and ran to Henry.

I winced as I saw the gash over his eye. He still hadn't come around

He's gone into shock," Mr. Gallagher said. "We've got to get him to a doctor, fast!"

Chapter 14

I held onto Henry's hand as he was carried on a stretcher to the fire pumper.

Officer Belden of the Carmel police approached Mr. Gallagher. "After these young hooligans are bandaged up, I'll need to speak to them down at the station."

"Not going to get much out of them, Belden." Mr. Gallagher yanked his thumb over his shoulder toward Nathalia, lying across the seat of the fire pumper.

I approached her. "What have you done?" My voice caught before I could complete the sentence.

Florence pulled me back. "Come away. We've got to get out of these wet clothes or we're going to freeze to death."

I spotted Ruth and Miss Addison carefully making their way down the icy embankment to shoreline. "Jay!" they yelled, arms locked. "Where are you?"

"Ruth! There's been an accident!" Florence and I helped them down so they could speak with the police officer.

"Margaret, give this poor girl your coat. Her lips are blue!"

Ruth removed her own sable and wrapped it around my shoulders while Miss Addison draped her winter wool around Florence. Ruth covered her mouth with her gloved hands as we tried to explain what happened.

"Are the kids badly hurt?"

"We think the boy broke his arm, but we're not sure of anything," Officer Belden explained. "I'm sorry Ma'am, but the water damage to the engine will never allow it to run right again. I'm afraid you're out a car."

"What would ever possess a bunch of youngsters to steal my car and drive it into a lake? Someone could've been killed! Jay, please tell me you had nothing to do with this!"

"Oh no, Ruth! Why was the roadster doing parked at Haviland? You must have left your keys in the car."

She smacked her forehead with the heel of her gloved hand. "That's where I left them! I was driving down from Albany, and I met Margaret here for dinner at the Lakeside Hotel before it was time to pick you up from the dance. I parked the car by the gymnasium and we took hers."

Miss Addison was interviewing Officer Belden.

Ruth continued. "We couldn't find the car anywhere. Then we heard all the commotion down here. I never would've imagined this!"

"Excuse me miss, but we'll need to get some information from you for the police report. Would you mind coming down to the station?" Officer Belden had stepped away from Miss Addison, who was now speaking to some of the dance guests.

"Yes, Officer, of course, but then I have to get these girls back to the dorm to warm up."

❈

"Why did he go off with her, of all people?" I sank down into the three hot water bottles Lydia had tucked in around me under my quilt. Florence sat on Evangeline's bed, her teeth chattering, wrapping both hands around a mug of steaming broth.

My party dress was drying on the steam radiator. The bodice was stained with blood from the cut over Henry's eye. "If Nathalia's trying to ruin my life, she's succeeding!"

"You know how low minded she is. Wait until you hear what Henry has to say for himself. He's gone and gotten himself into a whole heap of trouble stealing that fancy car."

The small mercy of sleep eluded me for much of the night. I couldn't warm up, and I kept hearing the awful screech of the roadster's tires, barreling down the entranceway. I longed for Sullivan's soft fur to console me.

I planned on sleeping all day Saturday, only to be woken by a knock on the door. Groggily, I answered it.

"You look awful!" Florence handed me a cup of coffee. "Mrs. Bumford fixed it the exact shade you like it, with plenty of cream and sugar, just like me."

I took a sip and set the cup down on my desk. "What time is it?" I asked, falling back into bed.

"Get up, Hayseed. What are you going to do, hide in here all day? Nathalia wins that way. Here, I brought you something, Special Edition." She took a folded copy of *The Courier* out from under her arm. "The crash made the front page."

Miss Addison had printed a photograph of the Saxon Six partially submerged in the lake. She must have stayed up all night at the printing press to finish the exclusive edition. The ink smudged when I touched it.

It read: "Fire Captain Gallagher, who is also Head Custodian at Haviland Seminary, was quoted as saying it was, "*by the grace of God that the youngsters' injuries weren't more serious. The two joy seekers were both treated for hypothermia. The only broken bones were suffered by Brewster Fire Captain Henry Harkin's boy, namely a few ribs and his left arm.*" The rescue of the youngsters in the car, which was submerged in the icy waters of Lake Gleneida, was courageously undertaken by the Brewster Bears baseball team and the ladies of the Haviland Seminary, valiantly led by George Addison and Josephine McKenna, both of Brewster, until the Carmel Fire Department arrived at the scene."

"At least you made the paper."

"She just printed that because George is her kid brother."

"Doctor Stanley Birdsall was quoted as he set Henry's broken arm. "*Sitting on the sidelines watching his teammates play ball this spring might give him time to think about getting in a stolen vehicle with a female behind the wheel.*" A shaken Miss Ruth Lefkowitz, of Lake Mahopac and Manhattan, owner of the luxury vehicle, was quoted as saying she wasn't interested in pressing charges, but wanted to know who was going to reimburse her for the loss of her roadster."

I handed the paper to Florence. "I don't want to read anymore."

"Suit yourself." Florence picked up where I left off and read the remainder of the article aloud.

"In a statement obtained by a school official, the driver of the vehicle, 15-year-old Nathalia Ormsby of Riverdale, New York, was unable to comment as she was said to be, "*heavily sedated and under the care of the school nurse at Haviland Seminary for Ladies, where she is a boarding student.*" There was no comment available from the girl's parents, who are reported to be vacationing in the Florida Keys.

Police officials were quoted as saying simply that the accident was under investigation."

❧

Thursday, February 20, 1919

"One day's suspension for stealing a car and driving it into a lake! That's a vacation, for heaven's sake. Mother is writing a stinging letter to Doctor Wisdom!" Evangeline was holding court as we walked back to the dorm after dinner. She hadn't felt up to returning to school until that morning.

"Nathalia said Henry forced her into the car, so he should be responsible for the cost of replacing the roadster," said Mercy.

"Her parents cut a check for Ruth the day they arrived home from vacation," I said. "Mary Agnes, what did Nathalia say at the dance when you went after her?"

Evangeline stopped in her tracks. "You went after Nathalia? Why didn't you tell me?"

"I forgot about it. I don't remember what Nathalia said." Mary Agnes walked ahead of us.

"Who do you think got hold of your, uh, things, Evangeline?" I asked.

"I can't figure out how in the world someone could've pulled off such a dirty trick! Who could've stolen my Perry Dame catalog order? You were with me, Jay. I picked the boxes up myself and brought them back here. And how could anyone know about Clarence? I've never told a soul, except you, Jay!"

"Don't look at me, Evangeline!"

A flicker of suspicion ignited in the pit of my stomach. "I'm going for a walk around campus. Look, it's still light out."

Florence and I passed the remaining weeks of winter walking at dusk each night through the stubborn patches of snow to our spot where we took comfort in the views of the thawing lake. We scanned the shore for any sign of the first weeping willows.

"Have you heard from him?" Florence asked during one of our ventures. Our boots crunched through the stubborn ice on the sides of the creek.

"No, and I never want to see him again." My heart had shriveled into a dark pit.

"If you want to lose your man to Nathalia, go right ahead. I know I wouldn't give him up without a fight. But that's just me. You want to hang on to all that resentment until it swallows you whole, be my guest."

"She tricked him into letting her drive Ruth's car, I know she did!" I felt the anger surge up in me, threatening to snap me in half. "But why wasn't he strong enough to resist her? How could he betray me like this?" Meddlesome tears filled my eyes as they had every day since the dance."

"You need to look at the role you played in all this," Florence said.

"Me? What did I do?"

Florence ticked off on her fingers as she explained. "That boy drove you to school, watched your dog, mucked out your barn, kept your livestock alive, and you couldn't even take the time to write him a thank you note or even give him the time of day. What do you expect?"

"Don't hold back, Florence," I mustered up all the sarcasm I could. "Just speak your mind. Don't worry about my feelings. I've just thrown away the most perfect man on earth."

Oh, look at that!" said Florence. We had come upon a small garden which had lain dormant over the long winter. A clump of purple crocuses were poking their heads through a layer of dead leaves.

❧

Wednesday, March 5, 1919
Miss Chichester asked me to stay behind one day after class.

"I wanted to let you know, Miss McKenna, that based on the results of Nathalia's academic evaluations, effective immediately, she will be switching to the less strenuous classical program of study."

"Does that mean I don't have to tutor her anymore? I don't know anything about still life painting or elocution lessons."

"You don't have to tutor her anymore. And I'd like to applaud you for bringing to my attention your correct suspicion that Miss Ormsby has reading difficulties. I don't know if I would've recommended that she be evaluated if it hadn't been for your foresight. I'm thinking you've the makings of a fine teacher."

"Thank you, Miss Chichester, but I'd like to pursue social work."

"A very admirable career for a young woman. Good day, Miss McKenna.

❋

Saturday, March 9, 1919

Lydia had joined me for a sunset walk as Florence had gone home for the weekend. We were on our way back when we saw a shiny, black Columbia Six roadster waiting at the dormitory entrance. Florence got out of the passenger side of the car and ran to me. "There you are! You've got to come with me."

"Is something wrong? I thought you were visiting your mother."

"I am, but you've got to see what I've found. Lydia, I think you should come too!"

❋

The Crane house was coming into view to the left. It sat atop a huge expanse of lawn, which afforded a breathtaking view of the Middlebranch Reservoir.

"Come inside," Florence said. "I'll tell you the rest once we get upstairs to my room."

The interior of the house was lavishly decorated, but way too dark. The parlor was filled with mahogany furniture and velvet sofas. Someone should've pulled back the heavy drapes and thrown open a window to let in some air. The smell of roasting chicken permeated the house.

"Mama!" Florence led us into the kitchen. "Come meet my friends."

"Hello girls! Florence has told me all about you." Mrs. Bright was very pretty. Her skin was a much deeper shade than Florence's, and her eyes were dark brown, not light green, like her daughter's. She was wearing a grey uniform dress with a ruffled white apron. On her head sat a starched lace cap.

"And I'm Mrs. Crane." Violet's aunt came into the kitchen to oversee the dinner preparations. She wore a round collared pinstriped dress buttoned up to her collar. "Father is ready for his tea, Charlotte."

"Come with me. I've got to show you something." Florence led us toward a stairway that led up to the servant's quarters. On the way, we passed the nursery where two little girls sat playing by a dollhouse. A nanny, in an apron stained with pabulum, sat rocking a baby while a toddler boy tugged at her skirt, crying. The characters of Little Boy Blue and Mary with her little lamb graced the soft blue and pink papered walls. It was the only pleasant, airy room in the house.

Once we climbed to the top of several flights of stairs, Florence led me down a narrow white hallway until she reached the last door on the right.

"Whew!" I was winded. "You do this every time you sleep here?"

"Yep." Florence opened the door to a sparsely furnished room with two iron-railed single beds. "A little different than the parlor, wouldn't you say? We can talk in private up here."

"I prefer this room," I said.

"We can sit on my bed." Florence opened the top drawer of the single dresser and pulled out a book. She laid it on the bed.

"That's just last year's yearbook," Lydia said.

"It's not the book I want to show you. Look." She opened the cover to reveal two pages of notes with the greeting. "Dear Shrinking Violet."

I opened my mouth in a circle. "Violet's yearbook! Did you find something?"

Florence turned the back cover and revealed a flattened stack of envelopes, tied together with a purple silk ribbon.

"I wasn't snooping in Violet's private things, mind you. This book was in the drawer of the nightstand next to my bed. I figured maybe it used to be in Violet's room, and no one checked the drawers before they moved it into this room. I was on my way downstairs to give the book to Mrs. Crane, when the notes fell out of the book. I did read them, I admit, but I think God will forgive me when you see what these letters tell us."

Tucked beneath the ribbon was a tiny bouquet of pressed violets. Florence gently untied the ribbon, and sacredly placed the pressed flowers back among the pages of the yearbook. I held my breath as she took a delicate sheet of stationery paper from the first envelope and began to read it aloud to us.

> "My dearest Violet,
>> Soon I'll walk beside you, proudly,
>> Two hearts will beat as one, my dearest.
>> No more discord, secrets, or shame,
>> Only harmony.
>
> Yours forever,
> Eugene"

I heard those words before. "Discord, secrets, shame. Those words were in Violet's poem."

Florence read on. "There's sixteen letters here, all promising Violet that this person and she will, "be as one," someday, but it never seemed to happen."

Florence thumbed through the stack of envelopes until she came to one in particular. She unfolded the note within and handed it to me. "Read this one."

> "Dearest Violet,
>> How unfair love can be,
>> While others cannot see that
>> Two so unlike
>> Can be so devoted
>> So much more
>> Than a humble pedagogue
>> And an earnest seeker of knowledge,
>> Only man and woman
>> Forever entwined

172

Soon, my precious one.
Soon.

Yours always,
Eugene"

"What's a pedagogue?" I asked.

"I looked it up," Florence said. "It means the same as teacher."

"A teacher was sending love notes to Violet!" Lydia exclaimed. "Isn't that against the law?" Suddenly, she clapped her hand over her mouth. "Oh my God. Florence, give me the yearbook, quick!"

She flipped through the pages until she came to the faculty portraits, and focused on the distinguished portrait of Doctor Eugene Propper, Professor of Biology. His wavy, light colored hair was combed back to reveal a high forehead.

"Oh, Violet." Lydia's eyes grew watery. "She was very fond of Dr. Propper. She did so well in science, and she talked about him all the time. I never in a million years thought that there was more to it than that."

"Why isn't he teaching at Haviland anymore?" I asked.

"I don't know. Remember Miss Chichester told us she joined the faculty just a week before school started?" Lydia said.

"A week before school started. Just days before Violet died." I put down the letter and looked at Lydia and Florence. "What if she jumped out of the plane when she found out he wasn't coming back to Haviland? Did Violet kill herself because Dr. Propper broke her heart?"

There was a knock on the door.

An elderly servant appeared, bearing a silver tray of sliced chicken, mashed potatoes, gravy, and biscuits. "Your mother sent this up for you and your friends." Her gaze went directly to the pile of letters we were poring over, and a scowl darkened her lined face. "You shouldn't be going through Miss Violet's personal belongings, Florence."

"We were just looking up a picture of some friends from school. We'll be careful, and put everything back, I promise. Don't tell Mrs. Crane, please, Gertie?"

Gertie set the tray down on the dresser. She reached to take the letters from Florence's hands. Florence pulled them back.

"Those letters caused a lot of misery for Miss Violet. She wouldn't want you girls picking apart her private property like scavengers. Now give them here."

Florence held tight to the letters.

"What kind of misery did they cause her?" I asked.

"That's none of your business, miss. Put those letters back where you found them."

"If you know something, Gertie, you owe it to Violet to tell someone. Dr. Crane is trying to find out how she died. What is it?" Florence asked.

The old servant sat down on Florence's mother's bed and rested a minute. "Suppose it's all water under the bridge now that it's all said and done. Some irate woman came pounding on the front door a week or so before poor Miss Violet died. Thought she'd take the door clear off its hinges. She had two little ones with her, a boy and a girl. All her hollering was scaring those poor little children. I opened the door, and she burst in without even being asked, demanding to see Violet Crane."

"Who was she?" I asked.

"I'm getting to that part. Miss Violet came running downstairs, and this lunatic started waving a bunch of letters just like the ones you're holding right there. She starts spewing all sorts of nonsense, demanding that Miss Violet leave her husband alone."

"Dr. Propper's wife?" I asked.

"She was someone's wife, that's for sure. When she called Miss Violet a home wrecker, I ordered her out of this house. I had to threaten to call the police before she took leave. Poor Miss Violet ran out of the house after her and wouldn't come back no matter how loud I called to her."

"Why didn't you tell someone?" said Florence. "You should have called the sheriff."

"I'm getting to that part." She passed us each a plate of food. "Here, eat this before it gets cold. I didn't carry that heavy tray all the way up here to have the food just sit."

I pushed the plate away. I wanted her to finish her story.

"Didn't see much of Miss Violet those next few days, always holed up in her bedroom, or sitting out in the gazebo for hours at a time, just staring into space. And then, the next thing you know, Mr. Crane comes home and tells us that that poor girl's dead." She wiped her eyes with a dirty handkerchief she took from her pocket. "It was all that crazy woman's fault, I tell you," she cried. "Now hand over those letters to me, please! I owe her that much."

"No," Florence said. "I'm giving these letters to Dr. Crane. You should've told him this yourself, months ago!"

The old woman broke down. "I know, child, but I couldn't. I wasn't even supposed to be at the house that day. Mrs. Crane left instructions for me to travel clear up to Danbury to pick up an order of frocks for the little girls." She rubbed her shoulder. "My neuralgia kept me up all night. I woke up exhausted that morning. After the family left on an outing for the day, I had a wee drop, and fell back to sleep. I didn't wake until I heard the banging at the door. I had no idea that Violet had stayed home."

"But, how did you explain not having the clothes order when Mrs. Crane arrived back home?" I asked.

"I should've cut my wicked tongue out for telling such a lie."

"What are you talking about?" Florence asked.

"I was so afraid for my job that I told Mrs. Crane Charlotte Bright offered to pick up the dress order so that I could visit my sister for the day, and that she must have forgotten all about it. I figured they'd believe me because she was new and all, and well, she was...."

"Colored!" Florence spat the word out. "You blamed the new colored cook, because, well, we're known for being lazy and unreliable. Isn't that right, Gertie?"

"I couldn't tell them about that crazy lady's visit or they'd have known I was lying!"

Florence's lips were quivering. "Go downstairs now and tell them what you did or I'll tell them myself."

The family assembled in the suffocating parlor. Mrs. Crane sat stiffly in a Windsor chair. An older man, dressed in an elegant burgundy robe and mono-grammed slippers, was seated in a worn leather chair that seemed out of place.

The stuffing was coming out of the armrest through tears in the leather. A beagle slept in the man's lap. This had to be the elder Mr. Crane. He was still quite handsome, with his neatly combed white hair and jewel-toned cravat tucked into the front of his robe. He wore a family crest ring on his pinky finger as he sipped cognac.

Florence sat with her mother. Lydia and I joined them on a red sofa edged in gold tassels.

"Gertie has something to tell you all," Florence began.

The old lady repeated the tale she told us upstairs.

"This house has a curse upon it!" yelled the elder Mr. Crane. "I should have never come up here!" He struggled to stand up on his spindly legs. The beagle woke and jumped down off his lap. It lunged at Mrs. Crane, biting her ankles.

"Keep that wretched beast away from me!" Mrs. Crane swatted the dog with a lace handkerchief. "You know how much he hates me!"

Old Mr. Crane collapsed into a coughing spasm that wracked his frail body.

"We never should have come up here, Charlotte! Let's go back to the city, now! I want to go home."

Florence's mother settled him back in his chair and topped off his cognac. "Don't go getting yourself all excited. You have a weak chest, remember?"

The old man removed his smudged spectacles and placed them on the arm rest of his battered chair. I looked at the yellow coronas that encircled the pupils in his light green eyes.

Chapter 15

Thursday, March 13, 1919

"What a creep this guy must have been, carrying on with Violet when he had a wife and children at home. No wonder he resigned from Haviland. Maybe Violet's father can press charges." I was walking with Florence through the gardens on the first warm day of March. Robins pecked at worms on the grass, still flattened and yellow from the tough winter.

"I don't think so," said Florence. "It's not like he pushed her or anything. She hired that pilot to take her up in the airplane. Still though, at least the investigator can question Dr. Propper, wherever he snuck off to. That old fool Gertie could have prevented Violet's death if she hadn't blamed Mama for her mistake."

"Do you think the school knew anything? Do you think they found out and fired Dr. Propper?"

"Possibly. I wonder if they knew what was going on and deliberately kept it from the investigators so they wouldn't be held liable for Violet's death."

"Do you think Miss Chichester would tell us why Dr. Propper left? Probably not, I know, but I don't have any other ideas."

"I would do anything that would help me figure this whole mess out."

Violet came to me in a vivid dream that night. She was writing a letter, tears falling from her eyes, spreading the indigo blue ink in blotches on her paper. She fanned the paper to dry the ink, folded the parchment, and tied it in a purple silk ribbon. She tucked a single violet beneath the ribbon. She scrawled the name Dr. Eugene Propper on the front of the envelope. She whispered to me, "*Remember.*"

My pillow felt damp under my head when I awoke. I was bathed in sweat. Dr. Propper. Where had I heard that name before? I blinked to clear my mind enough to recall that snowy day at the creek when Lydia told us that Violet tutored Nathalia Ormsby in science and math last year. If Miss Chichester had taken over for Dr. Propper, then Nathalia would have had him for those classes.

❧

Tuesday, March 18

"What can I do for you, Miss McKenna? I was just taking tea with Mrs. Westcott." Miss Chichester set out a tray of olives on a lace tea towel.

"May I ask you if you've heard anything about Dr. Propper, the teacher you replaced?" I was impressed with my own forwardness. Back in September, I was barely able to make eye contact with any of my teachers.

Mrs. Westcott answered for Miss Chichester. "Dr. Propper was a wonderful teacher. What's your interest in him?"

"I'm just wondering if you knew anything about why he left."

"I'm not sure if it's appropriate for you to be asking such questions, but if you must know, I believe in his letter of resignation he stated that an immediate move to upstate New York was required of him to deal with a family emergency. Of course, we were very sad to see such an esteemed colleague leave, but we've consoled ourselves with the delightful company of Miss Chichester."

Mrs. Westcott took the radish finger sandwich offered to her by Miss Chichester. "Is there anything else I can help you with?"

"Do you know if Nathalia Ormsby needed a tutor in Dr. Propper's class last year?"

Miss Chichester interrupted. "Miss McKenna. Have there been any further incidents with Miss Ormsby? Because if there have been, you must let me know immediately."

"No, Miss Chichester."

Mrs. Westcott took over. "Miss McKenna, kindly enlighten us. Precisely why are you asking about Miss Ormsby being in Dr Propper's class last year?"

"Because something terrible happened to someone who was tutoring Nathalia last year in Dr. Propper's class."

"Who?"

"Violet Crane."

Mrs. Westcott's teacup fell out of her hand, sending jagged chards of china shattering across the highly-waxed wood floor.

"Sit down and explain what this is all about. Miss Chichester, would you be so kind as to fetch Doctor Wisdom? And get Mr. Gallagher to sweep up the broken pieces, please."

❊

Wednesday, March 19, 1919

Classes the next day were interrupted by a steady parade of students being called down to Dr. Wisdom's office.

"I think Miss Biddle is going to have a nervous breakdown," Florence whispered to me in social studies.

"Maybe there's some kind of cheating scandal," Mercy said to Helen.

"I'll bet there's a new outbreak of Spanish flu in the school," said Evangeline.

When I was called down, two men were seated alongside the headmistress. A tall man in a grey tweed vest greeted me as I took my seat.

Dr. Wisdom's usually pressed jacket and skirt was today a wrinkled mess with dark perspiration stains under both armpits.

"Miss McKenna, this is Chief Investigator Knapp and Doctor Raymond Crane. Investigator Knapp would like to speak to you."

Violet's father had those same soulful eyes as his daughter.

The tough, square, jaw of the investigator's pockmarked face softened a bit. He extended his massive hand toward mine. "Pleased to meet you, Miss McKenna. I wonder if I might ask you a few questions about what you observed on the day of Violet Crane's death."

"Tell the investigator everything you know, Miss McKenna." Doctor Wisdom looked defeated.

❊

A few days after talking to the investigator, I was coming back from watching the sunset. To my delight, I noticed daffodils starting to come up in the gardens.

The town of Carmel below was punctuated by church steeples and the stoic white columns of the courthouse.

I smelled a bonfire. Mr. Gallagher often burned one for light when he was called on to make repairs on buildings after dark. I walked over for a visit.

"Good evening, Miss Jay. Beautiful night, isn't it? Can I ask you to tend the fire while I go fetch my toolbox? Got a jammed window over there on the south wing of the building."

I agreed and stood watching the fire burning in a barrel. The skeletal remains of the logs were mesmerizing. I loved the way they turned bright blue deep down into the fire. I often wondered how many thousands of degrees they must be. It took a moment before I realized I wasn't alone.

"I knew you'd come!" Mary Agnes rose from a bench and approached me. "Oh, I thought you were someone else." She shrank back to her seat.

"What are you doing out here?"

"None of your business."

"Did you get called in to Dr. Wisdom's office?"

"No."

"Oh, I thought you might. I remember how you tried to find out who played that awful prank on Evangeline at the dance."

"I said I didn't get called in."

"I hope they finally catch whoever is behind all these horrible pranks, or whatever they are, so no one else gets hurt." I poked at the fire with a stick.

"They won't."

"Why do you say that?"

She hugged her bony knees.

I tossed a log into the barrel, sending up a shower of sparks. A chorus of peepers serenaded us.

"Everybody thinks Nathalia is behind all the pranks. I can't figure out how she does it, though. She'll get caught, eventually. Someone will talk."

"You honestly believe Nathalia is capable of carrying off everything that has happened? I figured you to be smarter than that"

"Why do you say that?"

"I don't know."

"Well, if that's the case, then I could think of two people who would help her. I figure Helen and Mercy would do a lot of her dirty work for her. Other than that, I don't know, really."

"And you think among the three of them they can bring so many people down, create so much havoc, and find out so many personal details about girls they barely even know? You really think they can do all that?"

I poked at the fire to keep it going. "Now that you put it like that, no." The force of a heavy log I turned over sprayed embers around us.

Mary Agnes's eyes looked hollow in the firelight. I stayed quiet for a while, listening to an owl hooting above the peepers.

"Does it bother you, the way Evangeline treats you?" I finally asked. "Why don't you stick up for yourself?"

"Believe you me, I got back at her in a way she'll never forget as long as she lives."

"It was you."

She said nothing.

"Nathalia had nothing to do with the box of underwear for Clarence. Evangeline said that I was the only person she told about her kissing a mirror and pretending it was Clarence. But I wasn't. Friday, February 7, You were in the back of the car. You heard the entire conversation. And you'd certainly know about her Perry Dame underwear order. You just had to swipe it from her closet. Who else could it have been?" It all seemed so simple now.

I circled around the fire and Mary Agnes. "The question now, though, is why would you go to all the trouble to stage such a vicious public act, just to have Nathalia get all the credit? Evangeline will never figure out you were behind the whole thing. Why not just tell her? Maybe she'll think twice before she says something mean to you again."

"She owed me."

"Of course. She owes you a big apology. That's why you should ..."

She cut me off. "I don't care what that blowhard thinks of me."

"Well then, who are you talking about? Who owes you?"

She stared into the fire.

My mind began to race. Random dates and events began to form a common thread: The quarantine notice, the whiskey bottles, the arrest warrant, the unpaid bills. What had Mr. Gallagher said when Mary Agnes ran back into the building to get her French assignment that night back in September?

"Hey you, there, little girl. Haven't I caught you sneaking in and out of classrooms and the front office after school hours at least a dozen times? What are you up to now?"

"Friday, September 20. You weren't going inside to get assignments you supposedly forgotten. That was all a hoax so Evangeline would drive you back to school when no one was there. You were rifling through people's things, looking through student files, trying to get your hands on any dirt you could. You're working for Nathalia!"

"I'm not working for anybody!" Mary Agnes's face contorted in indignation. "We're friends. She needs me. She's too dense to get anything herself! She couldn't have pulled off half the things I've done for her. And now she…."

"February 14. Why was Nathalia yelling at you at the dance? What did you do, break a rule?"

"After all I did for Nathalia, I wanted this one to be all mine."

"All yours? What are you talking about?"

"I had been fighting her battles for her since I started at Haviland. Nathalia was furious that people at the dance thought she had given Clarence the box with Evangeline's underwear. She's cut me off now, won't even talk to me anymore. She said she never wanted my help! But she can't get along without me!" She punched her thigh with her closed fist.

"How'd you come to work for Nathalia?"

"As I've already stated, I don't work for her; we're friends. I met her during placement exams, you know, the ones we had to take in order to get into Haviland."

I guessed I was exempt because of the scholarship.

"I saw Nathalia trying to copy my answers. She said she'd make it worth my while if I didn't tell. She said we could be best friends."

"And you believed her." Mary Agnes was as gullible as I was.

"I started writing papers for her when I realized she could barely read or write. She used choir practice as an excuse for getting out of homework. We started meeting right out here on this bench after dark so no one could catch me giving her the assignments I'd completed. The best part was that Evangeline didn't know anything about me being friends with the most popular girl at Haviland."

I bit down on my tongue.

"Everything was going well until Dr. Propper accused me of writing Nathalia's science papers for her. Boy, was she mad at him for ruining our arrangement! I promised her we'd get our revenge. I guess we got him good." She broke into a small grin.

Tiny beads of sweat had gathered on my forehead as a result of standing too close to the fire. I brushed it off.

"I knew Nathalia was depending on me to come up with a new plan. I figured out that if Nathalia applied for a tutor, she could figure out a way to have somebody else write her essays for her. Lydia Penny got the job, so I told Nathalia to pressure her to write the paper. Of course, Lydia fell for it."

"But Mary Agnes, I've never seen you and Nathalia together. Why did you think you were friends?"

"She wanted us to keep our friendship private. We had to keep things secret so she wouldn't get in trouble for having people do her work."

"That's not friendship. She was using you. Don't you see? If you get caught, nothing you've done can be traced back to Nathalia. She can claim she didn't know anything about anything you've done."

"I know that now. But she said we were friends. She's the only person who has ever wanted to be friends with me. She told me she needed me. And I wanted to keep our friendship private, too."

"Why?"

"Because if Evangeline found out about us, she'd squash it. She's ruined any chance of happiness I've ever had."

She stood up and studied me, possibly calculating the meaning of my silence. I guess somehow she interpreted it as a sign of my willingness to listen to her side. I had to convince this monster to keep talking.

"If I'm to tell you any more, I want you to promise you'll nail Nathalia's hide to the wall. You better be sure that investigator can get her, or I'll deny ever speaking to you. I swear it." Her look was cold, void of remorse.

I swallowed, almost afraid to speak. "OK."

"I promised Nathalia I would dig something up on Lydia Penny once she started refusing to write assignments for her. It was easy. I found her application for R.A. Her mother's last name sounded familiar. I followed it up by finding the newspaper articles about her stepfather."

"Mary Agnes, did Nathalia specifically ask you to dig something up on Lydia?"

"No, but she didn't try to stop me, not until later. She seemed happy with what I was able to accomplish. She told me I was very clever." Mary Agnes grinned, baring sharp, yellowed teeth.

"And you, Jay, were a piece of cake. After your brother died, the quarantine notice was a cinch to get. You could swipe one at any public health office, along with masks, what with the influenza epidemic raging last fall."

I couldn't let her know what a sick, twisted minion I felt she was if I was to glean more information. I had to control my sense of revulsion, no matter how much this pathetic girl sickened me. "And again, Nathalia had no knowledge of this?"

"No, it was all me. I could tell she was impressed with that one."

"But how did you gain access to private documents? Surely someone must have asked you what you're doing when you were rifling through files in public health offices."

"Easy. I'm invisible, just like you. Nobody pays any attention to me."

"Doesn't it bother you to know you have caused so many people so much pain? Aren't you afraid of getting in trouble?"

"You see any witnesses to this conversation out here? I told you I'll deny everything unless you get Nathalia. Do not dare mention my name. I mean it, Jay."

'Did Nathalia ever try to stop you?'

"Yes, she told me people thought she was behind the pranks. She even got her mother to call the school and demand Miss Chichester stop accusing her of copying lab reports. She said she could handle herself, but I knew she didn't mean it. I just tried to be more careful so as not to leave a trail that led to her."

I imagined a handful of puzzle pieces scattered across a game table. How could I get them to interlock? "September 21, the night of the Pot Luck. Evangeline said the Mitchell Six ran out of gasoline that evening, and you just happened to know that I lived on Brewster Hill. You had only just met me. Did the car actually run out of gas, Mary Agnes?"

"It did after I drained most of the tank when we got home. I needed information on you. I thought you might be useful to Nathalia. Turns out, I was right, wasn't I?"

"You went over to Salmon's to use their phone. You told me to go back to the party. What did you ask Mrs. Salmon?"

"She is one nosy neighbor. She all but gave me a financial statement on your family's money troubles. Turned out I didn't need her though, did I, if you're so smart?"

"No, you didn't need her, because when I introduced Evangeline to Da, he told her that your father arranged the loan for the ice house."

"He might as well have given me the key to the bank's filing cabinet where the financial records are stored. You should tell him to watch his tongue when he's been drinking. Every business in the village has receipts that can be swiped when someone turns away for a minute. Turns out your Dahas unpaid bills stretching from Brewster to Mahopac!"

I had an image of Mary Agnes slinking around the village like a snake.

"And then I met Henry. I had a feeling Nathalia would like to get to know him better. Easy on the eyes, that one."

My hand itched to slap her, but I stayed quiet for a few minutes, carefully planning my next question as I tossed another log on the fire.

"What did you do to Violet?

"I didn't do anything to her." For the first time all night, she looked vulnerable, maybe even a little afraid.

"Well somebody did. Somebody as good as pushed her out of that airplane. I know she was tutoring Nathalia last year in Dr. Propper's science class."

"If only Violet would've written science reports for Nathalia, she might be alive today. You ought to remember that if you know what's good for you."

"Did you expose Violet's affair with Dr. Propper? Did you steal Violet's letters and give them to Dr. Propper's wife? Did you threaten to blackmail Dr. Propper unless he resigned?" It took a moment for me to comprehend the malice this creature might be capable of. "What did you do to cause Violet to take her own life?"

Five solid minutes passed in silence.

"There was no affair between Violet and Dr. Propper. He was married with children, for goodness sake. She was fourteen years old at the time. Really, Jay, you've quite the imagination."

"I've got proof, Mary Agnes. What about the letters he wrote to her? What about the letters that she wrote back to him?"

She looked at me as if I was a very simple child. "Dr. Propper never wrote Violet any letters."

"Then who …?" I stopped and put the final pieces of the puzzle together. "You wrote the letters."

"You actually believe Nathalia could write a letter?" Mary Agnes coughed up a low, guttural laugh. "Nathalia couldn't write a grocery list! You figured that out. She gets by through memorizing."

"I realize that now, but how has she been able to rely on memorizing stuff all this time?"

"By charming people to do her work for her with that velvety drawl of hers. When that fails, that's where I come in."

"Let's get back to the letters."

"They had to be convincing. Dr. Propper is, after all, a professor. The letters had to be good enough to fool Violet into thinking they were authentic."

I pieced everything together. "Violet thought Dr. Propper had feelings for her. She wrote back. You delivered Violet's letters to Dr. Propper's wife, probably by intercepting them at the front desk. Mrs. Propper showed up at Violet's door to confront her. Dr. Propper was forced to resign. Violet decided the only escape from her shame was to take her own life on September 2, on my farm."

"You're some kind of idiot savant with dates, aren't you?"

"Yes, I am. And you're a sadistic bully who humiliated an innocent girl to death! You all but pushed Violet off that plane! That drab little Mary Agnes act was just a smokescreen for your malicious sins! How do you sleep at night?"

Something close to pure evil blazed in her eyes. "Like a baby."

I had read that sociopaths are incapable of remorse. I was pretty sure I was looking at one right now. "And this was all payback for Violet not writing Nathalia's paper when she was her tutor?"

"Pretty good, huh? Think you've got enough on Nathalia to bring to the investigator?"

"I'd say that's more than enough. Let's go now while the details are still fresh in our minds." Only I hadn't said that. Miss Chichester was standing behind me, in trousers and a work jacket. A chilly breeze blew up from the lake.

"Miss Chichester! I didn't know you were standing there."

"I realized that, Miss McKenna. I was spreading mulch in the garden for spring planting. Mr. Gallagher came by and told me I ought to come up and listen to the conversation you and Miss Sprague were having up here by the fire. Isn't that right, Mr. Gallagher?"

Mr. Gallagher appeared, holding his cap in his hands. "I've been keeping my eye on this one, sneaking into the school building night after night with one excuse after another. I never bought that story about her going to get some homework assignment, Miss Jay." He stoked the fire. "She was a nice girl, that Miss Violet. Never hurt a soul."

Chapter 16

Monday, March 24, 1919

Lydia choked on her scrambled eggs. "Mousy little Mary Agnes was behind everything!"

"Sadly, yes. She's the last person I would have suspected. She orchestrated all of it, quite well, I'm afraid."

"What a monster! And we were convinced Nathalia was the bully."

"Nathalia's no innocent in any of this, but once again she's managed not to get her hands dirty."

She looked away for a moment. "I never would have suspected that Mary Agnes exposed my stepfather's arrest in order to get me fired as RA. Never in a million years."

I took her hand in mine. "I'm sorry, Lydia. I wish there was some way you could stay on here."

She smiled and gave my hand a squeeze. "I know you do." She wiped away an errant tear and exhaled. "So what happens now?"

"Mary Agnes's mother has pulled her and Evangeline out of school. They've gone."

"I can't believe I'm saying this, but why pull Evangeline out too?"

"Mrs. Sprague threatened to withdraw Evangeline if Dr. Wisdom expelled Mary Agnes. I guess she lost that argument."

"You've had quite the weekend! You've solved the mystery of Violet's death."

"Sadly, I did. Such a waste. I can't see Mary Agnes not facing some kind of manslaughter charges, even though she's a minor. Little comfort that will provide for Violet's family, though."

"I wish you had met her, Jay. She was such a gentle soul."

"I wish I had too. This whole thing has further convinced me that I want to fight for women, and children, and the underprivileged. There's just too many bullies in this world." I paused to finish the last of my tea. "Oh, I knew there was something else I wanted to tell you. I got some more good news at the Women's Party meeting yesterday afternoon. Ruth asked me if I would be interested in being a page in Governor Smith's Albany offices this summer. She mentioned the idea when I stayed with her over Christmas, but I never thought it would actually happen!"

"Really?" Lydia asked. "I thought only boys could be pages. They run errands and do odd jobs, right?"

"Ruth thinks girls can do just as good a job as boys. And Al agreed with her. I imitated his accent. *'That kid has enough spunk to go undercover in factories so we can check if they are following regulations! Hire her, Ruth.'* Those were his exact words!"

"In Albany?" Lydia asked.

"Yep, in the capitol building," I looked around the dining hall. "Where's Florence? She needs to hear this!"

❧

Thursday, March 27, 1919

It was three days before Florence came back to school.

"Where've you been? So much has happened here!"

"So much has happened to me, too. But I don't want to tell you here," she said. "Let's walk down to our spot."

We followed the stream through the woods where it widened into the brook. The spring thaw sent water roaring down from the mountains, turning brown and foamy as it churned up earth from the thawing ground. Florence held her arms out at her sides for balance while she navigated the slippery stones. "Mr. Crane, the old one, died the other night."

"I'm sorry." Chickadees the color of wood splashed in the rushing water. "Is your mother out of work now?"

"Nope. The will was read yesterday. You're not going to believe this." She maneuvered her way over to the downed tree where she joined me to sit. "He left a third of his estate to yours truly!"

"Holy Moly!" I stared at the sunbursts around her pupils, remembering the old man's eyes. "Why'd he do that?"

"I always had my suspicions that Mr. Crane was my daddy because of my light skin and eyes. When I was summoned to the reading of his will, I figured things out real quick."

"Why didn't you just come out and ask your mother if it was true?"

"Who am I to judge what choices she had to make to put food on our table?" Her voice softened a bit. "I'd like to think maybe the old coot really loved her. I guess he had to wait until they put him in the ground to tell people about me. And boy, did he tell them." She giggled. "Get this. Mrs. Crane passed out stone cold, right there in the lawyer's office! She came around when the talk turned to how much money was left to her husband. And get this, my new-found sister-in-law has taken to introducing me as, "Dear Cousin Florence from Manhattan."

"So let me get this straight. You're Florence Crane, part owner of the Crane House?"

She made a face. "I'm not changing my name, and I don't want that big old house. Mrs. Crane can stay there as long as she wants!"

"But seriously. What are you going to do now with all that Crane money?"

"Make sure Mama never has to cook another meal in her life. She wants to go back to the city."

"You're not leaving Haviland, are you?"

"I'm not sure what I want to do."

"Come to Albany with me this summer."

"Albany? I don't think so."

"Ruth wants me to be a page at Governor Smith's offices in the capitol building. Come with me. We'll have so much fun together!"

"A colored office page in Albany? Have you lost your mind?"

"Ruth and Al would love you!"

"Oh, so it's Al now? There'll be no talking to you once you're hobnobbing with all the higher-ups in Albany!"

"Think about it at least. Now sit down. I've got to fill you in on Mary Agnes."

"Mary Agnes? The one who's afraid of her own shadow? What could you possibly have to say about that little mouse?"

I filled Florence in on her confession.

"You could knock me over with a feather right now!" Florence said when I'd finished. "Mary Agnes? What about Nathalia?"

"Oh, it seems, by pure coincidence, Mrs. Ormsby is going to be sponsoring a Golf Tournament Fundraiser for Haviland next month. Unbelievable!"

"But what about Violet? I mean, at Mr. Crane's wake, I heard Dr. Crane had filed a lawsuit demanding the school be held liable for, what was it again? Oh, yes, I remember, *'Gross negligence in creating a school environment conducive to bullying students.'* Someone has to be held liable for Violet's death."

I shrugged. "I do hope Dr. Crane presses charges and has Mary Agnes arrested. But all the money in the world isn't going to bring Violet back."

❈

Thursday, April 3, 1919

"Ladies, I am delighted to announce that due to a generous donation, we, here at Haviland, have decided to start a committee designed to revise the current Honor Code to include some new amendments preventing students from being coerced into complying with cheating."

"There's no pressure to cheat around here, is there Jay?" Florence whispered. I elbowed her to be quiet.

"A revised school mission statement will be adopted, which reflects the aforementioned amendments, and from September forward, parents will have to sign off on such policies before their daughters are admitted to our school." Another round of applause greeted this statement.

I felt conflicted. I prayed Miss Chichester could change our school climate. Her committee certainly sounded like a step in the right direction but, like everything else, it was tainted by money exchanging hands. Time would tell, I supposed.

"I would like to publically acknowledge the persons responsible for making these changes reality. First, I'd like to thank our newest faculty member for bringing her idea to my attention. Miss Chichester will be heading this committee." My teacher stood to a hearty applause.

"Secondly, I would like to thank the person responsible for funding the revisions and printing of the revised Haviland Honor Code student handbooks, which will be available for all students by the start of the next school year. Will Mrs. Thaddeus Q. Ormsby please rise to be acknowledged?"

Nathalia's mother, in flowing tiers of pastel chiffon, rose like a butterfly among the drab browns and grays worn by the faculty, except for Miss Chichester, of course. She received a polite smattering of applause.

We walked back to the dormitory after the assembly.

"Oh, I almost forgot." Florence took a letter from her coat pocket. "This came for you today. Betty Cornish asked me to give it to you when I saw you."

The stationary was embossed with the Borden's seal. I had to stop and read the message twice before my brain would allow the words to sink in.

"What is it?" asked Florence.

"My scholarship's been cancelled due to my repeated behavioral offenses."

Chapter 17

"Who's that guy pounding on the door?" Florence asked as we neared the dormitory.

My heart stopped. "What's Jimmy Joe doing here?"

"There you are!" he yelled. "Da's had a stroke. It's bad."

I threw a few things in my valise, slung my book satchel over my shoulder, and jumped in the truck.

"Felix and Ernie are back working for us part time." Jimmy Joe said as he steered the truck around Lake Gleneida. "Ernie's also taking on work making linen deliveries, and he ended up dropping off an order at the poor house over in Kent. He thought he saw Da there, all crippled up, looking half dead. I take a ride over there, and wouldn't you know it, it was him!"

"Jimmy Joe, why is your hand shaking like that?"

"Damn, these tremors. They started when I was overseas." He sat on his hand.

"You should see Doc about them."

"Don't you even want to know how Da ended up at a poor house, for God's sake?"

"I guess so." I was more concerned with what I was going to do with the rest of my life. I guess it was back to the village school for me.

"Turns out a cop brought him there as an indigent a few month ago, they told me. Had him out working with the cows. They said one day he just went and keeled over, massive stroke. Left him paralyzed on his right side. Didn't even know who I was."

I wished Da didn't know who I was. I pretended to listen while I watched a fisherman scrubbing the winter grime off the side of his boat. Would I ever see

Florence again after June? What about Ruth? It felt like my life was over when it had only just started.

"Can't talk or walk. Brought him home this morning. Doc said he ain't got long, so Mam figured you might want to say goodbye."

"I don't know."

"What do you mean, you don't know?" He stubbed out his cigarette on the floor. "He's your da, isn't he?"

"You weren't here that day last October, Jimmy Joe! You didn't see what went on here. He was crazy mean, out of his mind! He beat Eileen, and took her away. He pushed Mam to the floor, and look what he did to me!" I held up my mangled fingers.

"I know, Jay. Eileen and Mam told me everything. They had mixed feelings about my bringing him home too, especially with the little one coming soon. So I'll tell you what I told them. Do it for yourself Jay, not for Da."

"Huh?"

"It does a soul good to make your peace and say goodbye to folks before they meet their maker. I didn't have that chance with a lot of my buddies over there."

"I know. I never got to say goodbye to Christie."

❈

"Eileen, you're as big as a house!"

Why thank you, Jay, you're looking very well yourself! " Eileen's face looked swollen. Her nose had widened and her lips were all puffed up. She rested her hand on the small of her back as she walked, sway backed, to greet me. "Bet you've been dying to say that your whole life!"

"I have. How're you feeling?'

"Like a hot air balloon. Can't even fit in my shoes anymore." She lifted up her night shift to show me her bare feet. "Mam swears it's going to be a girl, because she says girls rob your beauty. Wasn't that nice of her to say?"

"You look much better than the last time I saw you. Have you seen Da?"

"He looks like he's already dead."

"I don't know what to say to him. The way he …"

"I know. I can't even go in there. Mam's holding some kind of vigil, but I can't pretend that nothing happened." She lifted my chin with her hand. "You do it, Jay. Tell him I said goodbye, will you? Your better with words than I am."

I didn't want to, but Eileen had enough to worry about. I looked around. "Where's Sullivan?"

"Mam sent him over to Harkins because he keeps trying to attack Da."

"Oh," I said. Henry. I pictured his perfectly symmetrical face in my mind.

I stalled as long as I could before turning the handle on the door to Mam's bedroom.

"Come make your peace with your Da, Josephine." Mam's back was to me. A tray bearing an untouched bowl of soup and a cup of tea sat on the bed.

I steadied myself on the bed railing because my legs had gone all wobbly. One of Da's eyes was almost fully closed, and his mouth drooped down on the left side. I didn't think he could see me. Mam was holding one of his hands; the other lay useless at his side. His fingers had atrophied into a curled fist. He was emaciated, and he had least a week's growth of whiskers on his face.

Ma got up and took the tray. "I'll leave you to say your goodbyes. It won't be long now."

Years of suppressed pain rose up from deep inside of me. When they surfaced, I felt exposed, raw, and torn, unable to utter a word of comfort. I wanted to hate him for the way he treated us, but looking at him now, sick and helpless, I couldn't.

Walking slowly toward his bed, I looked at his one open eye, to see if he recognized me. "Da, wake up. It's Jay."

Nothing. He looked straight ahead.

I couldn't bring myself to embrace or even touch him. Remembering Jimmy Joe's warning about making peace with my father for my sake, I tried to go back in my memory to think of a time he showed gentleness, maybe even love.

His songs, I thought. He used to sing Irish songs all day long while he was working. They seemed to make him happy. How did they go again?

I could sing those songs to him. Maybe he could hear me, even if he couldn't respond. My voice came out all squeaky and weak at first, but grew in strength as I sang the lyrics to, "Danny Boy," "The Wild Rover," and his favorite, "Black Velvet Band."

I squeezed my eyes and tried to remember the good times, before life had robbed him of his livelihood and his son. I thought about the days when there had been money for extras, like those fall weekends when he would pile all of us in the back of the rig and drive up to the Danbury Fair.

Keeping my voice to a whisper, I sang every song of his I could remember until the sun set. He didn't show any recognition of any of them. When I couldn't think of any more songs, I looked down at his paralyzed face. A tear was sliding down his cheek.

❁

Friday, April 4, 1919

Ma took over for me in the kitchen the next afternoon. "You look like a blood donor. I can get along without you for a bit. Go up and see Bridie's calf. Born four days ago. The fresh air will do you good."

"Okay, just let me grab a sweater."

The sun was shining through the window and gleamed off a new picture frame as I passed through the parlor. I walked toward the mantle. Christie, uncharacteristically serious in his Marine uniform, gazed at me from a sepia-tinted portrait. He looked out of place among the tintypes of long-dead Irish relatives.

The farm was quiet, just a few birds chirping in the gnarled apple tree. A ruby red cardinal, perched on a branch, serenaded his modestly adorned mate. I thought the brilliant male was Christie's spirit coming to visit me. My thoughts were interrupted by the sound of horses coming and Sullivan's barking.

"My baby!" He ran to me, leaping up into my arms, wiggling and kissing me all over my face.

"Hi Jay." Henry was driving the rig one handed around the back of the house. His broken arm was bound to his chest in a sling. He took Sam and Martha up to the barn so they could drink from the trough. After bringing them some greens in a bucket, he walked down to the porch steps.

I said nothing. Let him talk first, I thought.

"I'd have been by sooner, but my pa hasn't let me out of the house except for work and school. Until today, that is." He was scuffing the tips of his work boots against the bottom step.

"Why?" I asked, staring at the bare spot where a long scar ran through his left eyebrow.

"Pa said your father's dying. I asked if I could come and pay my respects, and to thank you for saving my life, and to uh, apologize, Jay, and to see if ..." he struggled, "if, maybe you'd maybe talk to me again someday." He looked at me with an intensity that took my breath away. "Pa said you'd probably slam the door in my face."

"Mam thinks Da's trying to hold on until Packy gets home. We're expecting him any day. The hospital fitted him with an artificial leg."

"That's got to be tough."

"Don't feel too sorry for him. He married his nurse at the hospital. He's bringing her home with him."

"Good for him." Henry looked around the farm. "This place looks great. Who planted those rows of apple trees?"

"Jimmy Joe sold off some of the land to Mr. Salmon to pay off the mortgage on the farm and the ice house. He's gained ten new milk delivery customers since he's been home." I walked with him toward the rows of tiny trees. "He said farms need to diversify now, so he wants to start selling apples, peaches, and potatoes to Frank Maher, the greengrocer in the village."

"I see. So, should we keep discussing the farm, or can we talk about what happened to us?"

Stay strong, I told myself. "Sure we can talk about us, Henry, if you can tell me why you left with Nathalia and allowed her to drive you into the lake. She almost killed you." I swallowed hard. "No matter how badly I may have taken you for granted, I didn't deserve that."

His face reddened. "They told me you had ditched me, Jay. Honest."

"What? I didn't ditch you, Henry. I pulled you out of the car before it sank to the bottom of lake!"

"George told me." His index and middle fingers were tobacco stained, and his nails were bitten down to ragged skin.

I took his hand, holding his fingers up. "When did you start smoking?"

"Never mind about that." He pulled his hand away. "It's been hell these past two months."

"Tell me about it," I said, more sarcastic than I intended.

"Will you let me try and explain, for Pete's sake?"

"Go ahead." I threw a stick for Sullivan.

"Some girl came up to me at the table and said you had left with one of the fellows from Carmel. Said you were telling everyone you couldn't believe that sucker actually showed up after you'd been trying to give him the brush off for weeks."

"Why would you believe one word out of Nathalia's mouth?"

"Nathalia didn't tell me that, Jay. It was some girl with dark hair. She asked me to walk outside with her so she could explain what was going on."

"Mary Agnes. She didn't miss a trick, did she?"

"I was about to leave in my dad's truck when the girl walked over with Nathalia. She told me Nathalia's date had dumped her as well, and she needed consoling." Henry picked up a pile of pebbles and started pitching them toward at our barn. Sullivan chased after them. "I felt sorry for her. I figured out too late that it was all a setup."

"Whatever possessed you to get into a stolen car with her, Henry?"

"It was an idiotic dare." He threw another pebble, a bigger one now, more like a stone. "Nathalia asked me to teach her how to drive the Saxon Six. Said she had one just like it home and knew her way around the gears. When I told her I wouldn't get into someone else's car, she called me an imbecile."

"So, what? You took a joy ride in a stolen car, which just happened to belong to a good friend of mine, because Nathalia called you an imbecile?"

"She, uh, she told me if I didn't teach her how to drive, it probably meant I was an imbecile like my brother." Henry wiped his eyes with the sleeve of his shirt. "How she knew about Ambrose, I've no idea."

"Mary Agnes saw him at the Pot Luck."

"I had to prove to her that I could drive, that I wasn't like Ambrose. Once I realized it was all a hoax, it was too late. She lost control of the car, and well, you know the rest. I guess I am an imbecile."

"I am so sorry for hurting you like I did." His voice cracked.

I stayed quiet so I could listen to Florence's voice in my head telling me not to be a fool and lose him again. "You did hurt me, Henry, but I hurt you as well when

I took you for granted. I should have written you to tell you how much I appreciated your taking Sullivan and looking after the animals after Da abandoned the farm. I realize how selfishly I behaved toward you, and for that, I apologize."

"And I apologize for every stupid decision I made at the dance that night." He looked over my shoulder. "I, uh, see your mother peeking out the window. Maybe I ought to be getting back, this being my first time out in so long."

"Want to see Bridie's new calf?"

"I'd like that more than anything."

The ring of the telephone Jimmy Joe had installed jolted the both of us.

"Josephine." Mam had pulled the window up. "Someone from the school is asking for you on the telephone!"

"I'll wait here for you." Henry's uninjured hand lightly brushed mine as I passed him on the porch steps.

"Am I speaking with Miss Josephine McKenna?" Miss Biddle's voice was hard to hear amid the crackly static coming through the earpiece.

"Yes, Miss Biddle, this is Josephine McKenna."

"You'll have to speak louder, dear. I'm afraid we have a bad connection."

"This is Miss McKenna!" I shouted.

"Miss McKenna, I apologize to be calling during your time of mourning, however..."

"He's not dead yet!" Mam shouted into the receiver.

I motioned for Mam to go into the parlor. "I apologize, Miss Biddle. Please continue."

"As I was saying, I must let you know that fall registration and course selection is due today, and I see you have not signed up for any classes."

My heart sank. I hadn't yet told Mam my scholarship had been discontinued. Henry either.

I tried to speak softly so no one could eavesdrop. "I can't register for the fall, Miss Biddle. I lost my scholarship."

"I'm aware of that, Miss McKenna, but nonetheless, your Fall 1919 tuition, room, and board has been paid in full. I must insist you come in as soon as possible to register or there will be no seats available in any of the classes you need for your junior year. We've had an unexpected boost in enrollment now the war is over."

"Wait. There must be some mistake. How can my tuition be paid? My folks, I mean, my mother doesn't have money to pay for me."

"Let me see here, Miss McKenna. Ah, here it is. Your tuition has been paid in full for the 1919-1920 academic year by a Miss Ruth Lefkowitz. The check is from a bank in Albany."

I had to sit down. Ruth. My mentor, my inspiration, and now, my heroine. How would I ever repay her?

"Now, give me one minute here while I check something. Your room has been selected and paid for in full by a separate account. Here it is. Room and board paid in full for the 1919-1920 academic year from the Estate of Horace Crane in trust for Florence Bright. Please, Miss McKenna, you must be at my desk by 7:30 tomorrow morning so I can enter your course selections."

"Uh, okay," was all I could manage at first. Then, "Yes, Miss Biddle I will be there."

"Very well, then. Good evening, Miss McKenna. I'll keep your family in my prayers." The telephone line went dead.

I sat, stunned into silence at the profound acts of generosity shown by my two best friends, Ruth and Florence. They had given me my future back. I vowed to repay each of them someday.

I stepped out onto the porch and explained my good fortune to Henry. After visiting Bridie and her newborn, we walked up to the stone wall and admired the sunset, which set the horizon on a fire of deep pink, purple, and coral. A veil of mist hung over the mountains, now shaded that perfect spring-green. Cow bells and wind chimes signaled the day was coming to an end.

The cows were parading in a single file back into the barn. The tops of the mountains, where dark green pine trees etched a silhouette against the darkening sky, resembled a pen and ink drawing.

Wounds were healing. I was going back to Haviland, and Henry was once again part of my life. Packy and his bride were on their way. So was Eileen's baby. I'd made my peace with Da, the best I could. Life was beginning to renew itself.

From the darkening mountains, I heard the strains of "Pavane, Opus 50," by Faure. That beautiful music would always invoke Violet's spirit for me. Now that her story was known, she could, at last, be at peace.

Author's Note

An archival newspaper photograph of a group of girls at a private school in Carmel, New York, inspired me to write The Girls of Haviland.

Al Smith was elected as Governor of the State of New York four times. My character, Ruth Lefkowitz, was inspired by Governor Smith's political advisor, Belle Moskowitz.

General John Pershing led the American Expeditionary Forces in Europe during World War I. David Lloyd George was the Prime Minister of England during this war.

Alice Paul and Lucy Burns fought for Women's Suffrage. They picketed in front of the White House in an attempt to draw President Woodrow Wilson's attention to their cause.

Theda Bara, Lillian and Dorothy Gish, Fatty Arbuckle, and Mary Pickford were all popular entertainers during 1918-19.

Edith Diehl, a native of Brewster, New York, was commissioned to run a Women's Land Army Experimental Station at Wellesley College during the summer of 1918. My character, Margaret Addison, was inspired by Marjorie Addis, who was an editor for *The Brewster Standard* newspaper and attended Edith Diehl's Women's Land Army camp at Wellesley. *The Putnam County Courier* was, and is still, in circulation.

The Lobdell family operated a dry goods and grocery store in Brewster. There was indeed a Borden's Condensery in Brewster as well. All of the other characters are products of my imagination.

References

Alcott, Louisa Mae. *Eight Cousins*. 1874.

Cohan, George M. "Over There." Leo Feist, Inc., NY. 1917. Sheet Music.

Crosby, Fanny. "Blessed Assurance." *Palmer's Guide to Holiness and Revival Miscellany*.1873

Crosby, Fanny. "To God Be the Glory." *Brightest and Best*. 1875. The Clancy Brothers and Makem, Tommy. "The Wild Rover." *Recorded Live in Ireland*. 1965. Album.

The Dubliners. "Black Velvet Band." *A Drop of the Hard Stuff*, 1967. Album

The Dubliners. "Molly Malone" *Live From the Gaiety*. 2003. Album.

Egan, Raymond B., and Whiting, Richard A. "Till We Meet Again." Jerome H. Rennick & Co. 1918. Sheet Music.

Faure, Gabriel. "Pavane in F sharp Opus 50." 1887.

O'Hara, Geoffrey. "K-K-K-Katy." Leo Feist, Inc. N.Y. 1918. Sheet Music.

Palgrave, Francis Turner. *The Golden Treasury Selected from the Best Songs and Lyrical Poems in the English Language*. MacMillan & Company. London. 1861.

Weatherly, Frederick. "Danny Boy." 1913.

Young, Joe, and Lewis, Sam. "How Ya Gonna Keep 'Em Down at The Farm, Now That They've Seen Paree?" Waterson, Berlin, and Snyder Company.1919. Sheet Music.

Young, Joe, and Lewis, Sam. "Rockabye Your Baby with A Dixie Melody." Leo Feist, Inc., NY. 1918. Sheet Music.